PENGUIN BOOKS
SECRETLY YOURS

Vikrant Khanna is a captain in the merchant navy. He is the bestselling author of *When Life Tricked Me* and *Love Lasts Forever*. Apart from writing, he is fond of composing songs and playing the guitar. He lives in New Delhi.

He can be contacted here:
Facebook: www.facebook.com/writervikrant/
Twitter: www.twitter.com/_VikrantKhanna
Instagram: www.instagram.com/vikrantkhanna/

VIKRANT KHANNA

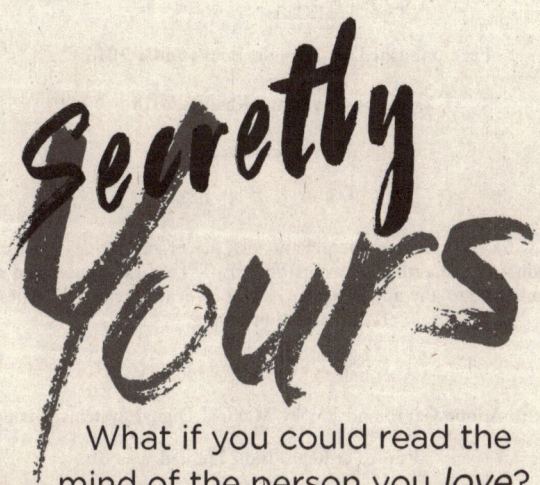

Secretly Yours

What if you could read the mind of the person you *love*?

PENGUIN BOOKS

An imprint of Penguin Random House

PENGUIN BOOKS

USA | Canada | UK | Ireland | Australia
New Zealand | India | South Africa | China | Singapore

Penguin Books is part of the Penguin Random House group of companies
whose addresses can be found at global.penguinrandomhouse.com

Published by Penguin Random House India Pvt. Ltd
4th Floor, Capital Tower 1, MG Road,
Gurugram 122 002, Haryana, India

First published by Penguin Books India 2016

ISBN 9780143425915

Typeset in Adobe Garamond Pro by Manipal Digital Systems, Manipal

Printed at Repro India Limited

www.penguin.co.in

MIX
Paper from
responsible sources
FSC® C047271

To Ma, Pa, Tutu and Amyra—
god knows how much I love you all

Prologue

Life can be a great teacher, particularly when you've been a bad student. Not the whining, self-righteous sort, but someone who knows how to come around and straighten you out.

When Monica told me, 'There is a journal maintained somewhere upstairs, which lists all our deeds, good and bad, and we'll pay for all our sins,' I knew it was time.

But it wasn't Monica who provided me with a fresh perspective towards life, it was Anya—the only girl I ever fell in love with. And now, whatever I'm planning to do, it is all for her. If I don't, they will kill her and I can't let that happen. I've lost enough loved ones already and can't afford to lose another.

I realize I might lose my life in the process. But it doesn't matter.

It's amazing what one is willing to do when in love.

1

Beginnings

My name is Sahil and I am seventeen years old. My mother died a few minutes after giving birth to me and my father, unhinged by the sorrow, committed suicide by slitting his wrists and bleeding to death a month later. My grandmother packed our bags and moved from Delhi to Shimla, with me and my elder brother, Ayush, who was six years old at the time, to live with her younger son.

We live in the northern part of the city, in Krishna Nagar, a neighbourhood which is a stone's throw from the popular tourist destination, the Ridge. It's an open space in the heart of the city lined with shops and restaurants. Even during the off-season it bustles with frenzied activity. When winter sets in, the area is submerged in clumps of fresh snow, restricting people indoors.

On that particular day, I was crossing the Ridge, bag slung over my shoulders, on my way back home from school. Although it was a few minutes' diversion, I took the Ridge route often.

The place was teeming with people—rich and poor, young and old, lovers, family, friends—and the afternoon sun was slowly heading west in the purple sky. I took a seat on a bench at the edge of the open space and placed my bag on my lap.

A few kids were playing football in the dusty playground to my right, their boots digging into the soft mud as they ran for the ball, leaving plumes of dust in their trail. Dead ahead I spotted a few tourists clicking pictures in front of the imposing Christ Church. It had a majestic appearance and stood towering in the distance, dwarfing the smaller buildings around. Vendors nearby were howling, beseeching passers-by to buy germ-filled eatables—*chana chat*, *bhel puri*, *kulfi*, ice cream. Some stopped, while others passed them without so much as a glance their way.

I crossed my arms across my chest and took a deep breath. Everyone appeared busy here, happy even, content with life, devoid of problems. A few metres towards my left, a young father was playing ball with his little daughter, who stumbled often, as his wife merrily looked on. They were happy; life, it appeared, had been good to them.

I got up and bought a cigarette. I lit it and took a long drag. I watched the white smoke twirl, rise and disappear. Wasn't life like that? We are born, twirl around life and then die. Why the hell are we born in the first place?

To suffer, I presumed. I took another drag and let the smoke disappear. Life never made any sense to me. It was boring and crawled away slowly. I wish we had a shorter life span, like that of an animal or an insect. One squish under a sturdy foot and it would be over.

My cigarette was spent and I bought another one. The wind had picked up and so had the noise in the air. More people had come out from their homes. I looked at my watch. I still had time.

I sat there cross-legged for an hour, moped around the streets and the shops for another hour, before making my way back home. Grandma had set a 7.00 pm curfew for getting back home.

Like I was some kid.

* * *

Our home was a three-bedroom flat on the second floor of an old, tawdry residential complex overlooking a garden with pine trees and untrimmed hedges. Grandma opened the door and looked at the watch. She never trusted me with time. She was in her mid-seventies but didn't look a year older than sixty. Her favourite pastime was to compare me to Ayush. In her opinion, there was no finer boy than him anywhere in the world.

'Where were you?' she asked, leaving only a little space for me to enter. I managed to squeeze by.

'Guitar class.'

'But you don't have music classes on Tuesdays.'

I had passed her by then. Without turning around, I said, 'The fest is coming up. I needed to practise,' and proceeded to my room.

I didn't pay attention to her grumbling behind my back.

My room was the farthest and to the left down the corridor. Once inside, I threw my school bag on the sagging couch in the corner. I picked up my guitar from its cradle and sat on the bed. After tuning it, I began to play.

After an hour of practising mostly smooth chord progressions, I placed the guitar back and picked up the book *To Kill a Mockingbird* that I had started reading the day before. Ten minutes later there was a knock on the door.

'Yeah, come on in.'

'Why aren't you ready yet?' asked Shweta, my first cousin, poking her head in. 'We're getting late, Sahil!'

Shweta was fair, moderately tall, with skin like a tomato. Her small eyes—the size of slits—distinguished her from the rest of the family. She had an attractive pixie haircut and never once was a strand out of place. She was always neatly dressed and sometimes, I felt, she carried herself with an air of overbearing self-confidence. She was our only sister and was well-acquainted with losing a parent at an early age. Her mother had died of a cardiac arrest ten years ago. Shweta was only eight then. Her father, a captain in the merchant navy, sailed for an appreciable amount of time in the year, leaving the three of us under the strict, and mostly annoying, tutelage of our grandmother.

Shweta was just a year older than me but never short of worldly advice. She liked to think of herself as a mature and sensible teenager—been there, done that—and I was the exact opposite.

'I'm not feeling too well,' I said, not trying too hard to hide my lie. 'You guys carry on.'

Shweta sighed and then rolled her eyes. 'Why are you never interested in meeting people?' She paused. 'It's *our* family we're talking about.'

'I get bored, Shweta. Besides the Malik family is the most sinfully uninteresting bunch of people ever.'

'You are a Malik—Sahil Malik!'

'I'm sorry,' I said. I had made plans with my girlfriend that night. It wasn't often that I had the whole flat to myself. 'Please close the door behind you, and tell Grandma too. I know she'll be pissed at me.'

'Why shouldn't she be?' she said spitefully, and then she was gone with a violent shake of her head.

I never confronted her much because of her father. He was a decent man who had ensured we had a good living and never differentiated between the three of us.

* * *

DAV Public School in Lakkar Bazaar, where I was a student in the twelfth standard, was a mere ten minutes' walk from my home.

I took a sip of the coffee that I had bought at the canteen and slowly walked along the periphery of the school playground. I had been working on a fantasy novel for the past few months. It was the story of a boy who dreamt about the events of the following day the night before, and planned to alter the future on waking up.

I had written a couple of chapters but found myself hitting writers' block lately. I had to bring more clarity to the plot and the protagonist. Just as my mind was reeling with a million thoughts, Mayur—my classmate, friend and the drummer in our school band—came strutting along down the narrow passage to my left.

'Hey,' he said, hands thrust in the pockets of his skin-tight trousers. 'What're you doing here?' He tipped his head slightly and held out his hand. I took it and raised my cup.

'Some coffee?'

He shook his head. He had a very ugly habit of bobbing his mouth repeatedly, not unlike chewing. He thought it looked cool. I found it really annoying.

Mayur was tall, a few inches above six feet, and was inordinately proud of it. His eyes were set too close together under his thick, bushy eyebrows. Below them an unwieldy nose nestled itself above a pair of full, overgrown lips. He was average looking but his hairstyle seriously damaged the outcome. It was handpicked from the 1960s films—a thick mass of hair peeking out from the rest of the neatly combed, gel-glued hair.

We walked together towards our class when he fired his next question.

'So did you guys do it?'

Everybody knew Mayur loved girls and was hell-bent on losing his virginity by the end of the year.

I gave him a sly look and smiled. 'What do you think?'

He brought his hand to his mouth a bit dramatically and said, 'You did it! You bastard, you did it with another one! Mansi Keswani has been popped. God! I wonder how many girls he has bestowed upon you.'

Mansi was a sweet-looking girl with wheatish complexion and long, brown hair. We were in the same class but different sections. We'd been together for the last three weeks.

Mayur and I rounded the corner and took the stairs to the first floor.

'You are one lucky bastard,' he said. 'You know that? Some guys have all the luck.'

We'd reached our class by then and we spotted Nishant, a good guy, a little restrained but unpretentious. His looks perfectly complemented the academician in him: old-fashioned glasses nestled on his nose, deep-set and alert eyes behind them, neatly combed hair that didn't manage to hide the bald patch right in the middle of his head, and a perpetually neat and clean-shaven face. He liked to think of himself as a well-organized and sensible guy. I thought so too.

'He did it with Mansi,' was the first thing Mayur said to Nishant.

'And good morning to you too,' Nishant said to him. Then, to me, 'So how'd it go?' Even if he was interested in knowing, he didn't show it.

'It was all right; finally had the whole flat to myself,' I said. 'But, towards the end, she left crying.'

'What happened?'

'Nothing,' I said. 'She said she was falling in love with me; I said I was not.'

'Ha!' Nishant snorted. 'That explains it.'

'Good morning class!' Deepika ma'am, our class teacher, entered the room, an air of authority around her. 'Settle down there.'

We all scrambled to our seats and girded ourselves for the next hour of boredom. I hated history class first thing in the morning.

* * *

After school Mayur and I trotted down to Musica—our music academy, which I secretly considered my real school as I was an aspiring musician. The annual Shimla festival was around the corner and we'd be representing our school in the music competition. Our teachers were pinning their hopes on us and we on our music teacher, Rajiv Rockwell. Rajiv had a swarthy complexion and hoarded a scraggly bunch of hair under his chin. He could play almost all musical instruments deftly but was most fond of his flute. His surname was just perfect for the musician that he was.

I had composed a couple of songs with Sammy, our classmate and the third member of our band, and Rajiv helped us develop these songs. Sammy was from Mizoram and, like most Northeasterners, had exceptional skills with the electric guitar. He was the lead guitarist of our band. Sammy frequently bunked school and mostly hung around at the academy.

Over the next hour, Rajiv gave us his take on our songs, worked with us on the lyrics, honed the rhythm and tonality, and gave me tips on how to sing them better. We followed every bit of his advice and incorporated his suggestions in our performance.

After our class, as was customary, we hung out for a while at Sita Ram, a small eatery in Lakkar Bazaar, famous for its *aloo tikki* and *chole bhature*.

I bade my friends goodbye after some time and made a pretence of going home. As it wasn't seven yet, I hung around Mall Road, failing miserably at developing the plot of my story further.

2

Wounds

Ten minutes after settling down in my room with a book, the
door creaked open. It was Ayush.

Although he was just two inches taller than my six feet, he
towered over me. He was big and burly, the kind of guy you
wouldn't want to mess with. Despite his young age, he had a
receding hairline and the silver in his hair was not inconspicuous,
in spite of his many attempts to hide it. His slight paunch went
unnoticed thanks to his huge frame.

Ayush was pursuing medicine from Indira Gandhi Medical
College and, from what I heard Grandma regularly say, he was
the best student there.

'What are you up to?' His voice was loud, shrill and hurt
my ears.

'Reading,' I said, not looking up.

'So what happened yesterday? Shweta said you were not
well. Bullshit, right? You just want to avoid people.'

'Look, Ayush,' I said, not in any mood to have an argument,
'I had some work to do, and that's why I couldn't make it
yesterday. Let's just leave it at that.'

Ayush shook his head. 'You know, I don't give a shit about your tantrums. It's just that Grandma, as usual, is pissed at you. She told me to check on you; if you were really ill. Not that she believed you but, you know, just in case.'

He came forward and took a seat on the couch near the bed. 'Anyway, let it be. I wanted to tell you Mehek and I are completing five years together, so to honour that, we're throwing a little party for some friends of ours at the Chinese restaurant on Mall Road tomorrow evening. She was asking about you. Just wondering if you'd want to be a part of it?'

My expression softened. 'Congrats man, five years? Wow! But they'll all be your friends, right? I'll get bored there.'

This was a lie. In fact, I preferred his friends over him and even my own friends for that matter. His friends were pretty chilled out guys and, to his surprise, I connected with them really well. Some of them were into music and books unlike Ayush.

Last year, they had a get together at one of his friends' places and I was invited. A little while into the party, a few drinks down, I was having an amazing time. One of Mehek's friends was really into me and we were having a conversation about our favourite books. She was a lovely girl and I'd thought of asking her out after the party. Then, to everyone's surprise, Ayush played spoilsport and turned off the music.

'It's close to midnight,' he'd said. 'Come on, Sahil, let's go. Grandma would be waiting.'

I didn't want to leave and everyone pleaded with him to stay. Ayush had such an unbelievably authoritative quality that half an hour later I found myself tucked in my bed at home. He'd literally dragged me out of the party when I'd refused to budge.

The next morning he'd told Grandma about my 'fondness for alcohol' and my 'loss of surroundings after drinking'. I got a massive rant from her and decided I would never drink in his presence again.

Ayush made a face now. 'But you like my friends, don't you?' he said, smiling. 'If you want, I'll call Mayur and Nishant too.'

'Thanks, but no. You know with the fest and all, we're really busy over the next few days.'

'Okay, man, whatever.' He rose and headed out. Just when he was about to disappear through the door, he turned, and, as an afterthought, said, 'Sahil, music is good, but I hope you are taking your studies seriously too. You know, Grandma is really worried about you these days.'

'I know,' I said. 'When is she not? See you at dinner.'

* * *

Dinner, generally, was a low-key affair. The four of us sat at the small round table in front of the TV and wouldn't speak much. I always felt the others never spoke too much in front of me.

Ayush was watching a documentary about birds on National Geographic. Despite the sound of the TV, there was an eerie silence that hung over the table. I could feel two pairs of eyes boring stealthily through me. Something was up. Grandma and Shweta, I felt, were itching to say something about yesterday.

And then it came, after a little clearing of her throat.

'You want to tell me why you didn't come along yesterday? Everyone was asking about you,' said Grandma, her eyes shooting daggers at me.

I stayed put, my eyes lowered.

'It was Taya and Tayiji's fiftieth wedding anniversary, Sahil.' It was Shweta's turn now. 'You should've come. What were you doing alone at home anyway?'

'I'm sorry, I had to practise.'

Grandma snorted. '*Uff*! This music!' She shook her head in disgust. 'Music won't take you anywhere. You need to study, do well like your brother and join a good college.' She turned to Ayush. 'Why can't you drill some sense into him?'

Ayush turned the volume of the TV down. 'What do you want me to do? Just let it be, he won't listen.'

'No,' she said, her voice gaining strength, 'I can't let it be! Sahil, you barely passed last year. Do you know I had to convince your teachers to let you move to the next class? It was only when I reminded them that you were Ayush's brother did they agree.' She paused for a sip of water, her eyes firmly rooted on me. 'I want you to follow in his footsteps.'

'Why do you want me to follow in his footsteps?' I cried. 'I have a mind of my own. I know what to do with it.'

'Really?' she exclaimed. 'So what is it?'

I let out a frustrated sigh.

'Why can't you listen to her?' Shweta asked, exasperated. 'What's your problem?'

I said, resignedly, 'I don't know.'

Ayush had turned the volume of the TV back up, a little louder than before.

'Know this then,' said Grandma. 'It's not easy for an old woman to raise three grown-up children all by herself. Rakesh is sailing all the time and . . . Sanjeev . . . he . . . he is dead.' Before lowering her head, she added in a soft whisper, 'Thanks to you.'

The floor slipped from beneath my feet and the four walls caved in on me. Suddenly I had a searing headache and my heart began pumping hard. Goosebumps prickled my skin. Those last three words felt like a strong icy wind slamming across my face on a brutally chilly day.

'Why "thanks to me"?' I couldn't believe my voice was shaking; the words came out in a broken gasp.

'My son committed suicide because he couldn't take the fact that his wife was dead!' she replied unflinchingly.

Ayush muted the TV, and both he and Shweta peered stolidly at me.

I was panting now and tears came rolling down my face. 'So what has that got to do with me?' I yelled. Suddenly I dreaded the answer. I shouldn't have asked that question.

Grandma stood up. She leaned forward, her eyes dilated, her teeth clenched. 'Your mother died because of you! Because you were in a damn hurry to come out into the world! Couldn't you have waited a few more months?'

At the sight of Grandma's tears Shweta rose and nestled her head in her chest, patted her back and intoned, 'It's okay! It's okay!'

But Grandma wasn't done. She sniffled and I heard another muffled scream, 'My son . . . he . . . he would have been alive today had your mother not died that day.'

'Please take back those words!' I begged her, through my sobs. 'Please take them back, please.' I turned to Ayush. 'Please tell her to take back her words. You know more than anyone it's not my fault.'

Ayush had a solemn expression on his face—no pity, no sympathy, just blank eyes staring back at me. 'You know she doesn't mean it. She's just sad.'

'She meant every single word of it!' I roared, my entire body shaking. 'Every single word! Just look at her! She's mad at me! Why?'

'She's not. She didn't mean anything,' he said and buried his face in his hands.

As Grandma continued to sob, Shweta kept patting her and Ayush continued feigning concern. I couldn't take it any more. I dragged myself out of the chair, which fell with a thud. I bolted to my room and slammed the door shut.

I immediately started playing a CD of the Brazilian heavy metal band Sepultura—the one with all the head-banging shit and loud, foul language. Sammy introduced me to this genre of music. I turned the volume up high. I dug out the rum bottle I had kept buried beneath the mattress and took a large sip. Not able to calm my nerves I took another large gulp. I lit a cigarette and inhaled a few, quick puffs. The shrill voice of the singer reverberated through the room: *What a fucked up place! What a fucked up world!*

She had done this a few times before. I know whatever Ayush might say, Grandma genuinely believed I killed my parents. I would never be able to redeem myself. Never!

My breathing grew heavy and I failed to calm my shaking hands. Another big gulp of the rum and a few drags of the cigarette followed.

What a fucked up place . . . What a fucked up world . . .

Still nothing. No relief from the pain. No relief from the tears. I knew what I had to do. From the drawer I pulled out a blade that I had kept hidden for days like these. I rolled up my left shirtsleeve and gulped down the rum with quick, staggering breaths until the bottle was empty.

I took a deep breath and shut my eyes. Cutting was the only way I could distract my mind and take off to a distant place—a place devoid of emotional pain, a place where only physical pain existed. I opened my eyes and took the last drag of the cigarette before dropping the stub in the empty rum bottle. I steeled myself and began counting . . .

THREE! *What a fucked up place . . . What a fucked up world . . .*

TWO! *What a fucked up place . . . What a fucked up world . . .*

ONE! *What a fucked up place . . . What a fucked up world . . .*

At first I grazed the blade slowly over my skin. Then I went deeper. When the blade tore through my skin, I screamed my lungs out, so hard I could hear myself over the loud music. I dug deeper and watched the blood spurt from my veins in a quick, staccato rhythm. I was someplace else. Nothing else mattered here. There was only the pain here . . . deep, piercing, agonizing pain.

I clenched my teeth and continued cutting myself at different places on my arm until the pain finally washed over all the depression and anxiety that had been building within me over the last couple of weeks.

I threw the blade away and looked at my arm. Blood continued oozing out.

The last thing I remembered before falling asleep in a daze was wiping my eyes and contemplating bleeding to death.

3

Murders

The annual Shimla festival was a two-day affair. It was an opportunity for Shimla-dwellers, especially the youngsters, to get together and celebrate two days of music, contests and entertainment at the historical Gaiety theatre located on Mall Road. Hundreds of students from various schools, colleges and universities gathered to cheer for their friends who were participating. More than a dozen bands from Shimla, Chandigarh and the surrounding areas got a chance to showcase their talent on an open platform. Apart from music there were competitions for dance, dramatics and creative writing.

More than a dozen bands had already performed on the first day and on the second day of the fest came our turn. All afternoon we'd been pretty excited about the crowd turnout, though no one from my family had come. I wasn't expecting them to anyway. Grandma and I hadn't been talking for the last four days, since our face-off; Shweta would just silently smile at me—she probably felt a bit sorry for me—and Ayush had come up to my room the previous day for a talk.

After knocking, he asked if he could come in. 'You aren't naked inside or something?' I heard his short laugh.

'No, come in.'

I was practising the song that we'd finalized. To improve the rhythm Rajiv had incorporated some augmented and suspended chords—the ones with really difficult and awkward finger positioning—and I was having a tough time perfecting them.

'All set for tomorrow?'

I nodded, my eyes on the fretboard.

'All the best, man,' he said, his strong arm suddenly patting my shoulder. 'And . . . um . . . I want to come but . . . Grandma, she . . . she has given me some work and . . .'

'Don't bother giving me an explanation. She doesn't want you to come, I get it.'

He let out a sharp breath. 'You've got it all wrong about her, that's not . . .'

I stopped strumming and peered at him. 'Really? You think so?' He dropped his gaze. 'She thinks I killed our parents. God, I didn't even get to see them! You at least were lucky enough to have spent six years with them. I didn't even get that chance. And, as if that isn't tragic enough, I'm blamed for their death . . . I . . .' I trailed off.

Ayush looked at me with a firm gaze. 'She lost a son!' He paused. 'Losing your child when you're alive is the hardest thing one can endure. Ask any parent and they'll tell you this. She doesn't blame you, she's just really, really sad on the inside with one son dead and the other not around.' He scooted closer and placed his hand on my face. I was looking down and a couple of tears managed to find their way out. 'She's lonely, man. We're all she has.'

I shook my head really hard and ran a clumsy hand over my eyes. 'No, you're lying. She thinks I killed them.' My voice was hoarse. 'She thinks I killed them both. She's told me that so many times now, so many times.' I jumped out of bed, banged my guitar on the wall and stormed out the door.

'Sahil! Sahil!'

I didn't answer his summons and left the house only to return for dinner.

To hell with her 7.00 p.m. deadline!

* * *

Sammy, Mayur and I had been waiting outside the theatre for the past half an hour for our turn to be announced. The entire theatre was pulsating with the rich reverberations of electric guitars, keyboards and drums. Outside, we could feel every bit of the excitement. A few minutes before, on Sammy's insistence, Mayur and I had a few gulps of whisky.

'It drowns the performance pressure and brings out the musician in you,' he'd told us.

Sammy lit a cigarette and offered me one. Although not in the mood, I accepted it to assuage my anxiety. When I reached out for the cigarette, the cuff of my shirt slid back, exposing a few scars on my arm. Hurriedly, I pulled down my sleeve.

People often asked me the reason for my obsession with long-sleeved shirts, especially in the summer. I told them I loved them. I didn't. It was the only way I could hide my scars.

This habit of cutting myself every time I felt hurt had begun two years ago. I had read an article in the local newspaper about how disturbed teenagers would self-inflict injury to get relief from emotional pain and pressure. I didn't think much of it at the time. A week later, when Grandma launched a tirade at me about her usual shitty subjects—irresponsible, foolish, killed your mother, why can't you be like your brother?—I'd debated if I should give it a try when my eyes fell on a paper cutter on the desk in my room. I'd stared at the cutter for a long time. On an impulse, before the weaker part of my brain could react, I scraped it across the skin of my forearm. It was very painful, but it felt good.

Cutting was a way to alienate myself from all the misery, emptiness, longing, and also a way to calm myself, for however short a period of time. Since then, it had become a habit.

Glancing away, I forced the thoughts out of my mind and took a long drag of the cigarette. It was then that I first saw her. Pretty, definitely, but it was her striking eyes that caught my attention. One moment they appeared relaxed, grounded, at peace, and the next moment a wave of trauma seemed to possess them. She appeared in a bit of a hurry, frightened maybe, which came across as odd. She was alone and ambled away from the theatre. Not here for the contests then, I figured.

She couldn't have been more than seventeen, eighteen tops. She was tall and had an attractive, wholesome figure. Her black, shoulder-length hair glistened in the sunshine and, even from a distance, I was certain she was easily one of the prettiest girls I'd ever seen. Her eyes cast me a faraway glance when she crossed my line of sight, and that's when I realized I'd been gawking at her. I jerked my vision sideways but couldn't miss the narrowing of her eyes at me. And then she was gone.

Sammy and Mayur caught me off guard when they both asked me why I looked so lost. I evaded their question and said nothing. Mayur stubbed his cigarette and pulled out another one. I turned around to catch the last glimpse of the pretty girl but I couldn't find her. I couldn't fathom why she looked so hassled but I was sure she'd made her way out of the theatre in a huff. Either she was bored of the music or an emergency had forced her to leave.

My mind was jerked back to the present when I realized it was our turn to go up on stage. I quickly fumbled with the bottle and took one last gulp of the whisky.

I never thought performing under the influence of alcohol could be so effortless. One moment we were on the stage setting up our instruments and the next thunderous applause filled the theatre. The time in between seemed transient, as though it never existed, although I did remember the dynamic crowd joining us in the chorus. Then I took off to a higher octave, straining my vocal muscles while Mayur supported me on the drums and the applause intensified. It was the most unparalleled and awesome feeling—the feeling of being appreciated. Sammy did a brilliant job with the lead guitar and Mayur was terrific too. We'd performed a song with both English and Hindi lyrics, and that did it for us.

For some reason, the face of the pretty girl I'd seen outside the theatre flashed a couple of times in my mind while I was singing. It was those eyes that had entranced me—those calm, unfettered, confident eyes and then the sudden panic in them. But before I could give it any more thought, the applause had begun.

The three of us thanked the audience for being so passionate and supportive. A few of them shouted 'Once more' much to our delight.

At that moment a high-pitched scream interrupted us. Initially we thought it came from the crowd, from a well-wisher or a fan perhaps.

'Someone's been killed,' screamed a voice.

Within minutes, panic engulfed the entire theatre. The audience that once was peaceful and orderly, now leapt from their seats chaotically towards the exits. There was commotion all around. We hurriedly packed our instruments, stepped off the stage and sprinted to the nearest exit.

The hallway was splattered with the bloody footsteps of people hysterically running helter-skelter. We were later told by the frightened people around us that not one but two boys had been murdered. In the washroom. Somebody had discovered their dead bodies on the bathroom floor, which had precipitated the scream. But they were not just murdered, we learnt later.

They were castrated and their limbs mutilated. Somebody had not just murdered them but tortured them to death.

When the police arrived, none of us were allowed to leave the premises without being interrogated first. The classmates of the dead boys informed the police they were Cottonians, students of Bishop Cotton School. No one could posit a simple, logical explanation for why those two boys were chosen. Their classmates also said that the victims weren't involved in a spat in the theatre nor were they the belligerent types. Instead, they were bright students, best friends and usually kept to themselves.

The police couldn't find any evidence at the scene of the crime, the murder weapon or a motive. Finally, much to their apparent dismay, they had to let us leave, albeit one by one.

Outside, the perimeter of the theatre had been barricaded with black and yellow tape. There were more than a dozen police vans parked, sirens wailing, lights flashing. A few other vans were parked further in the distance with dish antennas on top, reporters bursting out with their fancy cameras and ancillary equipment.

Sammy, Mayur and I quietly walked down the street, away from all the commotion. We didn't want to give any statements to the reporters. I couldn't tell if it was because of fear or shock.

Two students, teenagers like us, had been murdered in cold blood not too far from where we were performing. No one saw the crime being committed or the killer. What seemed to baffle me was the fact that someone chose a crowded place like Gaiety theatre during the festival to kill those two boys, when the crime could easily have been committed afterwards, outside the theatre, maybe in a desolate area, when the boys were alone.

Something was terribly wrong. And if that wasn't weird enough, the killer actually took the time to castrate them, mutilate their limbs and risk being caught by taking so much extra time with the bodies.

Like many others, I had thrown up at the sight of the corpses swamped in a pool of their blood. Their arms were pulled out from their sockets and lay at a distance, the blood continued dripping from them; their trousers were lowered to their knees, revealing the bloodstained hollow spaces between their legs—what had been there, now lay a couple of feet away, drenched in blood.

Whoever the killer was, he definitely was a psychopath and needed to be put behind bars immediately. I wiped the sweat off my face and cast a sidelong glance at Mayur and Sammy. I could tell they were as horrified as me.

4

The First Meeting

I woke up with a start the next morning. I couldn't escape the morbid images of the mutilated bodies even during my fitful sleep. I sat upright on my bed for a few minutes, thinking about nothing in particular, still trying to accept what had happened the day before. It was only when I got out of bed did I realize that my heart was racing.

At the dining table, three startled faces greeted me. The previous night I'd just gone straight to bed, without having dinner and without telling them about the events of the evening.

'The twin grisly murders of Shimla' read the headline on the front page of the *Shimla Times*.

'What happened yesterday?' Grandma howled. 'Are you okay?'

This was the first time she'd spoken to me since her accusation five days ago.

I shook my head and took a seat. 'Two boys were killed brutally.'

'Were you there?' asked Ayush.

I nodded. 'Just a few metres away. We were performing on stage when this happened.'

'Oh god!' he said. 'You are okay, right?'

I nodded again.

'Thank god.'

'But . . . but . . .' Shweta shook her head. 'I don't understand. The article doesn't say anything. Why were they tortured like that? Did they do something wrong?'

For an answer, I gave her a feeble shrug.

'What is the world coming to?' asked Grandma. Then to me she said, 'Pramod wants to speak to you about yesterday. He has some questions.'

'Why me? I don't know anything.'

'You were there, so he wants to talk.'

I made a face. 'Grandma,' I said, 'he's the deputy police commissioner of Shimla. He can interrogate anyone he wants. Why me? Please, I don't even want to think about yesterday.'

She was applying butter on a *parantha* and dropped it on my plate. 'Okay, okay,' she said. 'Eat something first. You haven't had anything since last afternoon.'

I took a small bite. 'But please, tell him no.'

'He doesn't want to talk as a policeman, but as your uncle.'

'Grandma,' I said, and stopped chewing. 'Please. He's your brother and he's exactly like you, so nosey; he asks so many questions.'

'Sahil!' Ayush said, the index finger of his right hand jutting out. 'Watch your words!'

'Sorry, Grandma,' I said, 'but please. It was very disturbing. I don't want to relive those moments again.' I took another parantha from the casserole, rolled them both and took off to school.

* * *

At school, everyone fired questions at the three of us, students and teachers alike. I knew they all meant well but eventually it got on our nerves.

Finally, during the lunch break, when we were by ourselves, Nishant came over. He glanced at the three of us. Normally, at school, you wouldn't find Sammy with us. He sat with his girlfriend Gracy in a classroom by the window, overlooking the playground, and they strictly kept to themselves. They'd giggle and murmur amongst themselves all day; never bothered with what went on outside their bubble—there could be a fire or a bomb for all they cared. They hardly spoke to any other students and if they were absent, you wouldn't notice it. Also, if Gracy was absent, Sammy would be too; you never found one without the other.

But now Sammy was with us and Gracy sat alone, motionless, staring at the wall in front of her.

Nishant cleared his throat. I could tell from his expression that he was measuring his words. He'd seen Mayur's outburst at one of our juniors in the computer lab when he'd tried to pry earlier in the day. 'Did . . . did you actually see . . . I mean . . . the bottom . . . testicles . . . were they all out?'

'Fuck you!' Mayur had said. 'Go read the paper!'

'You guys,' said Nishant gingerly. 'Are you feeling okay now?'

Sammy shook his head slowly from side to side. Then he said, 'Man, it was like one of those American movies, *Saw* or *Hostel*—you know what I'm talking about. Ew! Still gives me the creeps.'

'True that,' I said.

'Who the hell would do a thing like that?'

Nishant's question hung in the air without any answer. I'm sure Pramod uncle and his juniors were working hard to crack the case.

The rest of the afternoon proceeded uneventfully. Post lunch, two maths classes were followed by two lectures on history. Time crawled its way through the entire afternoon and, by the end of it, I was so drained, I decided not to head back home. I convinced Mayur to join me for a practise session at Musica.

Just when the day promised to be dreary, the strangest thing happened at Musica. There were new admissions to the academy, two precisely. One was the pretty girl I had seen outside the theatre a day earlier and the second was a boy accompanying her. I could study the girl's features from up close now. She had chocolate brown eyes that burnt with a confident and happy gleam. Her hair was shoulder length, ebony coloured and glossy. I noticed the slight hint of a potbelly sticking out of her light blue jeans that she wasn't conscious of at all.

A very faint smile played at the corner of her lips when she caught me, yet again, staring at her. I shook my head quickly and turned to Mayur.

As they settled across from me, I studied the boy who'd accompanied her. He was short and gaunt, had pockmarked cheeks and his clothes loosely draped his body. He appeared uninterested as though he'd been forced to join a music course. His hair was messy and he had a centre parting, twentieth century style; his eyes were dull and tired, perhaps due to lack of sleep. However, there definitely was a boyish charm about him, the kind that could attract girls with ease. The thought of him dating the pretty girl crossed my mind twice.

Both of them looked around in apparent confusion. The room where the class was held was modest. In one corner, a drum kit had been set up; in another sat a Casio keyboard. There were a dozen chairs along the periphery of the room for the students. Rajiv would sit in the middle imparting music lessons. The funny thing about the academy was that it consisted of just this one room. All the instruments were taught in this single room. Apart from Rajiv, there was one more teacher who was equally skilled and, together, they managed all the students and instruments.

I was one of the better guitar players and invariably Rajiv would leave me with the beginners for guitar training and disappear to run errands. I had a feeling he was about to do the same by the way he was conversing on his phone. My intuition was proved right when he introduced me to the new students— Anya, the pretty girl, and Sameer, the short and gaunt boy.

'They are here to learn the guitar,' Rajiv said to me, still on the phone. 'Just tell them the basics. I'll be back soon.'

I made my way towards the new admissions, pulled up a chair and sat facing them.

'Hello,' I said, offering my hand to Anya. 'I'm Sahil.'

Her hand felt soft against my own. I faced Sameer. He had a lethargic handshake, I realized, as his limp hand pressed against mine.

'I'm not as great a guitarist as Rajiv just suggested, but I'll try to help you.'

'That'll be wonderful,' said Anya, smiling, exposing a perfect set of white teeth. A little dimple appeared on her left cheek with that smile.

I began with an explanation of the basic anatomy of a guitar—the base, neck, the six strings and the fretboard. Then I taught them how to tune it using a tuner, some basic finger exercises, the notes of the first string and stopped when it was apparent I'd been going too fast.

'So, what made you want to learn the guitar?' I asked Anya.

'I've been wanting to learn for a long time. I've just been putting it off, I guess,' she said, continuing the finger exercises with extreme difficulty, getting most of them wrong, as was usually the case with all beginners.

'You do know it's a very difficult instrument to learn.' I reached for the ring finger of her left hand and stretched it so it reached the correct fret. She had small hands with stubby fingers and well-manicured nails.

'Yeah, of course,' she said, trying hard to get her little finger in the correct position. 'But nothing comes easy in life. Isn't that so?' She smiled when she completely failed to stretch her finger, which helplessly drifted everywhere but on to the correct fret. 'This is so damn difficult!'

I returned the smile. 'Trust me, it's even more difficult than you think. I always tell everyone, "You need to have the three Ps if you want to learn this instrument."'

'What are they?' Sameer asked with an apparent lack of interest. He appeared agitated, like he wanted to get the hell out of there.

'Passion, practise and patience.'

Anya placed a lock of hair behind her ear. It was pointless; her silky hair flew back over her face the next moment. Then she said, 'I have the first one, will try for the second one and I highly doubt I'll achieve the third.'

'What about you, Sameer?'

'Honestly,' he glanced at Anya before facing me, 'I'm really not interested in this. I'm just giving her company.'

I nodded. Perhaps I wasn't wrong in assuming they were dating.

Mayur continued pounding his drums in the corner. I could feel his eyes burning a hole in my back. I was sure that with a new girl around he would want to try his luck with her.

The lesson continued for an hour. We spoke a bit, though Sameer was mostly quiet. I learnt they were from the same school and lived in the same neighbourhood in central Shimla. I told them a bit about myself too.

An hour's practise later, they stood up to leave. For homework I gave them three finger exercises to be practised for all the six strings till the eighth fret. I followed them outside and scheduled the next class. When I came back inside Mayur smiled at me. There was a hint of scorn in that smile.

'What?'

He stopped playing. 'Why do you have to make it so obvious?'

'Why do I have to make what so obvious?'

'That you like that chick.'

'Oh, somebody is jealous.'

He began pounding the drums again. Just when I was about to leave the room, he said in a tone that was supposed to sound like concern, but came off as plain jealousy, 'I'm concerned, asshole. She looks like a nice girl, that's why I am saying this. I know you are an insensitive bastard. Just make sure you don't do to her what you do to the others.'

'Do what?' I hissed.

'What you did to Mansi: fuck and forget.'

5

Hesitation

I've always hankered for a good friend. Mayur's remark stung the entire evening. After dinner, as I lay on my bed thinking about the protagonist of my story, I promised to give him a great friend. That's something I've always wanted.

Mayur didn't give a damn about what he'd said. I don't think he was concerned; he just didn't want me to date Anya. If he had his way he would screw everything that moved, without giving a damn about feelings or whatever it was that he pretended to show concern for. And, for the record, Mansi and I just kissed that evening at my home; we didn't go all the way. I couldn't when she said she was in love with me and I realized that I didn't feel the same.

Come to think of it, Mayur and I were friends but we never talked heart-to-heart with each other; superficial, over the surface, inane conversations maybe, but never about our deep, inner thoughts.

Nishant, on the other hand, was a restrained and serious person. He was a good guy, was mostly into his books, and generally kept his thoughts and desires to himself.

Ditto with Sammy. He was a person lost in his own world that consisted of Gracy and music.

I couldn't discuss anything personal with them. They didn't even know Grandma accused me of killing my parents or that I drank alone at home sometimes or that I cut myself.

Ayush, on the other hand, had loads of friends. He had at least three best friends and another dozen good friends. His girlfriend, Mehek, was another great person in his life.

Sometimes I felt jealous of him and wondered what it would be like to have friends like that—real friends, friends whom you could go up to and say just about anything without any thought, any concern and know you'd emerge lighter.

But in this world of pretence, I believe, having friends like that is a rarity.

The first thing I did the next morning was to walk over to Mansi's desk. She was startled to see me. 'Hey,' she said, 'what's up?'

I brought my hands together and let a sharp breath escape. 'Okay,' I said, 'I'm sorry, I'm really sorry that I hurt you.'

Her lips curved into a tiny smile. 'Why are you sorry?'

'I don't know . . . because . . . I . . . I don't feel that way for you.'

'I understand.'

'Really?'

She nodded. 'Really, I mean . . . why are you sorry if you don't love me? It's not your fault.'

I took a step forward. 'Thanks for understanding.'

A silence, not uncomfortable though, hung between us for a while. Then she looked up, smiled and said, 'No, thank you.'

* * *

On Wednesday, after school, I was pretty excited as I sauntered towards the academy. I was looking forward to seeing Anya.

Despite meeting her just once, I thought she was the sort of person you could have long conversations with, losing complete track of time. When we spoke for the first time, it was such an easy conversation; not forced or artificial, just easy. It didn't feel like it was the first time we were talking.

She'd caught me staring at her, like a slob, twice; she only smiled at that, not in a haughty, proud way, but in a way that suggested she appreciated me admiring her. She was definitely aware that she was pretty and had no airs about it.

When I entered the academy, Anya was inside rehearsing. Rajiv was missing again and I couldn't locate Sameer. Mayur and I were going through a bit of a cold war, so he had skipped today's class. Sammy was on a hiatus since the festival. Now, even his evenings were spent with Gracy. There were a couple of kids practising in the corner, and a lone girl was softly tapping the keys of the piano behind Anya.

'Hey there,' I said, placing my guitar on a chair in front of her.

'Hi Sahil,' Anya said, offering me her hand. I took it. 'How have you been?'

'Good,' I said. 'So . . . um . . . where's your friend?'

'Oh, Sameer. He's busy. He had some chores to do.'

'All right.' I pulled up a chair and sat down.

She demonstrated a few finger exercises I'd asked her to practise and, to my surprise, she had nearly perfected them.

'I'm impressed,' I said. 'Really!'

'I was up the whole night practising.'

I raised my brows. 'The whole night?'

'Yeah.'

'You don't sleep or what?'

She stopped her finger movement across the fretboard. Glancing at me, she seemed to hesitate a bit, before finally answering, 'I'm a very light sleeper.'

The next words were out of my mouth before I could stop them. 'That doesn't come as a surprise judging by your dreamy eyes.'

I clenched my teeth and immediately regretted what I'd said.

She gave me a cheeky look, and then smiled a subtle, graceful smile. Thankfully, she didn't think I was hitting on her.

'Are you hitting on me?' she then asked coyly.

I was taken aback. 'Do you read minds or what?'

'No, I don't. Why? Were you thinking that I was thinking that you were hitting on me?'

'No, that's what you were thinking.'

A sly smile appeared on her lips. She leaned back and studied me. 'When you said dreamy, in what context did you say it? You know dreamy can have different connotations—vague, lost in thought, soothing, gorgeous or desirable.' She paused, her expression suddenly serious. 'Gorgeous or desirable, one of the two, right?'

I shifted uncomfortably in my chair. It made a screeching sound against the floor. 'No . . . No, I . . .'

She laughed softly, her eyes twinkled. 'Don't bother answering that; it was just a joke. You should've looked at your face though—all red!'

I wagged a finger playfully at her. 'You bad, bad, girl.'

She trained her attention to the next set of finger exercises I showed her. These were a little more difficult than the first ones, I told her. Her fingers seemed comfortable now and easily reached across the fretboard, and once again I was impressed. Either she was very passionate about learning the guitar or she was very determined.

Over the next hour I taught her the notes to 'Happy Birthday' and 'Congratulations'. She was so thrilled when she managed to get the tune right—although it was extremely broken—that she threw herself at me, giving me a tight hug.

She settled back and continued playing those two tunes over and over again. My mind was busy framing the right way to ask her out.

I finally got it and gathered the strength. 'Hey Anya, I was wondering if you'd like to have a cup of coffee with me later.'

Her expression turned grim and I knew I'd made a blunder.

'I'm sorry,' she said, her face growing dark, 'but I don't drink coffee.'

'Um . . . tea, then?'

'Oh, I don't drink tea either.'

'A soft drink?'

I might have made a really contrite face, maybe a funny one, because, at that, her mouth tore open into spluttering laughter. It startled the little girl playing the piano, who turned around and, realizing nothing significant was happening, turned back again.

'I'm sorry,' she said, amidst a fit of giggles. 'I was just kidding. I'd love that but I'm busy with Sameer today.'

I gave her an understanding nod, first relieved that I didn't annoy her, then annoyed that she was busy with Sameer! So were they a couple? Judging by the fact that she'd turned down my offer for him, it seemed likely.

'By the way,' she said, 'were you asking me out?'

She got me again. I grew a little nervous.

'Relax,' she said. 'Girls like it when they are asked out. You should have seen your face though. You know sometimes I wonder why all of us hesitate so much before conveying our feelings. We try to convey them through little codes, scrambled messages, we wait for others to go first, we wrap up our true feelings inside boxes of pride and ego and vanity.' She stopped and narrowed her eyes. 'I believe, just say what you feel. Let your heart do the talking. The world will be a better place then.'

'Okay,' I said, all perked up, holding out my hand, 'so Anya . . .?'

She took my hand. 'Sarin. Anya Sarin.'

'Anya Sarin, I'd really, really like to take you out.'

She let out a pretty giggle and I smiled with her. 'Better,' she said, 'much better. Way to go, but sorry for today.'

The smile drained from my face. 'All this bluster for nothing?'

'This is your first time asking out a girl, right?'

'Only the fifth time,' I muttered under my breath.

'Sorry, what?'

'Yeah, first.'

'I thought so,' she said, rising from her chair. 'Okay, so dumbo, since this is your first time, I won't disappoint you. Where are you taking me?'

6

The First Date

We walked a few hundred metres down Mall Road, before settling on a local café overlooking the hills. The café was on the first floor and, after ordering coffee and muffins, we sat on the wicker chairs placed on the narrow balcony. Although it was usually warm in the month of August, it was a bit cool today owing to the northerly winds. The ubiquitous hills of Shimla were dotted with houses and plantations, doling out a serene setting for us to gaze at.

The café was moderately occupied for a Wednesday evening and the streets below us were relatively quiet. I normally do not notice much around me and that's when I realized that I felt a bit ill at ease with her at the café. I couldn't say the same for her. It was the easy way she smiled at me whenever our eyes met that made her appear quite in control of herself.

The coffee arrived with the muffins. Anya pointed out to the waiter that we'd ordered a chocolate muffin and not the raspberry one that he had got us. The waiter apologized and quickly exchanged it. She nibbled at the muffin before sipping her coffee.

'So you haven't told me much about yourself,' she said, white foam from the coffee smudging her lips.

'What do you want to know?' I asked, adding sugar to my coffee.

'All I know is that you are a great guitarist. So I guess pretty much everything else.'

I smiled. 'I didn't realize you were the prying type.'

She made a face. 'I'm not. I'm just generally interested.'

'I'm kidding,' I said, moving my chair back a few inches to allow for some legroom. 'Okay, let's see. Where do I begin?'

It's not that I was averse to the idea of sharing my life with others; I just hadn't done it before. Ever. But with Anya this wasn't the case. For one, she was a very good listener; it appeared as though she really cared about what I said, with her eyes fixed on me and the subtle variations in her expressions evoking concern, sadness, sometimes anger. Secondly, she didn't jump to unbidden conclusions. One thing led to another and before I realized it, I'd told her everything about my pathetic existence.

I also told her about the book I was working on and she was fascinated by it.

'Wow!' She leaned forward. 'You're writing a book. That is so cool! What inspired you to write one?'

I thought for a few seconds and shook my head when I couldn't think of the inspiration. 'I guess it was boredom, coupled with angst. What is there to do in this world, anyway? It's so bloody boring. I think it's better to live in a fictional world than a real one.'

'Do you really think so?'

'I just told you about my family. Grandma thinks I killed my parents; Ayush and Shweta, for all I know, feel likewise. I just can't make any true friends—'

'Wait, hold on.' She held out her hand. 'Do you really believe your grandmother thinks you killed your parents?'

I nodded.

'Are you serious?' She was scowling. 'No parent would ever think like that, you dumbo!' Then she shook her head slowly and tutted. 'You know, sometimes, you remind me of myself from a few years ago—angry, rebellious, I hated the world I was in, I thought my parents hated me. Get this: no parent can hate their child. Parental love is the most unconditional and pure form of love in this world. Have you not heard of real life stories of parents protecting their kids and being killed while doing so? Yeah, parents go that far.'

'So, what are you implying?'

'That you are an idiot.'

I waved a dismissive hand at her.

She gazed at me for some time, slowly sipping her coffee.

'What?' I asked, turning back to her, her gaze still steady on me.

'Um . . . why do you wear full-sleeved shirts in the summer?'

'I like them. They suit me.'

'Would you mind rolling up your sleeves for me,' she said. 'I find it very distracting.'

'Why?'

'Because I'm telling you to.'

I looked at her carefully, then did as told. It struck me as a pleasant surprise the authority she asserted over me.

'What are those scars?'

I waved another dismissive hand. 'Oh, you know, there is this cat in my society. She . . . she leaps on me from time to time.'

'You cut yourself, don't you?' Her look was stern, unwavering.

For a while both of us said nothing.

'How'd you know?' I finally asked, my voice low and shaky.

She laid her cup on the round table in front of us and bent down to slowly roll the jeans of her left leg up till the knee. She thrust her leg out and I saw them there. Scars. A lot of them on the calf.

I scrunched up my nose. 'Oh, my god! You do that, too!'

A weak smile, one that expressed sadness, slowly lit up her face. She nodded. 'Yes . . . I mean I used to. Not any more.' She lowered her jeans and settled back. 'Now I wonder why I did that to myself.'

'To find relief, of course,' I spoke instantly. 'From strain, sadness, anger, whatever.'

She shook her head. 'I don't think so. It did nothing. It just became a habit, a very awful habit.' She picked up the muffin and absently bit into it. 'Like I said, sometimes you remind me of what I was like a couple of years ago. But I have matured now, everybody does . . .' She trailed off and looked away.

I took a long sip. 'So what brought about the change in you?'

'I met some good people along the way,' she said. 'They changed my perception.'

'Like Sameer?'

'Like Sameer,' she replied. 'Ironically, you know he . . . he used to . . . cut himself, too.'

'Really? Sameer? He doesn't look like the sort who'd do that.'

She cleared her throat. 'I could say the same about you.'

'You like screwing with me, don't you?'

'I can't say no.'

A plastic football rolled over to her feet from her right. A small girl, with pink cheeks and cat-like eyes, called out for the ball. Anya picked it up, dodged the little girl a few times and finally handed it over. She kissed the little girl and got a kiss in return.

When she looked back at me her eyes shone. 'I think there's a beautiful world out there. We just need the right eyes to see it.'

'More muffins?' I asked.

She shook her head. 'You know, I think you've got a great life.'

'My parents are dead, remember? I didn't even get a chance to see them.'

'Fine, I agree,' she said. 'But we all have something that others around us don't have. The problem with the world is not only do we not realize that, but we always see what others have and we don't.'

'Okay? So what do I have that others don't?'

'At least you've got family, a home. And you are such a good-looking guy!' she said, her eyes shining again. 'I mean you are blessed with great height, Tom Cruise-like hair drooping over your forehead, a sharp nose, sort of chiselled features. I really like that little scar on your left eyebrow. You play the guitar, you are writing a book, you're a talented guy. I'm not trying to flatter you but I think you're so cool . . . and oh look, you're blushing now like a little girl.'

'I'm not blushing.'

'Yes, you are,' she said, with a sly smile. 'My point being, although this might sound clichéd, think about the good things in your life. Count your blessings.'

After taking a deep breath I said, 'Okay, fine.' I took a last sip of the coffee. 'And now, it's time for you to spill the beans. I have told you so many things I wouldn't discuss with my so-called best friends.'

She raked her hand through her hair and tucked a few strands behind her ear. It was pointless—her beautiful hair was back, framing her pretty face. 'There's really nothing much going on in my life that'll interest you.'

'Come on,' I said. 'Either you tell me or I'll ask questions.'

'Shoot.'

I perked up and crossed my right leg over the left. 'Okay, so this is going to be interesting. I'll start with an easy one. How many siblings do you have?'

'None.'

'Oh, single child, wow. So you must be the apple of your parents' eyes—loved and spoilt by them.'

Weeks later, whenever I recalled this day, I always regretted making that statement.

'Um . . . actually . . .' There was a quiver in her voice. 'They kind of hate me.' She forced a smile but it disappeared as soon as it came.

It occurred to me that I'd pressed the wrong button. This was the first time I realized Anya had a sad bone in her too.

'I am so sorry,' I said, genuinely apologetic. 'But why? You seem like a great girl.'

She shook her head vigorously. 'I'm not.' She continued shaking her head. 'Really, I'm not. I've been a very bad daughter.'

'It's okay.' My hand reached out to take her hand and I gently squeezed it. 'It's not your fault, trust me. It's the parents; they never understand us. All of us have the same problem.'

'It's not the same problem!' she said. 'We haven't even talked in the last six months! They just hate me. They have . . . they have abandoned me.'

I could see her hands curl into tight fists and it appeared as if she was trying very hard not to allow her tears, which stood right at the edge of her eyes, to run free.

'Then, where do you stay, with whom, I mean?'

She was staring at the floor. 'My . . . my uncle,' she said, hesitating, still staring at the ground.

Suddenly she shook her head, wiped her eyes and her lips curled into a forced smile. 'Just let it be; it's a part of me I don't like sharing with anyone. You can call it my dark side.'

'Big deal,' I said. 'Everyone has a dark side. Trust me I have hundreds of them.'

'So, how far have you reached with your book?'

'Don't change the topic. It's still your turn.'

She reached for her cup and, realizing it was empty, put it back down.

'Another one?'

She nodded.

I ordered two more cups at the counter and when I returned, her cheerful demeanour was back.

'So this Sameer, he's your boyfriend, right?' I said, settling back in my chair.

'What?' She smiled again, only this time it wasn't forced. 'Are you serious? Of course not! We're just good friends.'

'Really?'

'Really.'

I studied her and somehow figured out she wasn't lying. A frisson of excitement shot through me. We sipped our coffees quietly for a couple of minutes and that's when I remembered that day at the Gaiety theatre.

'Hey Anya, you were there at the theatre, right, on the second day of the Shimla festival?'

'Yes.'

'Was there something wrong? I was looking at you when you exited the theatre; you kind of looked worried or frightened or something, in a hurry perhaps. What happened?'

'N-nothing, I was . . . um . . . it was an emergency. My uncle had called, somebody in the neighbourhood, you know . . .' She shrugged.

'Oh, okay, everything all right?'

'Yeah, yeah, all good.'

'You know, I still can't get over what happened that day.'

'Me too.' She fumbled with her cup and stood up. 'Guess we should be leaving now. It's pretty late.'

'You don't want to finish your coffee?'

'No . . . no, I just realized I'm getting late.'

'Um . . . sure, okay.'

7

Love

When I reached home it was past eight; way beyond my deadline of seven. Grandma opened the door, her expression unwelcoming.

I had taken only a couple of steps, when I heard the door click and Grandma call my name.

'Yeah?' I turned round.

She took a step towards me, her face wrinkled in a frown. 'Did I not tell you to come home early after school? I had to collect my medicines from the pharmacy.'

'Sorry Grandma, but I told you I couldn't have missed my guitar class.'

Her frown deepened. 'So, what were you doing after your class?'

'I was with a friend.' Looking at her grouchy expression I added, 'Why didn't you take Ayush?'

She followed me into the dining room. 'Ayush was busy with his college assignments. He has important things to do, unlike you.'

I gritted my teeth and said, 'Not again! Please! When will you stop comparing me to him?' I stomped towards my room.

The television had nothing exciting to offer. I flipped over to a local news channel. The police were still investigating the twin murders at the Gaiety theatre. They were trying to find a match for the fingerprints and DNA sample they had found at the murder site. So far they had nothing.

I switched the television off after ten minutes, wrote for an hour and then dozed off.

The next few weeks passed by in a blur. School was boring but it was the thrill of guitar class afterwards and the meetings with Anya that kept me going. Anya was definitely improving with the guitar. She could already play some of the tunes I had taught her, and was ready to learn the chords and songs.

Sometimes after guitar class we'd go for long walks along the Ridge or drop in at a nearby café. Although Sameer did come to class once in a while, he never accompanied us after. He definitely wasn't Anya's boyfriend and I was happy about that.

Sameer had large dark circles under his eyes and he always appeared exhausted. When I asked him, he told me he couldn't sleep much. He was a quiet person and kept to himself. I appreciated that about him as it gave Anya and me a chance to become closer. They were family friends, I learnt, and both lived with Anya's uncle in the same house. Like Anya, Sameer wasn't in touch with his parents.

The first Monday of September, we skipped our guitar class and went to watch *Dhoom 3* at Ritz Cinema on Mall Road. When we returned to the Ridge, the sun was slowly disappearing from our part of the world.

'Look,' Anya said, nodding towards the retreating sun behind the hills, birds gliding past it. 'Isn't that the most beautiful sight in the world?'

The sky was a kaleidoscope of colours, variations of pink and purple dominating it. The sun, having lost its vigour, appeared to be an orange ball suspended in the sky.

'What's so beautiful about that?' I asked. 'It's an everyday sight.'

She continued gazing at the sky in admiration. Then she turned to me. 'Isn't that odd?' she said. 'Just because it's an everyday sight we don't appreciate it.'

'So?'

'Imagine if a blind person could see just for a couple of minutes. How would he feel about this sight?'

* * *

The next Friday we went out for a coffee after our guitar class to the same café where we had our first date. We sat in the same chairs on the balcony overlooking the mountains in the distance. A cool wind blew from the north. Anya was sitting in its direction. Her hair flew all over her face and she tried her best to put it in place. She couldn't. The final effect was stunning.

'Wow!' she said. 'Awesome, isn't it?'

'What's awesome?'

'Everything,' she said. 'The breeze, the surroundings, the coffee.' Then she closed her eyes, her head titled slightly backwards, and a smile slowly spread across her face. 'Everything,' she said again. She opened her eyes and went on, 'Don't you think so? And you say there is nothing to do in this world.'

I gave her a little shrug.

'It's good to be alive,' she said.

I shook my head. 'I don't think so.'

'That's why I call you a dumbo,' she said. 'My dumbo.' Then she grinned in a big, hearty grin, her dimple making an appearance.

I smiled back. The 'my' in 'my dumbo' felt good to hear.

Anya was a happy person, a very happy one. She loved her life. And somehow when I was with her, life didn't feel that bad after all.

It was somewhere in the third week of September that it first occurred to me that I was slowly but surely falling in love with Anya.

8

The Third Murder

On the last Friday of September, a school picnic had been scheduled to the Shimla State Museum, Christ Church and Jakhoo Hill, which was a two-kilometre drive from Shimla.

I wasn't thrilled about the idea as Mondays, Wednesdays and Fridays were the days for my guitar classes, and also the only days I met Anya. We weren't close enough yet to meet outside of those three days. There was no doubt that the little excursion would ensure I wouldn't be back by the scheduled time of the class and I'd lose the opportunity to meet her that day. I would only be able to meet her on the next Monday.

On Wednesday evening, after guitar class, as we made our way out, I wondered if I should ask her out for coffee again as it would be another five days before I would see her next. I decided I should. I was so sure she'd say yes when suddenly her expression took on a frantic edge.

'No, not today,' she said.

'I'll only see you five days later then.' I told her about the picnic.

She appeared tense and it was if she was desperately trying to figure out something. With her eyes shut, she rubbed her temples; her other hand was shaking nervously. She was trying to think but I got the feeling it wasn't about our coffee date.

A minute later she turned to me, her eyes elsewhere. 'I've got to go,' she finally said.

Before I could ask where, she was already halfway down the road, sprinting past people and jostling them out of her way. I was amazed by her speed.

I reached home at seven, after my usual few hours of loitering in the streets and parks of Shimla. My family sat glued to the television, watching the evening news.

Ayush looked over his shoulder at me. 'Another murder!'

Then Grandma said, 'Where were you, Sahil? We were worried.'

'And the same modus operandi,' Ayush finished.

'What are you talking about?' I asked. Shweta scooted over and I plonked down beside her on the sofa.

'Please increase the volume,' I said.

'. . . another tragic turn of events. Another man was found brutally murdered near Preet Apartments in Naldehra. Sources have said that the police are investigating if it is the same killer who had, last month, murdered two sixteen-year-old Bishop Cotton School students at the Gaiety theatre. Today's victim was also found castrated and his limbs mutilated. The police have identified the victim. His name was Harish and he was twenty five years old. The police are trying to put the pieces together and establish a link between the murders. They believe it will be crucial to nab the killer who has been absconding since last month. Now we take you live to the site where local correspondent Nisha will provide further updates. Nisha . . .'

Ayush muted the TV.

'Hey,' I said. 'I was watching that.'

'It's nothing,' Shweta said. 'They are showing the same pictures—blood on the walls and the floor, a cluster of policemen and worried onlookers. It's gory.'

'Why did you not speak to Pramod that day after the first murder?' said Grandma. 'I talked to him today. He was saying it would have been helpful. Maybe you could have given him some clues.'

I glanced at the three of them helplessly. 'There was nothing,' I said. 'I was inside the hall performing when it happened. I was as clueless as all the others there.'

'Still,' she went on, 'Pramod was saying had you spoken to him, maybe it could have averted today's murder.'

I rose in exasperation. 'Okay, now go on,' I said. 'Go on and blame me for these murders as well!'

'No,' said Shweta. 'that's not what she is implying, she's just . . .'

I turned and wagged a finger at her. 'You shut up!' I was yelling now. 'I'm not talking to you!'

I don't know when it happened but suddenly I felt a sharp pain on my cheeks. Ayush had risen and planted two slaps across my face.

'This is no way to talk to your sister!' he barked.

Infuriated, I grabbed him by his collar, shook him a few times before pushing him hard. He lost his balance and crashed onto the sofa. His right leg struck the edge of the glass centre-table and he grimaced. He cradled his shin, his teeth clenched and he appeared in deep pain.

With an agility that belied her age, Grandma was in front of me in a flash. She slapped me. 'Is this is any way to behave?' she screamed. 'You've got no respect for your elder brother!' Then she and Shweta were at Ayush's side comforting him.

I stood there shaking my head. 'I hate you,' I cried. 'I hate you all!'

I needed to be lost. In my room I took out the bottle of Old Monk from under the mattress and gulped it down in quick sips till it burned my throat. This shouldn't have happened. I didn't deserve this. I wish mom and dad were alive; they would have taken my side, and truly and unconditionally loved me. I missed them so much.

I picked up the photo frame from my bedside table and stared at it. It was an old picture of my parents smiling into the camera, the Taj Mahal in the background and a young Ayush crawling on the ground beneath them. They looked so happy. I ran my hand over the photo. My mother was beautiful. She would have loved me so much. She would have loved the songs I wrote and would be so excited about the book I was writing. My father would have never hit me. He had such an adorable and guileless face. The photograph became blurry and I slowly wiped away the tears that had fallen on the frame.

I must have forgotten to bolt the door because Ayush stood at the threshold a few minutes later and slowly made his way in. He was limping and peering down at me.

'What?' I said. His eyes were on the bottle in my hand. 'Yes, I drink. Go tell Grandma that. I don't care!'

'Look, I'm sorry,' he said. 'I shouldn't have slapped you.'

I took a deep breath. 'You know,' I said, 'I could have slapped you back. I just pushed you, I didn't mean to . . .' I pointed towards his leg on the bed.

'I know,' he said, sitting down, his face contorting as he rested his leg.

'And look what Grandma did.' I shook my head. I was agitated.

'I'm sorry for her too,' he said. 'But I've told you before, Shweta is our only sister. Don't talk to her like that.'

'Why? She was taking Grandma's side. And you heard what Grandma said.'

'I know, but this is Shweta's house,' he said. 'We owe it to her father. Rakesh uncle treats us like his own children. He's given us everything.'

I continued drinking.

'Why the hell does Grandma always blame me for everything?'

He rested his large hand on my shoulder. 'She doesn't,' he said. 'Although I agree it comes across like that. She has a bad mouth sometimes, but her heart is clean and it beats only for the three of us. You've got to understand she's old, she's lived her life. That's the way she is, she can't change now.' He paused and I took another sip. 'But you're young, you can change and try and accept that flaw of hers. All of us have flaws.'

I wiped my mouth. 'You know what, just leave me alone. You'll always take her side.'

'No Sahil—'

'No, I get it. It's always my fault. Now please, leave!'

'Sahil, listen,' he said, slowly getting up. 'There's no point holding grudges. They make life difficult. Learn to forgive, man, learn to let go.'

'I said out of my room. NOW!'

As he hobbled out, I picked up a William Faulkner book from my collection—his longest. The longer the book, the longer you spent in another world.

And that's exactly what I wanted now.

9

The School Picnic

On Friday morning our classroom resembled a fish market. It was the day of the picnic. We'd chucked our school uniforms and, instead, we were wearing our favourite casual clothes. I was goofing around at the back of the class with Nishant and Mayur. Sammy and his girlfriend Gracy, as usual, sat in the front, whispering and giggling among themselves, oblivious to their surroundings.

I was hoping the picnic would end as scheduled and that might leave me with enough time for my guitar class and Anya. I was itching to ask her about Wednesday and what the whole rush was about when Geetika ma'am, our English teacher, walked in. She was extremely obese with red, plump cheeks and I always wondered how she managed to squeeze her body through the narrow doorway. She greeted us and informed us that it would take another hour for the transportation to arrive and then promptly left the class, but not without warning us to keep silent.

When she left we adhered to her advice for a full minute. Mayur was the first to break the silence.

'It's got to be Pallavi,' he said, leering at her to his left.

Pallavi was an auburn-haired girl who'd migrated from Canada last year. She was extremely fair and had a Canadian accent. Boys used the word 'fast' to describe her and girls called her 'bitchy'.

'Before the end of this year, I'll be a man,' he finished. Then he straightened his back, cocked his head to one side, moved his jaw animatedly and his hands went in his pockets; his eyes continued burning a hole in Pallavi's bosom.

Nishant chuckled. 'Look at his style,' he told me.

'Stop with those lewd stares, Mayur,' I said. 'Just go and talk to her, be nice and polite; ask her how she's doing.'

He turned to me, his jaw still moving. 'I don't care how she's doing. I just want to take her to bed. She's the easiest target.'

I shook my head. 'That's not the right way, man. Show some respect.'

'Oooh respect,' he imitated. 'As though you have something else in mind with Anya.'

I didn't deign to answer that.

'What do you think, Nishant?' Mayur asked him.

'What do I think about what?'

'About girls.'

Nishant smiled and adjusted his glasses. 'I don't know,' he said. 'I'd rather study hard for the next five years, get a good job first and then think about them. They are a waste of time and money anyway.'

Mayur arched his brow. 'Yeah, well, and grapes are sour.' He winked, then turned to me. 'So . . . Anya, huh?'

'Anya what?'

The look he gave me then—half sneering, half insinuating— was so annoying I had to snap my face away from him.

'Aren't you and Anya a couple?'

'No,' I said. 'We're not.'

Mayur gave Nishant one of his trademark 'Are we really his friends?' look.

'Let it be, Mayur,' Nishant said. 'If he doesn't want to talk about it, it's okay.'

'No, really,' I said to Nishant. 'We are not a couple.'

'But you like her, don't you?' Mayur prodded.

'Who doesn't like a pretty girl?'

Both of them nodded.

'So tell me about this girl,' Nishant said. 'This is your third girl in the last four months, right?'

I nodded.

He continued. 'No, I actually want to know about this girl because her name brings that smile, that spark, to your face, which I have never seen with your ex-girlfriends. What is so special about her? Mayur tells me even during your music class you can hardly keep your eyes off her face.'

I glanced at Mayur and punched him playfully. 'You can't keep anything to yourself, can you?'

So I told them everything about her—that she was pretty, responsive, smart and blah, blah, blah. Of all the adjectives that I used for her I surprised myself by including 'strange' in that description.

* * *

The Shimla State Museum had nothing exciting to offer. It was Shimla within Shimla. It had succeeded in firmly ensconcing the cultural heritage of the city with collections of miniature Pahari paintings, sculptures, bronzes, wood-carvings, and also costumes, textiles and jewellery from the region. Outright boring. Ditto for Christ Church. I wouldn't deny this—it had an absolutely majestic appearance from the inside, but it was not a good choice for a school picnic. I don't know what goes on in the minds of teachers when deciding on a place for a picnic.

I couldn't say the same for Jakhoo Hill. I'd been there plenty of times and it was a wonderful place to visit.

'Looks like you are going to miss Anya today,' Mayur said, casting me a sidelong glance.

We'd been trekking up the hill amidst the dense deodar forest for about an hour, on our way to the Hanuman temple. Although it was just two kilometres from the Ridge, where our school bus was parked, the walk seemed tiring. Our teachers, though, had hired ponies for the ride and had already reached the top.

'Yeah, looks like it.'

Although a Shimlaite, I wasn't used to the steep terrain. I had a family history of asthma and my air-stricken lungs found the climb difficult. I stopped in my tracks, grabbed the bottle of water from Nishant and took a big sip. I tried relaxing and took in the surroundings. Sunlight was trapped between the deodar trees but peeked at us from time to time when a slight wind rustled the leaves. I took another sip. Much ahead of us, our classmates continued the climb and we trailed them by at least fifteen minutes.

'Okay, let's move,' I said.

Although steep and tiresome, the climb is rewarding once you get to the top. The Hanuman temple at the top of the hill was the highest point in town and offered fine views of the surrounding valleys, peaks and of Shimla itself.

A couple of hundred metres later, the steps that led towards the temple were visible. Our classmates were out of sight and I figured they were done with the temple and were hanging around. Nishant and Mayur were a few metres ahead of me and were busy talking. I walked slowly behind them, taking in the crunch of the leaves beneath my feet.

'Hey,' Nishant said, looking behind his shoulder at me and both of them stopped. 'We were talking about that murder that happened day before yesterday.'

'What about it?' I reached them.

'According to last evening's news,' said Mayur, 'it is the same killer. The one from the theatre. The fingerprints, or whatever, matched.'

We continued the walk together.

'It doesn't surprise me,' I said. 'It had to be the same psychopath bastard.'

'What's more,' Mayur went on, 'the victims weren't related. They were complete strangers. So now he's just killing people randomly?'

'What did your uncle say?' Nishant asked.

'Who? Pramod Uncle?' I asked. Nishant nodded. 'I didn't speak to him, Grandma did. They're still investigating.'

'Why don't you speak to him?' questioned Nishant. 'You'd get first-hand information, even before the news channels. Mayur—' He turned to him. 'You could probably impress the girls then.'

'I like the sound of that,' Mayur said.

They were both looking at me now.

'No!' I said. 'Pramod Uncle is exactly like Grandma. He wanted to speak to me after the first set of murders. I'll tell you exactly how the conversation would have played out: "Did you happen to see anything out of place that day?"

'"No, Uncle."

'"Anything at all?"

'"No, Uncle."

'"What were you doing there?"

'"I was participating in a music contest."

'"Oh, you still wasting your time on music?"

'"No, Uncle. I love music."

'"You should study. Like your brother."

'"Sure, Uncle."

'"So you didn't see anything that could be of help?"

'"No, Uncle."

'"Hmm . . ."

'"Any other questions, Uncle?"

'"No, but study, huh, study! Go!"'

Both of them were in peals of laughter by the end.

'Oh, you're good,' Nishant said, guffawing. 'You should be a stand-up comedian, man, with your funny imitations and expressions.'

A giggle escaped me. 'Trust me, he can be more annoying than Grandma sometimes.'

Mayur was holding his stomach, the sound of his laughter coming out in quick, staccato bursts.

After the hysteria had passed, I wished Anya had been around. We'd have talked along the way and I would have taken some pictures with her.

Suddenly, ahead of me, I saw Anya. I could have asked for a million things more and got them all today, I thought. She was sitting on the pavement next to the steps that led to the temple. Sameer was standing next to her, and there was another boy and a girl with them. I quickened my pace and trotted towards them. Anya smiled when she saw me approaching and I couldn't have been more pleased.

'Hey, what are you up to?' Mayur bellowed from behind me when I overtook him, brushing his shoulders in my haste.

'Anya,' I said to Mayur, looking over my shoulder.

He nodded and waved at her. Anya reciprocated and walked towards me.

'Hey, nice to see you!' I took a deep breath. Then another one. 'What are you doing here?'

'Nothing,' she said, smiling, appearing pleased to see me. 'Just hanging out with a few friends.' She glanced over her shoulder. 'Come, I'll introduce you to them.'

I followed her. Sameer offered a handshake and I couldn't miss his bloodshot eyes. He definitely hadn't slept since the last time I saw him.

'How are you doing?' he asked.

I said I was doing fine, but didn't ask him the same question.

'Sahil, this is Monica and that's Aditya. Monica, Aditya, my friend Sahil.'

A couple of handshakes and hellos later, I sat with them on the pavement.

Aditya was tall and muscular, had short, cropped hair, a sharp nose and sparse eyebrows that somehow made his eyes look bigger than they actually were. It was the flitting way in which they moved that told me he was an impatient guy or, perhaps, a very observant one.

Monica was a tiny, cute-looking girl with jet black hair pulled back tightly in a ponytail. She was no more than five feet tall but what she lacked in her height she more than made up for with her tongue.

'So Sahil,' she said, 'where do you live?' Her hands were deep inside the pockets of her jeans and she stood with one leg thrust out.

'Krishna Nagar.'

'Which school do you go to?'

'DAV Public School,' I answered.

She nodded for a second. Then, 'So what are your hobbies?'

'I like music, I like books, in fact I'm—'

'Do you have any girlfriends?'

I looked at Anya; she was smiling, slowly shaking her head from side to side.

'No Monica,' I said. 'I don't have a girlfriend.' I looked at Anya again. 'At least not yet.'

'So how many people are there in your family?'

I gave her the answer. She fired a few more questions, one after the other, almost every time without waiting for me to complete my answer. She was definitely a firebrand.

Finally, while I was answering her question about books and why I liked them so much, Aditya cleared his throat.

'Ever been to Samra, Sahil?' His question was sudden, without any preamble, his gaze was intense, fixed and didn't waver.

'I . . . I . . .' I looked at Anya. 'No. Where is it?'

'About two hundred kilometres north of Shimla, near Kullu valley.'

'No, never been there. Why do you ask?'

He held his icy gaze. It was malicious. His eyebrows had converged and the skin of his forehead crinkled above them.

'You sure?' he questioned, anger creeping into his voice now. 'Think again.'

'Yes,' I said. 'I'm damn sure. Why are you asking me this?'

He continued studying me in a threatening manner. I glanced at Monica, who avoided eye contact, then Anya, who hastily withdrew her gaze from mine. Finally, I looked at Sameer. He was looking somewhere else. It was as if he weren't even there, as if he didn't even exist.

I turned back to Aditya. Suddenly, he flashed me a smile, baring his teeth. He came forward and patted my shoulder. 'No,' he said, smiling a little more now. 'I was just curious. You look familiar. I thought I'd seen you there last month.'

I shook my head. 'No, never been there.'

Suddenly, the tension in the air vanished and all of us smiled, except Sameer who didn't even look our way. He was lost.

'Okay, guys,' Aditya said. 'We'll leave now.'

I asked Anya to stay a little while longer. She darted a look in Aditya's direction before saying yes. It evoked a long 'Oooh' from Monica. She nudged Anya and winked at me.

'So, do you want to walk and talk?' Anya asked, a slight smile playing at the edge of her lips.

'Of course,' I said.

10

No Drugs, No Cutting

'What the hell was that all about?'

The question was out of my mouth before I even realized it. I turned around and was relieved that the three of them were out of earshot.

'What?' asked Anya.

'That guy, Aditya,' I said. 'Why was he asking me that question in such a . . . scary . . . you know . . . intimidating sort of manner?'

'He said he thought he'd seen you there.'

'Okay,' I said, 'but it was as if I'd done something wrong.'

Anya dismissed me with a slight wave of her hand. We started walking downhill towards a snack shop in the distance.

'He is like that, though,' she said. 'You know, strong and forbidding. He can scare people.'

'He didn't scare me,' I said immediately, my chest tightening. 'Even though he tried to.'

'Ha, ha,' she said. 'Did I awaken the man in you?'

'Yeah, whatever.'

As we continued walking downhill, I was very aware of my school mates dispersed all over the hill. The birds were chirping and the dense Himalayan trees reaching the sky. Anya was looking sensational in a pair of beige trousers and a blue T-shirt that fit her well. Her beautiful hair was loose and a few strands blew in the wind like the waves of an ocean. I slowed down a little, came up behind her and sniffed the air around her hair. It smelled like strawberries and vanilla and fruit cake.

'Hey,' said Anya, looking over her shoulder. 'Where are you? You walk like a tortoise.'

I quickened my pace and joined her side, the fragrance of her hair still lingering in my nostrils.

We reached the snack shop. It was a makeshift hut with corrugated amber-green plastic sheeting overhead, supported by bamboo sticks that had been put up in a slapdash manner for support. There were a dozen chairs and a few tables sprawled outside, a menu scribbled on a blackboard with white chalk and a small counter in front for placing orders.

Anya and I took a seat on the wooden chairs that were surprisingly comfortable.

'So what'll you have?' I asked her.

She cast a cursory glance at the menu. 'A chicken sandwich, perhaps.'

'Right. In a minute.'

I returned with two cans of Coke, two chicken sandwiches and a pack of wafers.

'You know,' she said, over the crunching sound of wafers in her mouth, 'I'd like to tell you something.'

I gave her the cue.

'No, actually, I want to ask you something.'

'Go ahead.'

'Why do you think we are here?' She stroked a finger between us. 'You and me?'

It took a moment for the question to register. Did she mean it literally, like why were we here in this hut, or as a metaphor of us being together? At the prospect of the latter option I felt a spark flutter inside. 'I don't think I understand your question completely.'

'Okay, forget it, dumbo,' she said, sipping her Coke now. 'I'll tell you.' She picked up a sandwich, took a small bite and laid it down. She wiped the mayonnaise from her lips and caught my gaze. 'But first stop staring like an owl while I eat. It distracts me.'

A snort of laughter rose from me.

She smiled back, took another sip and then said, 'I believe everyone who comes into our lives comes for a reason.'

'So, you and I, what might that be?'

'We met so I could tell you life is a gift. Enjoy it while it lasts. You never know what's waiting on the other side.'

'Hell, you mean?'

'That's one option,' she said, 'yes.'

I grabbed the wafers packet from her hand and took some. After forcing a stilted smile, I asked, 'How old are you?'

'Eighteen.'

'So then why do you sound like a fifty-year-old woman who's seen everything, done everything?'

'Because,' she said, 'I've seen everything, done everything.'

'Really?' I questioned, narrowing my eyes. 'So what's your story?'

She leaned forward and snatched the wafers packet from my hand. 'Nothing much,' she said, popping one in her mouth. 'Yours is more interesting. There is so much scope for improvement.'

I shook my head. 'I don't think so.' I took the last few bites of the sandwich and drank some Coke. 'My family sucks. Do you know that day before yesterday there was so much of commotion in my house. Ayush hit me, then I hit him, then Grandma hit me and then . . . then . . . I can't forget the hatred, this deep-seated hatred the three of them had in their eyes . . .'

Suddenly I stopped. My heart felt heavy and, much to my chagrin, my eyes filled with tears. I was doing okay, feeling nothing, but, out of nowhere, this wave of emptiness and grief took over and swept me along. I sniffed and my hand reached out to wipe my eyes.

Anya was at the edge of her seat now squeezing my hand. Her eyes held nothing but sympathy, her lips curled. 'Go on,' she said. 'I'm listening.'

'I don't know,' I said, feeling embarrassed at my cracking voice. 'I'm not as bad a guy as I'm made out to be.'

'You're a good guy, Sahil.' She squeezed my hand some more.

'Then why do they hate me?'

'They don't.' She shook her head. 'They don't. Sometimes situations are bad, not the people placed in them. Everything's going to be okay.'

I didn't want to hear that everything would be okay because I didn't believe it. You couldn't tell someone to love you back. You couldn't tell life to make everything okay. Life, anyway, had never been on my side.

'I want an escape,' I said, more to myself than to her. 'Drugs maybe, they can help.'

She let go of my hand and anger took over from sympathy. 'Now where would you get a dumb idea like that?'

'It's true. Drugs help. They mess with your nervous system or something and make you forget things.'

'Sahil,' she said, anger now fully entrenched in her voice. 'We're not talking about this. Look at me. "Look at me," I said.' She shook my hands. When I looked at her she continued, 'Promise me you'll never do that. I want you to promise me.'

'Why? What is wrong with it?'

'Sahil, you donkey,' she said. 'Don't look for temporary fixes. It'll look like they're helping you in the beginning, but later you're going to regret it so much and there'll be no going back, trust me.'

'You say this as if you have experience.'

'Yeah,' she said, nodding. 'I have experience. Now promise me, please.'

'You're joking about your experience, right?'

'Whatever,' she said. 'You promise me now. No drugs, ever!'

I promised.

'And, by the way, are you still cutting yourself?'

'Not since the day you found out.'

She smiled. 'Good. So, promise me no more cutting as well. Don't ruin your life.'

I made her another promise.

'Now, coming back to your family,' she said, sitting back in her chair. 'Have you ever tried to resolve your issues with them? Have you ever tried to talk it out?'

'What is there to talk about?'

'Exactly my point,' she said. 'You don't have a right to complain about any damn thing unless you have done everything in your power to resolve it first.'

I slowly shook my head.

She continued, 'Go talk to them. Maybe your grandma and your siblings are just worried about you. Maybe behind all that that anger and those rebukes hide a great deal of love and concern.'

There was a deafening noise of thunder, like that of a roar from a tiger nearby, and instinctively our heads flew up. The sky had taken on a dark, ominous appearance, diminishing the light from the sun which was nowhere to be seen.

'Oh, it's going to rain,' I said.

It started with a gentle patter first. Moments later, torrential sheets of rain coupled with a strong breeze slapped everything in its way. I grabbed Anya by her elbow and hunkered, with little difficulty, inside the hut. People ran helter-skelter, some had flipped open their umbrellas that swayed everywhere but overhead, others hid beneath trees. Visibility reduced to just a few dozen metres and all I could behold in front of me was commotion. The trees danced in the wind, completely under its command, eliciting a deep, whooshing sound. There was another round of thunder crashing above and the sky tore open in a blinding white light.

The scent of wet sand filled the air, together with the enticing aromas of *adrak chai* and *pakoras* frying beside us. Anya placed an order for two chais and a plate of assorted pakoras.

The shack owner's wife, dark and frail, brought us two plastic stools to sit on. There were a few other customers huddled like us, smiles on their faces at the scene before their eyes, relieved all the same to have escaped nature's fury. There was the constant drumming sound overhead of rain hitting the roof, and little trickles of water managed to seep through the chinks and fell on us from time to time.

Anya brought her hands together. 'Wow,' she said, looking awed. 'What a wonderful, wonderful view!'

'Anya Sarin,' I said. 'I agree with you this time, indeed it's wonderful.'

The chai arrived in earthenware cups, hot vapour swirling above it. We wrapped our hands around the cups and slowly sipped from them.

I broached the topic of Aditya again. Anya told me he was employed with the Shimla branch of the State Bank and was a very intelligent guy. I told her I thought he was an arrogant asshole.

'And Sameer,' I said. 'He has got to be the most boring and uninspiring guy I've ever met.'

'You shouldn't make judgements about people you barely know.'

Then she said Sameer was shy and reticent because he had abusive parents and had been bullied at school a lot during his childhood. Those nightmares are what made him an insomniac.

The smile that descended upon Anya's face when she spoke about Monica was discernible. She was her best friend.

'Sometimes,' said Anya, 'I think just one good friend, one pair of good ears, is all you need to live a happy life.'

Then she told me something I found weird: Monica and Aditya also stayed with her in her uncle's house. They were also estranged from their parents. When I asked her the reason all she said was, 'What's weird about that? We're all friends.'

She snapped her fingers in my face. 'Where are you lost?'

I shook my head. 'Nowhere,' I said. 'Um . . . you've got this little . . .' I extended my arm and picked out a piece of grain husk from her hair, dropping it on the floor. A ripple of excitement shot through me; her hair was soft and smooth, and I allowed my hand to linger in her hair for just a moment longer.

Anya smiled coquettishly. 'Are you done, Sahil, or have you found something else?'

I retracted my arm. 'No, it's all done.'

She continued smiling, boring her confident gaze through me.

I averted her gaze for a moment, then cleared my throat, looking into those beautiful eyes. 'Anya, I feel very fortunate to have met you. You know when I'm with you, talking to you, I feel kind of happy.'

I needn't have said anything else because, at that moment, the way she smiled, her eyes twinkling with self-assurance, the slight shake of her head as if she'd just read my mind, I knew she knew what I wanted to say next: that I was deeply and madly in love with her.

11

The Accident

I should have said it. The three words were caught in my throat and I couldn't get them out. It was the perfect opportunity and the perfect ambience for a heartfelt proposal. We'd sat there for another hour munching on onion and aloo pakoras and sipping hot tea before the rain finally stopped and we made our way through the mushy ground, hitching up our trousers. Anya smiled all the way finding even this damn thing enjoyable. She was crazy.

Now, in my home, *The Fountainhead* lay in my hands begging to be read and I couldn't manage to read beyond the third chapter. Anya's thoughts had clouded my mind and seized full control of it like a captain in supreme command of his ship. Normally, it wouldn't take me more than a couple of hours to complete a book at bedtime and only then would sleep embrace me in its mercurial arms. It was some kind of deal, an unspoken agreement.

But now, I knew, sleep would be a commodity hard to find. I had to end this madness and opening my heart and soul to Anya was the only way.

For now I lay the book on the bedside chest, switched off the light, pulled the quilt over myself and braced myself for a sleepless night, only to get out of the bed an hour later when sleep refused to pay me a visit. I wrote for two hours straight, a few thousand words of anxiety spilling out of my mind and on to the page.

* * *

Three days later, after guitar class on Monday, Anya asked me to hang out with her friends. I wanted to refuse. Today was the day to tell her I loved her. But Anya was insistent.

Wandering around, looking for a place to unwind and failing at it, we just strolled along Mall Road. It was a dark, gloomy day, the sky threatening to burst open any minute. Despite the looming bad weather, there was a flurry of activity around us. The five of us walked past hawkers on the narrow pavement just outside the over-crowded shops; we crossed a couple of cafés and decided against going in. It felt good to just walk. Sameer and Aditya walked in front of us, while Monica, Anya and I trailed a couple of metres behind them. Monica was her usual self, blabbering on and prying about the details of how we met.

'Outside Gaiety theatre,' I said. 'On the second day of the Shimla fest.'

'No, wait,' Anya countered, nudging me in my ribs. 'We actually met the following day, during our guitar class. Outside the theatre, you were just gawking at me.'

'Oh, yeah, right.'

The air was heavy, filled with scents of *kebabs,* fried egg paranthas, tea, dust and sweat. People savoured street food in Shimla just as in any other city in India. *Chaat* counters and snack stalls were swarming, people jostling for space.

'It's weird, you guys dating each other,' Monica said, picking up the pace to catch up with us.

I found that odd. 'What is weird?'

'I know it's weird,' Anya said, 'but we're not dating, Monica. How many times should I tell you that?'

Monica didn't respond.

'Wait, guys, wait,' I said, a little confounded. 'Why is it weird? Why can't we date?'

I wasn't sure to whom my question was addressed.

Both the girls looked at each other almost imperceptibly, in a sneaky manner. Then, as if she wanted to say something else, Monica said, 'Because she's too good for you.'

I would have questioned them further when suddenly, ahead of us, something very strange happened. Out of the blue, Aditya scrambled towards a young couple and their toddler, and shoved them off the pavement towards an artefacts stall. The harried couple picked themselves up; the toddler frightened in his father's arms. They looked at Aditya, then looked at each other in surprise.

Not more than thirty seconds later, a car, seemingly out of control, veered sideways towards the edge of the road, right where the couple had been standing, and rammed into the pavement.

The driver died on the spot.

* * *

'So what happened out there?'

We were sitting in a Café Coffee Day, not too far from where the incident had occurred a while ago. A huge ring of people thronged the crash site moments after the accident. An ambulance and a couple of police vans had rolled in a few minutes later. A dusty fire brigade arrived soon after. Suddenly, the only sound we heard were the wailing sirens and the only thing we saw was the smoke billowing above the wreck. A high-pressure jet of water was aimed at the fire and the crowd slowly dispersed. The vitality of Mall Road had been replaced by an eerie disquiet.

Not wanting to be interrogated by the police, Aditya had pushed himself through the crowd and left in haste along with Sameer and Monica. Aditya had said before leaving, 'There's nothing worse than being questioned by rogue cops.'

Now Anya appeared surprised. 'Aditya saved that couple and their kid, what else? Road accidents, I tell you!'

'Yeah, I know that,' I said. 'But how did Aditya know something was about to happen? We all were there. No one saw that car coming. How did he anticipate that it was on a direct course towards that couple?'

'You're right.' She took a sip of her cappuccino. 'He has good foresight, that's all I can think of.' Her eyes didn't meet mine.

'Anya, are you hiding something from me?'

'No . . . no . . . why would you say that?'

'Are you sure?'

'Absolutely.'

Something felt wrong but I dismissed it with a shake of my head. Now was not the time for this. I steeled myself and let out a wisp of air through my curled lips. If I didn't confess my love now I would never be able do it. I blocked out any further thoughts.

'Anya,' I called out.

She looked at me in surprise. 'Yes?'

Suddenly there were a thousand needles pricking my body all over. My heart throbbed loudly against my rib cage, my hands and feet turned cold and I started sweating profusely.

'Yes Sahil,' said Anya, 'What is it?'

'I love you, Anya. I love you very much.'

She gave me a crooked smile, then sipped her coffee. 'Okay.'

My jaw dropped open. '"Okay"?' I exclaimed. 'What kind of response is that?'

'What else do you want me to say?'

I shook my head in surprise, shock, disappointment, anger—all at the same time. 'Anya I'm telling you that I really love you. You're always on my mind and I can't imagine a life without you. Please don't give me a lame "Okay" in response.'

She laid the cup on the table, pulled her chair closer, swept her hands over her hair and finally held an intense expression befitting the situation. 'You shouldn't love me.'

The wave of confusion hadn't passed yet when she continued, 'I'm going to say this one time and one time only. For your own good, don't fall in love with me.'

Then she rose and left without even a goodbye.

12

I Won't Give Up

I had been writing furiously for the past two hours. I had recently discovered writing as a medium to vent my feelings and inner turmoil. Writing is about pouring your heart and soul out on paper and feeling lighter at the end of it.

What else was I supposed to do anyway? When I came home in the evening, my family was hooked to the TV. They were watching a news show where journalists ridiculed the inefficiency of the police at nabbing the psychopath killer.

The three of them had ignored my presence and I had reciprocated, heading straight to my room. I shut out thoughts about the day's strange events and pulled out my journal and a pen, and sat at the desk. Initially hesitant, I finally gave in to the alcohol craving. I pulled out the rum bottle and poured a generous peg in a glass. Writing is better with alcohol—free and uninhibited. After that, I was completely absorbed in the story.

Once I reached a dead end, I put my pen down and that was when thoughts about Anya came whooshing in to my mind like a sudden rush of liquid.

For your own good, don't fall in love with me . . .

Was she in love with someone else? She would have told me if she was. When I told her I had no doubt she would say 'Me too'. I'd seen it in her eyes so many times, the same love and affection that I'm sure she saw in mine. Saying those three words was a mere formality. Hell, it already felt like we were dating. We hung out with each other like it was the most natural thing to do, like it was our destiny.

She said, "Don't fall in love with me." But I already was. It was too late now. And, anyway, you don't *plan* to fall in love with someone, you just . . . fall. That's why they use the word 'fall'.

The next day at school, I thought of sharing the recent developments with Nishant and Mayur. Perhaps I was thinking too much and a second opinion would help. During our lunch break in the canteen I told them everything. Nishant had a concerned expression but Mayur, that bastard, was actually smiling.

'Maybe,' he said, devouring the canteen's *idli–sambar*, 'it was a polite way of saying no. You know she's way out of your league.'

'Just try another time,' Nishant said, ignoring Mayur. 'I know you won't give up.'

I dipped my bread pakora in ketchup and thought about it.

'My advice is,' said Mayur, 'don't get so hung up on one girl. There are plenty of fish in the sea, man.'

The guy could really piss me off. 'Listen, you dimwit,' I said to him. 'That's the difference between me and you. Anya is not a fish. I love her.'

'Fine,' he said, 'but she clearly doesn't love you. Why can't you just give up?'

His question rang a bell. It took me back four years when Rajiv, my guitar teacher, had asked me the same question.

He'd said, 'You don't have an ear for music, Sahil. It's been six months now and you still can't play a single tune right. You should find another hobby. Music is not for you.' When I shook my head, he'd continued, 'Why can't you just give up?'

I said I couldn't, and pursued it relentlessly day and night. It was the only thing that mattered at the time. A few years later, I was his best guitar student. I learnt something profound then: with the right focus and enough determination everything is possible.

So now, I didn't reply to Mayur's words. Four words continued playing in my mind, over and over again, like a broken record: I won't give up, I won't give up, I won't give up.

* * *

During guitar class on Wednesday, I waited patiently for Anya to show up. Sammy was back, after his self-inflicted exile, and was demonstrating a perfect rendition of the song 'One Last Breath' by the band Creed on his electric guitar. Mayur had joined him; tapping on his drums softly and gradually increasing the intensity as the rhythm crystallized. Rajiv, with a perfect count, clapped along. A few other students had stopped tinkering with their instruments and watched in rapt attention. I wanted to join them on my acoustic guitar after I established the correct chords, but my eyes were fixed on the door. There was no sign of Anya or Sameer. It was twenty minutes past the scheduled time of their class and by now it had dawned on me that Anya was clearly avoiding me.

But why? Why was it so wrong that I loved her?

After they were done regaling the students, Mayur and Sammy requested for a practice session after class with me. We hadn't practised together since the festival and it was time to start jamming as a group again. Sammy had composed some tunes and urged me to give them a soul by adding lyrics. I hesitated. I was enjoying writing my story more than the songs. I asked Sammy for some time.

It was thirty minutes past their scheduled time when Sameer slowly made his way through the door, guitar slung on his shoulder. He was wearing loose fitted blue jeans and a red T-shirt. The colour of his face contrasted with his bright shirt. He appeared worn out, as always; the contours of his cheeks were specked with his ragged beard. I craned my neck and to my utter dismay Anya wasn't behind him.

'Where's Anya?'

Sameer offered a handshake. 'She won't come.'

'Why?'

'She's got some errands to run.'

'In the evening?'

'In the evening,' he said.

I slumped back in my chair. Mayur was eavesdropping. I didn't care much about it.

I turned to Sameer. 'Hey, could you give me your address? I . . . I want to speak to Anya.'

Sameer shook his head. He took out his guitar and put on a charade of tuning it. He clearly wasn't interested and I wondered if Anya had sent him. 'Look Sahil'—he scooted his chair closer to me—'there's something you should know.'

The intense expression on his face baffled me. 'What?'

'Anya can never fall in love with you.'

* * *

I met Aditya and Monica in the evening. It wasn't planned; I just ran into them at Krishna Bakery on Mall Road. I liked the *momos* they served. The others were gorging on sandwiches.

'Hi guys, nice to see you.'

Aditya stood up and offered a perfunctory hug. 'Same here.'

I shook hands with Monica; she shifted to her left and offered me a seat.

We talked for a bit about inane topics and then I asked Aditya about the day he had saved the couple. He wasn't interested in discussing it and just said he'd seen the car coming.

Impossible, I thought, but didn't push the topic. All I knew was he saved them that day and that should've been proud of it.

'So, where's Anya?' I asked. 'She didn't come for guitar class today.'

I tried to sound as casual as I could. I wasn't sure if they knew that I had told her about my feelings. Their subtle change of expression made it clear they knew.

Monica shrugged. 'Oh, you know she's like a bird. One day she is here, the other day she is somewhere else.'

Aditya corroborated, 'That's the way she is. Don't worry, she'll be back. I'm sure you are worried about her guitar lessons.'

I watched Monica and Aditya exchange a long glance, as if they were deciding on something, perhaps about how much they should be telling me. A faint nod from Aditya made it clear that they'd been considering something.

It was Monica who began first. She grabbed the bottle of water and took a sip. Placing it back down, she turned to me.

'Who are we kidding?' she said. 'You are in love with Anya, aren't you?'

I said, 'Yes, very much'.

She gave me a discouraging look. Aditya clasped his head in both hands. 'Oh, god!' he said to Monica. 'This is what I was afraid of. Didn't I tell you guys?'

Monica nodded.

'What?' I asked. 'What is it? What were you afraid of?'

Monica held my hand and gently squeezed it. Her expression was contrite. 'You can never get what you want, Sahil. Anya won't fall in love with you.'

Despairingly, I looked at Aditya.

'Never!' he said.

13

Suicide

'But why?' I asked.

I didn't realize I was almost yelling. A few people seated in front of us turned their heads to look at us. I raised my hand and apologized.

'But why?' I was much softer this time. 'Why does everybody keep saying that?'

Aditya looked at Monica. 'That,' he said, 'I'm afraid you'll have to ask Anya herself.'

My jaw dropped open. 'What?' I glanced at them back and forth a couple of times. Their expressions were stolid. 'Is she dying or what?'

A low shriek escaped Monica. 'No, ha, ha.' She looked at Aditya. 'No, hell, no. How can you say that? In fact it's the exact opposite.'

'What?' I threw my hands up in the air. 'What? What is that supposed to mean?'

'Nothing,' Aditya said. 'She's just screwing with you.'

And then they left me with my steaming hot momos. I couldn't even take a bite.

* * *

There are two kinds of thoughts that spawn in our brains. The first kind arrives politely, asks a few questions, raises a few doubts and, when satisfied with the answers and solutions, leaves promptly. The second lot is an arrogant and raucous bunch. They barge in and percolate their negativity within minutes. They keep asking questions without expecting answers and, by the time they are done adding fuel to the fire, it feels like our brains are about to explode.

Currently I was inundated with the latter and the searing headache was such that I felt my mind could explode any minute. It was Sunday evening, four days after my conversation with Sameer, Aditya and Monica.

Anya can never fall in love with you.

There were four possible reasons I'd conjectured:

1. Anya was a lesbian
2. She was in love with someone else
3. She was devoid of emotions
4. She hated me

I ruled out option number four as soon as I wrote it. Why would a sane, intelligent girl hang out regularly with a guy she hated? So which of the other three options could it be?

I didn't know the answer.

I was in my room, my back propped against the headboard, legs outstretched, staring at the wall ahead. Guns N' Roses played in the background. Anya had skipped the Friday class too. Given that she was so passionate about the guitar and hadn't missed any classes before, I had only one explanation: I screwed up.

Couldn't she have told me she didn't love me instead of all the untoward drama? I could have taken it. For two hours I'd been drinking rum like it was water. It was my only cure. It wasn't just Anya who perturbed me. Earlier in the day Grandma had reprimanded me for a number of reasons.

'What do you do in your room all day?' she asked sharply post lunch. 'Why don't you talk to anyone?'

'I have a headache,' I said.

She'd stood on the threshold shaking her head and possibly thinking of more reasons to scold me. She found another one. Apparently she'd never seen me studying.

'It's only your novels or your guitar that I see you with. Look at Ayush—he's always studying. What do you plan to do with your life?'

'Writer,' I said. The word just fumbled out of my mouth. It felt good so I said again, 'I think I want to be a writer.'

'That might not be such a bad idea, after all,' she said, her expression softening, but only a little. 'You're always lost in your own world!'

She'd left me then but not without another one of her taunts. 'And you better get a haircut today!'

I didn't; I didn't want to leave my room. Anya had brought some purpose and fun to my life but she took it away all too soon. Something told me this was not the way it was supposed to end. After swearing that I wouldn't give up, I finished my drink and heaved a sigh of frustration. Jumping to my feet, I turned to my second cure: writing.

* * *

In school the next day, the datesheet for our mid-term exams was released. The despondency spread like a viral flu through the entire room. By the end of that period, all of us had long faces.

After lunch, in maths class, I was daydreaming about confronting Anya, holding her arms and yanking them, asking her the reason for her erratic behaviour.

I had decided that if she skipped guitar class that day, I would find her damn place and get all my answers.

I continued firing questions at her in my mind when, suddenly, I felt something sting my cheek. My hand went up to feel it when I noticed a lot of heads staring at me. Our maths teacher's face was twisted in an ugly frown. 'Stand up, Sahil!' she barked. 'Stand up!'

I stood. My eyes fell on the piece of chalk, now lying on the floor, that she'd hurled at me.

'I have called out to you six times,' she said. 'Where's your mind? Are you time-travelling?'

The class burst out laughing.

'Silence!' she screamed.

'Sorry, ma'am,' I said. 'It won't happen again.'

* * *

There she was at the academy later that evening: all five and a half feet of her, smiling, bubbling with excitement, as I entered the class. My hand flew to my chest and relief washed over me. 'Thank god,' I said, under my breath.

She was dressed in dark blue jeans and a pink and chrome shirt, the sleeves folded back neatly till her elbows. Her hair was firmly held back by a blue band, exposing her wide and slightly pitted forehead. Her eyes were like the bright stars of a constellation in a cloudless sky. The dimple in her cheek was deep, the deepest I'd ever seen, and her lips parted to allow for a full smile.

'Sorry,' she said, holding up her hands as though I was approaching with a gun. 'I was out of town the entire week.'

A breath came whooshing out of me and I shook my head. 'I didn't even ask,' I said. Suddenly all those questions I was yearning to ask, disappeared. All that mattered was that she was here.

There was a distant relative's wedding in Chandigarh, she told me.

'But I took my guitar along,' she said. 'I never stopped practising.'

'Okay,' was all I could say.

She had lots of stories to recount: the idyllic drive through the hills before hitting the plains, the bumpy ride in the minivan, a *dhaba* they had discovered along the route and its finger-licking good food, but she mentioned nothing about the wedding. Sammy and Mayur had also joined us but I don't think Sammy was listening: his fingers continued plucking his guitar strings in a soft melody, a soothing background score to Anya's tales.

When she was finished, I told her candidly about how my week had transpired: slow and boring. She sensed what I was getting at and deftly avoided it by pulling out her guitar from its cover, and strumming the few chords I'd taught her.

'See,' she said, 'have I not improved?'

I responded with a nod inferring that she didn't want to discuss the reason for my slow and boring week, and let the conversation end. I taught her the finger positioning for a few more chords and she engaged herself in the task.

All this while Sameer sat by her side and didn't utter a word except to say an initial hello. He sat huddled, his head down, trying desperately to get a tune right that Anya had mastered four weeks ago.

Although Anya had come back and was all happy and smiling, our friendship seemed to have dwindled—like some kind of transparent wall had been built between us. I realized this when I told her about my week. Her eyes had moved swiftly, and immediately her guitar was out. It was a very subtle hint she'd thrown my way: please, I don't want to talk about it.

Up until this time, I could have discussed anything with her without the slightest hesitation, but now, with my feelings for her out in the open, I had to weigh my words carefully. I figured it could go downhill from here. This narrow crack of uneasiness might easily grow wider as the days passed, ruining our friendship, if I didn't handle it tactfully. A shiver of fear passed through me at the prospect and I allowed it do just that: pass. I told myself firmly I would never let it happen.

So Anya had drawn a line, a boundary for our discourse, and beyond that line lay a prohibited field of love; hell, there were always trespassers and I didn't mind being one.

Sammy must have seen a shard of sadness across my face because he stopped practising and asked me: 'Are you okay, Sahil? You look sad.' Then, his body bent forward and looking towards Anya furtively, he added in a whisper: 'She's here now.'

'I'm fine,' I said perhaps with a sigh of frustration because he then he replied, 'Why "fine", man? Why not happy?'

Anya's interest had been piqued and she looked at us.

I sighed again. 'Are you happy?'

'Yes,' he said. 'I am.'

'Why?'

He glanced at Anya before settling his eyes back on me. Then he shrugged. 'It doesn't take a lot to be happy; all you need is love in your heart and a goal in your mind.'

'And you have that?'

'Yes.' He nodded. 'I have Gracy and a goal to be the best guitarist in the country.'

'That's lovely,' said Anya. 'Sahil, do you agree?'

I was a little annoyed with her so I dismissed her question with a polite wave of my hand.

'What did I miss?' Mayur asked, completing his set on the drums and pulling up a chair to sit across from Anya.

'Nothing at all,' I replied.

Suddenly Sameer jumped to his feet, almost banging his guitar on the floor, and rushed out of the door in a hurry.

'What was that all about?' I asked Anya.

She made a gesture of ignorance by shrugging.

Ten minutes later, just outside the class, we heard someone screaming. Barring Sammy, everyone followed the sound and saw an exhilarated Rajiv hugging Sameer and pumping his fists in the air. Sneha, a girl from our class who played the violin, stood beside them; a restrained smile on her face.

'I can't believe it,' Rajiv was howling.

'You can't believe what?' I asked.

He came towards us. 'You won't believe what Sameer just did.' He turned to Sneha. 'Sneha was about to commit suicide. She was on the roof of the building, about to jump, when Sameer pulled her back and convinced her against it.'

There was a narrow, winding staircase just on the left of the door to our academy. I looked up and my eyes followed its long, curved ascent right up to the roof. I breathed a sigh of relief. Surely a fall from there would have been devastating.

'Good job, Sameer,' Mayur and I said in unison.

'Thanks,' he replied.

Anya walked up to Sneha. Holding Sneha's arms, she looked in her eyes. 'Promise us all you'll never do such a foolish thing again.'

She gave a weak, slightly embarrassed nod. 'After what Sameer told me, surely, I won't.' Then she left us.

When she was out of earshot, Rajiv asked Sameer: 'What did you tell her?'

He shrugged. 'I just told her about a theory that I'd read somewhere on how after suicide your soul wanders around helplessly, you can't talk to your loved ones, you can't sleep or be at peace. I told her it seemed a much worse place than the present and that she'd regret it every second of her afterlife.'

All of us were dumbfounded. Mayur was the one to break the silence. 'She bought that bullshit?'

'I hope she did,' he said solemnly, under his breath, and proceeded to go back inside.

When we were all settled, guitars back in our hands, something suddenly struck me. 'Hey Sameer, how the hell did you know she was up there?'

He breathed a theatrical sigh. 'It's a good thing I knew.'

14

Enjoy Your Meal

Obviously, I didn't believe his answer. So when I pressed further, he said that while the rest of us were busy with our instruments, he'd seen Sneha sneak out of the door, her face blotchy from all the crying. 'It's normal,' he said, 'all of us are so busy with our lives, we seldom see the suffering of others around us.'

What preceded the sobs, he told us, was a phone call, and the moment she disconnected the call, melancholy seized her: her hands shook and her face twisted in despair. Later, on the roof, she told him that her boyfriend had compromising pictures of her and that he was using them to blackmail her. All Sameer had seen was a fleck of her blue *dupatta* fluttering in the breeze as she ran out the door and he'd guessed.

It was the most brilliant guess, we told him.

Later, after class was over, another strange happened: Anya asked me to go out with her for a coffee. Was it a sympathy date? It didn't matter. I said yes.

* * *

Wake and Bake Café was a quaint little place located right opposite the Ridge, overlooking Mall Road. It was one of the most famous hangout areas in Shimla and held a cult-like status amongst youngsters.

After hanging out at the same café dozens of times, we thought, unanimously, that it was time for a change. Twenty minutes later, we were climbing the narrow staircase that led to Wake and Bake Café.

The waitress took our order of coffee, pita bread and lemon chicken. I'd always admired the modern appeal of the place: rich wooden tapestry, dazzling walls painted bright yellow with graffiti, and ornate lampshades casting oblong shadows. One could spend the whole day here just reading a book, looking out of the window and enjoying the view of the entire valley lit with hundreds of lights in the evening.

Anya was very fond of wearing different shades of blue and the turquoise blue T-shirt she came wearing looked very elegant on her. She looked like a calm, serene beauty, just happy to be herself.

'How's your book coming along?'

I was still looking around, admiring the place. We'd taken a seat by the window and the table to our right was occupied by a dozen or so students, still in their school uniforms, howling and having a ball, celebrating a birthday; their whooping loud enough to reach the extreme end of the room. The middle-aged couple sitting near them were clearly distracted.

As for the book, I told Anya, I'd managed to write half of it. I also wanted to tell her the majority of it was done last week, when she'd been missing, but then I remembered the boundary she'd drawn and kept quiet.

'Really?' she was clearly overjoyed. 'Wow! Tell me what happens in it?'

The protagonist, I told her, is a teenager who, at night, sees visions of the next day in his dreams. He is a lonely, disturbed guy and this gift is a blessing. He manages to improve his life gradually by planning his day in advance and that is what constitutes half the book. When everything seems hunky dory, one night, he sees himself killing someone.

She leaned forward in excitement. 'Wow, that's interesting,' she said.

'Do you like it?'

'Absolutely, when do you plan to finish it?'

The food arrived and we moved our arms off the small table to make space. When the waitress was done laying out the food, she smiled at us and left. I took a piece of chicken.

'Some day, soon,' I said.

Anya took a sip of her coffee. 'So, you're actually taking this seriously; this whole writing thing?'

'I don't know,' I said, absently chewing on the chicken. 'For now, I want to write the kind of story that makes readers cry and think, and perhaps change something in them.'

'That's good,' she said. After a couple of sips and a few bites of the bread, she said, 'You clearly have a passion and flair for writing. My suggestion is to evolve it into a dream or a goal— become a professional writer.'

I nodded and she kept pushing me further. Passion, she said, fizzles out, only goals remain. I wondered if she was genuinely concerned for me or if it was just another of her usual bombastic talks which had now started to annoy me. If she was so concerned, why couldn't she tell me her reason for not falling in love with me? That, after all, was the primary cause of my sadness.

She had stopped talking and was relishing the chicken. From time to time, she even licked her fingers.

'You really like it,' I said, 'don't you?'

'It's delicious.'

'Yeah, it's all right.'

'I wonder,' she said, still savouring the same piece, 'why don't you enjoy your meal, you dumbo? You eat as if it's a job. Take in the smells, savour the taste and flavour, chew it slowly and enjoy it.'

'I eat to live, not live to eat.'

'Ha, ha,' she said. 'Funny boy, now you want to sound wise!'

'It's a saying.'

'It is, but I don't agree with it. Tell me something: what is everyone running after—a good job, money, promotions, bank balance. But the fundamental thing all of that provides is food, and no one has time for it. Such irony, don't you think?'

After picking up another piece, she continued, 'Learn to appreciate these little joys if you want to be happy, Sahil.'

'Okay, you know what, Anya,' I said as I thrust a hand out, 'enough of your self-righteous talk. If you are so concerned about me, why don't you tell me why everyone keeps saying you can't fall in love with me?'

I tried and tried hard not to steer the conversation in that direction, but my curiosity and anger had surged so much, I needed to vent. I couldn't pretend any more that all was fine when it was not. I didn't like that I had to hesitate when I opened my mouth. I didn't like the wall that had come between us.

Anya tried her best to put on a neutral expression, as if to pretend that we hadn't had the conversation the previous week; that she hadn't abruptly taken off in the middle and that her friends hadn't warned me about her.

'I also know you weren't attending a wedding. You just wanted to avoid me, isn't that so?'

With the smile slowly disappearing from her face, placing the chicken piece down, she wiped her hands. Then she took a deep breath and said, 'Yes.'

'Why?'

'You won't understand.'

'Try me.'

She hesitated, then finally said, 'Because I wanted to protect you.'

I let out an irritated snort. 'Protect me? From what?'

I never thought I could be so angry with Anya. She kept silent, avoiding my gaze, perhaps thinking of a way to manipulate me. I had curled my hands into fists and only when I felt the slight pain of my nails digging into my palms, did I loosen my grip.

Anya was ready to speak. She looked at me. 'Okay, I'm sorry,' she said. 'I can give you the answers to all your questions, but then I can never meet you again. So you decide what you want: answers or my friendship?'

I grew angrier by the second. 'That is the most ridiculous thing you have ever said to me!'

Anya was steadfast, her gaze intent. 'Answers or friendship?'

I shook my head violently and slumped back in the chair. 'I hate you, you snotty bitch!'

She gave out a short laugh.

'And you find this funny?'

'Shh . . . wait a minute.' She held up a hand.

She closed her eyes tightly, deep furrows appearing on her forehead. She was trying to think hard. I looked around. Everything appeared normal. Her face contorted in a frown and I noticed the slight shake of her hands. The next moment she rose frantically and hurried down the stairs.

'What happened?' I yelled after her.

She didn't even look back.

15

The Fourth Murder

It's a strange law of nature that the more a thing eludes you, the more you are drawn towards it.

Anya, having told me I couldn't get the answers unless we never met again, had piqued my curiosity in her even more. That she was shrewd, I knew before, but shrewd in a cunning way, I realized only now. She knew I could have never chosen the answers over her and she'd manipulated me. But she didn't know me very well. Stubborn as I was, I'd find a way to get both.

The laws of nature don't only apply to things, they also apply to people. Would it be fair to say that my love for her had intensified because it was unrequited? I'd say yes. I was more in love with her than I ever was. It was acceptable to me that she didn't love me; my love for her wasn't so weak that it would wither. There are more unrequited love stories in the world than reciprocated ones anyway. But what didn't feel right was to not even get an explanation. She'd also taken the one thing that is instrumental when pursuing the impossible: hope.

And to top that, was the mysterious way in which it all transpired. Anya's uncanny condition—answers or her friendship—her friends discouraging me in strange ways and

Anya's sudden disappearances. It had happened twice now. Where the hell did she go? What was she hiding?

I'd read that women would always be a complex mystery to men, but a mystery to this extent? For a moment I wondered if I could find out the mystery surrounding her first, everything about her and then figure out my next move.

It struck me like a lightening. I suddenly knew what I had to do.

* * *

I could have never anticipated the news that would present itself when I reached home after a long, pensive walk on Mall Road after school: another murder. Grandma was frantic. She sat us all down on the sofa in the living room and urged us to not leave the house unless she spoke to Pramod Uncle about our safety first.

The murder had taken place a day before in Vikasnagar but the corpse was discovered only this afternoon by the neighbours. The police department was conducting a post-mortem to identify the time of death. The body was mutilated and castrated, but a police official said they would nonetheless run tests on the fingerprints and DNA samples found at the site to ascertain if it was the same killer who hadn't been apprehended for the previous three murders.

'Sir,' said the visibly anxious reporter in a raspy voice, 'this is the fourth murder! The victims have all been tortured and killed ruthlessly. Why is nothing being done in the case?'

Ayush increased the volume.

Pramod Uncle shook his head. The pressure was evident on his face. 'We are doing our best,' he said into the mic. 'We are as worried as the people of this city.'

'But sir, have you been able to establish the motive for these murders?'

'No.' He shook his head again. 'Not yet. There is no relation between the victims, they're chosen at random. We're trying our best.'

'Sir,' pressed the reporter further, pushing aside a lock of her hair, 'sources tell us your department believes it is some kind of satanic ritual, to honour a deity or an evil power. Is that true?'

'No more questions please.' Pramod Uncle brushed the mic aside and got into a waiting car, a throng of reporters with their mics and recording equipment pushing against the window.

'That was the deputy police commissioner of Shimla,' said the reporter, now looking into the camera, 'who clearly didn't have a lot of answers. With cameraman Ashok, this is Piya Roy for News Twenty-Four.'

The screen switched to a swarm of angry protestors gathered outside the police headquarters, hollering and holding placards indicating their annoyance at the incompetent police: 'Save our kids', 'Find and torture the killer', 'Shimla police is incapable', 'Shimla is unsafe'.

Two hours later, Pramod Uncle was at our doorstep. He was of medium height with broad, heavyset shoulders; his face was unyielding with a big nose and sharp, black eyes. His silver hair was neatly combed to one side. His paunch—a trademark in our family—had grown since I last met him.

The three of us bent down to touch his feet and he gave us a cursory hug. He proceeded to the chair beside the couch and plonked down. Shweta brought him a glass of water, Grandma returned a few minutes later with a cup of tea and a few Marie biscuits.

'Any clue about the murders?' asked Grandma, taking a seat across from him.

He shook his head and took a sip of the tea. There was a little clink when he placed the cup back in its saucer.

'I'm worried for my kids.' She gave us a quick gaze starting with Shweta, Ayush and finally me. 'It's becoming unsafe now. There have been four gruesome murders in less than two months.'

'It might be too early to say,' he said taking another sip, 'but I think we know what to do.'

The reporter, he said, was right about the satanic ritual. Currently they were collecting all the information on the four victims: their names, ages, the times and places of their births, sunsigns, times of death and the like. That it was the same killer committing murders with the same hatred and modus operandi was all too obvious. The best chance to nab him was to establish a pattern between the murders. If they could figure out the rationale for the ritual, it wouldn't be too hard to find out the 'who' and 'when'. Only this time the police would be waiting to arrest him.

Ayush nodded. 'Sounds like a decent idea.'

'But what kind of ritual?' Shweta probed.

'We don't know yet,' he replied flatly. 'Religion has always been a very complex and contentious subject: it raises more questions than it answers. It has done us more harm than good and has given rise to these fanatics who can't figure right from wrong.'

There was another weird edge to this case. The forensic team had confirmed the fingerprints and DNA samples found at the previous two murder sites were identical. The killer didn't try to smudge or distort them to conceal his identity or implicate someone else, as happens in most first degree murder cases. For the fourth murder that took place yesterday, Pramod Uncle said, they were sure they'd find the same pattern. But what baffled them was that they failed to find an appropriate match for the samples. How could that possibly be?

Then he spoke at length of his hatred for the media. The police couldn't have explained all of this on television. This would have made the killer cautious. It was better to project a picture of ignorance to elicit a casual and careless approach to his next murder.

'But they ask all sort of questions,' he said proceeding to the dining table where Grandma had laid out dinner. 'I have to plug the leak first in our department. Someone is talking to the media behind our back.'

Grandma asked him if he could provide some security for the three of us, despite our unwillingness. It impedes our privacy and—thank god!—Shweta and Ayush were with me on this one.

Uncle calmed her down and gave her his word that we'd be safe, and that they'd catch the killer very soon.

16

Secrets

The next week the same thing happened: a coffee date with Anya, discussions about love, the sudden panic and then she was gone in a jiffy.

Only this time I followed her. Asking her wouldn't have helped as she always gave vague answers.

Following someone is tricky. You can't be too slow, you risk being left behind. You can't be too fast either, you risk coming too close, and one tiny lapse in concentration and you're caught.

I was doing all right. Anya was about fifty metres ahead of me; she wove through the evening crowd on Mall Road, edging past them, stopping in her tracks frequently, looking around, and then again proceeding. She was confused and even from a distance I could make out she wasn't sure where she wanted to go.

She took a right towards the Ridge, walked past Christ Church and the state library, and then began running. She crossed the statue of Mahatma Gandhi and took another right.

I tried my best to keep up with her but lost her just after she entered a society. I trotted down the street, turning my head everywhere but there wasn't even a slight trace of her. I continued running some more. A minute later I had to stop to give rest to my lungs. I took a few quick breaths. I stooped a little, palms on my thighs.

Then one more three-sixty-degree view all around. Nothing.

Damn! I'd lost her. Now I'd have to wait for the next time to figure out the mystery about her sudden disappearances.

I walked back a few hundred metres when someone tapped me on my back.

'Yes?' I spun around and my jaw dropped open.

It was Anya.

She was panting. 'What the hell do you think you were doing?'

I swallowed. 'What?'

She was grinding her teeth. 'Don't act smart. Why were you following me?'

'I . . . I wasn't. I just um . . . came to—'

'No!' She thrust her hand a few inches from my face. 'Stop lying! I know what you were doing! Why?'

Her face was twisted in an ugly scowl. She was furious. Her eyes didn't waver, didn't blink and bore straight through me. I debated for a moment if I should tell her the truth. I decided I should. She deserved to know.

I told her everything then, that I loved her and wanted to know her secret. 'Maybe then, I could've got some answers,' I said. 'I don't want to be just your friend.'

She squeezed her eyes shut and shook her head in disgust. 'Oh god!'

I wondered what the big deal was, if she had nothing to hide. And then it struck me that perhaps she did have something to hide. Something profound, something she didn't want me or anyone else to find out. But what? And why?

A knife-like slap broke me out of my rumination. 'Who the hell do you think you are, huh?' She punched me in the chest. I fell back a couple of steps. 'I don't love you. I never will. You're a fucking nobody in my life. You get that? Who gave you the right to stalk me? You were just a damn friend, nothing more. And what fucking secret are you talking about, huh? I don't have any secrets.'

'Anya, I . . . I am really sorry!'

'Go to hell, Sahil!' she said. 'And never show me your face again! Whatever little friendship we had, you've screwed that up today.'

'I'm sorry, Anya. I really love you. I didn't mean to—'

'We're done! Leave me alone!'

'I promise it won't ever happen again.'

'Fuck you!' she snapped. 'Just go to hell!'

She spun around on her heels and a minute later was out of my sight. Tears stung my eyes as I walked back home.

17

Cutting

When you love someone with all your heart, you unwittingly render the key to your happiness in their hands. Like a puppeteer, they hold the threads to your life—manoeuvring and driving it. You give them the divine power to decide the fate of your life. If the feelings are reciprocated there isn't a better experience in this world, but if they are not, the world is a sad and dark place.

With Anya gone, I suddenly knew how it would feel if a bolt of lightning struck a man. The pain was unimaginable. I felt a terrifying heaviness inside and my breathing grew laborious as if someone had pricked holes in my lungs, draining them of all the air. Despite the evening light, a veil of darkness had spread in front of my eyes. Over the sound of traffic, I could hear Anya's deep, penetrating voice, 'You were just a damn friend, nothing more! We're done! Go to hell!'

By the time I reached home, the sun had gone down. I had allowed for enough time to compose myself. I sat in a park a few blocks away from home for over an hour. Huddled on the bench, my face buried in my hands, I cried till my cheeks burned.

Crying can be very indulgent, once you dive in a river of tears you find yourself going deeper and deeper. Suddenly I was crying about everything—my senseless life, my dead parents, my cold and distant relationship with my siblings and Grandma, my lack of friends.

Life, without meaningful relationships, is meaningless. But I guess some people are meant to live alone and die alone. Anya was the only silver lining, the only highlight, in my otherwise lonely life. With her in my life, I felt alive. I truly loved her and would never be able to love someone that way. My heart sank again and a fresh bout of tears emerged, shaking me as they made their way out. A few passers-by stopped and after getting no response to their interrogations, carried on.

When it drew close to seven, I got up to my feet and washed my face thoroughly with a garden hose. Before proceeding back home I took another detour to a liquor store and carefully hid the bottle of rum I purchased under my shirt, tucking it firmly inside my jeans. Shweta and Ayush were in their respective rooms and Grandma, after unlatching the door, proceeded back in to the kitchen. I quickly walked up to my room and locked the door behind me.

After putting on a heavy metal CD in the player, I wasted no time in gulping down the rum. I drank it undiluted and let it burn my throat. I needed some physical pain and that's when the thought of cutting occurred to me. I decided to finish the bottle first. I lit a cigarette and took a few large drags. After a few more sips, I began feeling heady.

I'd planned on spending the night wallowing in misery. Tomorrow would be a new day and I'd think about the whole Anya episode again. Giving up wasn't an option. As I saw it, I'd have to lie low for a while, perhaps a couple of days, may be a few weeks. Then go back to her, apologize and hope that time assuaged her anger. But it wouldn't be easy. Whatever little I knew of Anya, she sure wasn't a lousy, flimsy girl. If she said something, she definitely meant it.

But what seemed to perturb me all this while was the visceral reaction that I had evoked from her. Why was she so angry? Something odd was definitely going on with her and she sure as hell didn't want me to find out about it. Did Sameer or any of her other friends know about this? Were they involved, too?

As I pondered this there was a loud bang on the door. I shivered at the sudden sound, rose and quickly hid the bottle in the bedside drawer. I waved a few times to dispel the cigarette smoke before unlocking the door. Grandma stood outside, glaring at me, Ayush peeping out from behind her.

'What's happening?' she asked. 'Why is the music so loud?' She came close and sniffed the air around me. 'Have you been drinking?'

To this I said nothing. I might be a lot of things but I wasn't a liar.

'You have.' She scowled and slapped me. Then shot a sideways glance at Ayush, 'Did you know about this?'

He shook his head.

'So,' she said, counting on her fingers, 'you don't study, you drink alcohol, you lock yourself in your room all day doing god knows what, you don't talk to any of us, you don't help me out with household chores, you're lost in your own world, you've no idea about your future . . .' She trailed off and shook her head. 'Aren't you ashamed of yourself?'

I think I was. If I had managed to infuriate Anya, the girl who cared so much about me, 'ashamed' was a very subtle word to describe what I felt now.

Normally I would hate Grandma for lecturing me, but now I felt nothing—no emotion of anger or sadness. Oddly, her words felt right. I stood there, my head bent in shame, eyes rooted to the floor, absorbing her every word. Was I that bad? How do I manage to make everybody hate me?

'From tomorrow onwards,' she continued, 'I want to see a responsible Sahil. You will study for at least two hours every day, spend more time with us and help me out. And cut your hair! And you, not Ayush, will take me to the hospital tomorrow for my check-up. Is that clear?'

I nodded.

At her instructions, Ayush pulled out the rum bottle and dumped it in the dustbin.

'I never want to see you drinking again!' she warned with a firm finger wagging at me before leaving the room.

I locked the door and resignedly plopped down on the edge of the bed. It wasn't long before a blade was out and I slashed my forearm with it. The pain felt liberating.

I cut myself some more on the other arm. Throwing the blade away, I finally broke out in a fit of sobs.

* * *

The next day I decided to let bygones be bygones. I bathed and breakfasted on time and was ready to drive Grandma to Sanjivani Hospital, few kilometres south of our place, in our car. She was on medication for arthritis. She was pleased to see me waiting for her in the living room. I was pleased that, for once, I hadn't disappointed her.

I hadn't been able to sleep for even a minute the previous night and now my eyelids felt heavy.

It was Anya.

As I tossed and turned in bed throughout the night, my mood drifted to various stages: depression, anger, regret, acceptance and, finally, exploring the limited options to reconcile with her. After a few days, a sincere apology might work. I'd also made peace with her uncanny traits and sudden disappearances.

I didn't need the answers any more, having her in my life was far more important.

During the drive to the hospital, my mind continued drifting. Grandma sat by my side, fingering a rosary, her eyes shut. She passed one bead at a time with her thumb and recited a little prayer each time. I wanted nothing more than to close my eyes like her and take a nap.

After turning on the indicator, I swerved the car right towards the Ridge Sanjauli road.

I have no recollection of what happened next because one instant I was rubbing my eyes with my fist, shoving sleep aside, and the next moment a truck rammed into our car from the left. The impact was so strong that our car swirled mid-air and then crashed a hundred feet away with a deafening bang.

Then everything went black.

18

Grandma

'You bastard!' I could hear someone screaming. 'You fucking idiot! How could you do this?'

The room was filled with an unearthly, keening sound—like that of an animal crying in pain. I slowly opened my eyes and saw the blurred vision of a hospital room. I was being fed oxygen through a mask, needles pierced my hands and Ayush stood over me, howling.

'First you killed our mother, then our father and now you've killed Grandma! I hate you, Sahil. I fucking hate you! How could you do this?'

My heart sank. Shweta and Pramod Uncle stood on the other side of the bed, staring gloomily back at me. Shweta was crying with quick, guttural sobs.

I turned back to Ayush.

He fired a blizzard of questions at me, 'How were you driving? What happened? How could you do this, Sahil? How could you? You did this on purpose, didn't you? Tell me!'

I felt a piercing pain in my head, and instinctively my hand went up. There was a thick bandage around my head.

'You have suffered a head injury,' Uncle told me. I saw abject sadness in his eyes. 'Try to relax.'

Tears escaped my eyes as I tried to recollect the incident. A knot tightened in my stomach when the sight of Grandma crashing through the windshield appeared in my mind. She must have died on the spot. Oh, how I wished I had died with her too. I couldn't take the blame of another death on me, I just couldn't; I had already killed my parents, I had killed them both, and now I had killed Grandma.

I struggled for breath and my chest rose and fell. My fists clutched the bed sheet and my eyes filled again. I made a groaning sound and Pramod Uncle came by my side and pressed my hand.

'I will never forgive you!' Ayush was saying in a choked voice. 'I hate you! I really hate you!

I saw him turning and leaving the room, banging the door shut behind him. I could see a similar rage in Shweta's eyes and she stormed out of the room too.

Suddenly my eyes began to feel heavy and slowly the blurred vision dimmed into darkness. My body became stiff and cold. The sounds around me were slowly fading and seconds later they were distant.

I was in another world.

19

Coma

They said I'd been in hospital for two weeks now. I had no recollection of this. The only thing I remembered was the accident and killing Grandma, just like I killed my parents. I also remembered a teary-eyed Ayush and Shweta, their high-pitched sobs, the hatred in their eyes when they looked at me, them storming out of the room.

And Anya: the anger with which she broke all ties with me.

I am cursed. Either people around me die or they end up hating me. And now, like everyone else, I hated myself too. I'd always caused pain and agony to my loved ones. Grandma, despite her crude manner and blunt opinions about me, surely always wanted my best. She wanted me to study, do well and follow in Ayush's footsteps, and I never paid any heed. I never spent quality time with her, never had a real conversation with her; I wish at least on the last day that I'd been nice to her. Now she was dead because of me.

I should have also died that day with her. I didn't deserve to live; the world would be better without a reckless prick like me. Or maybe I *was* dead. Maybe this place where I was lying, without being able to move a muscle, was hell.

The air was heavy with the pungent smells of anaesthetics and medicines. My eyes were shut and I couldn't bring myself to open them. Other than the sound of faint beeps, presumably from the monitors behind me, there were hushed murmurs from somewhere outside the room. I want to call out, scream and ask them what the hell had happened to me but parting my lips to speak was a massive struggle in itself. I drove all my energy towards this seemingly Herculean task but failed after several attempts. Exasperated, I gave up. I was a soul trapped in a lifeless body.

I heard another sound then, that of a door creaking open and footsteps approaching me. I caught a whiff of a lady's perfume. It was strong and sharp and dominated the air for a while before being swept away by the odour of medicines. She tinkered with some instruments to my extreme right—snatches of metallic sounds reached my ears.

'I'll be giving you an injection now,' she said. Her voice was soft and mellow. 'This won't hurt.' I felt her cold hands on my skin, the soft fabric on my right arm being rolled up and then the needle going in. Normally I would twitch my lips with pain, but now I could do no such thing.

'It's all done. You can relax now.' She unfurled my sleeve. 'And you have visitors.'

It was Ayush and Shweta.

I heard Shweta's sniffle and she took my hand in hers. 'Is he going to be okay?' Her voice cracked.

'Of course,' said Ayush. 'He's going to be fine. Sahil, you hear me? You're going to be fine.' His voice cracked too and he broke out into a series of intermittent sobs. 'Promise me. I've lost so many closed ones, I can't afford to lose you. Please, please wake up.'

Then he began sobbing inconsolably along with Shweta.

I tried opening my mouth, moving my fingers, but it was as if my entire body was fastened and held back by a taut rope. I couldn't so much as twitch a muscle. I wanted to cry with them and apologize for Grandma. For our parents. Ayush had to suffer because of me. I wanted to bury my head in his broad chest and shoulders, and tell him I could hear his every word. He didn't deserve this.

'Please wake up, please,' he said in a broken gasp. 'It's been two weeks now. I know you are angry with me. I didn't mean a thing that day. I know it was not your fault, it was just an accident. I love you, brother. Please wake up.'

There was a soft knock at the door and then it creaked open.

'Good morning, doctor,' Ayush said, and blew his nose.

'Morning.' The doctor's voice was loud and raspy.

I heard their discourse. Both my siblings pressed him about my recovery. The doctor explained that I had suffered a head injury that had pushed me into a coma. A coma lasts at least two to four weeks. They had taken care of everything else: my condition was being monitored regularly, oxygen was supplied through a ventilator, through a feeding tube I was administered nutrients and liquids, a catheter had been inserted right into my kidney to assist in passing urine; from time to time the nurses shifted my body to prevent bedsores.

'We're doing our best,' he told them. 'Have a little faith.'

'Yes, doctor,' said Ayush.

'Hopefully he should be up in a couple of weeks.'

The worst part of being in a coma is not the coma itself. It's not being able to talk to your loved ones and tell them 'I can hear you'. It's more a punishment than a disease because you have to suffer all alone.

When Ayush and Shweta left, I pondered for a while if I really wanted to wake up. Wake up to what? Guilt, regret, melancholy, pain.

I had killed Grandma and I would have to carry that burden for the rest of my life. I didn't think I could do it.

Death, on the other hand, would set me free.

20

The Response

The next day I had another visitor—Anya.

She was accompanied by Sameer. For more than two minutes she said nothing. I could feel her eyes piercing my body. I wanted to apologize to her too. She had been a very good friend, better than I ever deserved, and yet I managed to disappoint her.

'That's the way I am,' I wanted to tell her. 'I hurt people all along the way.'

I surmised that Anya was a much better person than I would ever be. If someone had managed to anger me as much as I had angered her, I would never have cared what became of them. And yet, here she was, moaning, crying softly; shedding tears for someone who had hurt her immensely and betrayed her trust.

'I'm so, so sorry, Sahil,' she said. 'I miss you.'

Her words felt like a cool breeze from an air conditioner on a hot, steamy day. She ran her hand over my hair and tousled it; the scent of her was overpowering—it made my heart do a little dance. God, I loved her so much.

Here again I tried to move, speak, blink, anything that would give her an indication that I was alive and could hear her.

I couldn't and it was agonising. She wept and caressed my arm with her hand.

'You're the best thing that ever happened to me, Sahil,' she said. 'I want you to come back.' Then she gave a sharp sniff before continuing, 'I'm sorry for what I said that day.'

My heart did a little somersault, but in the next instant I was submerged in gloom when it occurred to me that those words were for a comatose Sahil. It was pity that had elicited them. And maybe guilt. The accident happened a day after her rebuke. She probably felt it was her fault, that her snubbing me led to all of this.

If she felt that way, she was wrong. But I couldn't convey this to her.

When I woke up, if I woke up, would she still feel I was the best thing that happened to her? I highly doubted it.

'Let's go,' Sameer said, his first and final words as they left the room.

Every day over the course of the next week, I had a few constant visitors. Ayush would try to be cheerful, recounting his day's events. At times, he would be contrite and assure me that Grandma's death was not my fault. No one thought it was. So if that was what was keeping me in the coma, I should rise. At other times he would be optimistic, talking about his plans, about a vacation to Goa, a new electric guitar that he had bought me, a party that he was planning to throw after my recovery. But mostly, he appeared normal and self-possessed. He would talk about his college, the snowfall that would soon be engulfing Shimla, my school, Nishant and Mayur's inquiries.

'I told them you were fine. You'll be joining them next week.'

Shweta, on the other hand, would always cry. She'd try being upbeat but tears would eventually find their way out, choking her. Then she would go quiet.

Pramod Uncle also paid me a visit once with Ayush. He spoke to the doctor who had nothing much to say other than to have faith. I was completing three weeks here and that had him worried.

I had but one endeavour: to convey that I heard them all. But I couldn't.

* * *

It was in the fourth week, almost a week after Anya said that I was the best thing that had happened to her, that I finally found the strength to twitch a few fingers. I gathered all the energy I could muster. A nurse was in the room. She had moved my body a little to prevent the formation of bedsores. After this she had proceeded to prepare an injection and, a few minutes later, I heard the crash of metal striking the floor; she must have noticed my twitching fingers.

'Doctor!' she screamed. 'The patient is responding!'

21

Hallucinations

Over the next week, the only activity I remember being able to perform, was responding to questions my doctor, Dr Mehta—a short, bespectacled, middle-aged man—asked.

His examination would begin with my eyes. He'd ask me to blink, close and open them, move them sideways. Then he would scribble something in his small diary. Next he would check my verbal response to a command, the usual 'Yes, sir' and 'No, sir'. He would jot this down as well. Lastly, he would assess my voluntary movements in response to a command. He told me and my family, Anya included, that these three checks constituted the Glasgow Coma Scale. The higher I scored, the better my chances of recovery without any loss of brain function.

On the first two days after regaining consciousness I managed an eleven out of a score of fifteen. When worried looks caught his gaze, Dr Mehta said this was normal.

'Recovery from a coma is usually gradual, with patients becoming more and more aware only over time. They may be alert and awake for a few minutes on the first day, but gradually they stay awake for longer and longer periods. They even regain brain function over time.'

By the end of the fourth week, Anya and I had resumed 'normal' conversations. I say normal, because again, a boundary between us had come up. I had no plans of transgressing it this time. I said sorry for the day I stalked her, she said it was okay and followed it up with a sorry too. Then we never spoke about it.

What we did speak about were her guitar prowess, movies and books, life, and about Sameer, who'd stopped visiting now, Aditya and Monica. Aditya had grown a goatee. Monica was the same.

When I told Anya that I could hear every word while I was unconscious she didn't believe me. When I insisted I thought I saw her blush.

'Everything?' she asked, her eyebrows angled to form a 'V'.

I nodded. I said eventually, 'So Anya, I'm the best thing that happened to you, huh?'

The colour drained from her face. She bit her lip and let the moment pass with a wide grin. Wagging a finger at me, she said, 'The asshole is back.'

I laughed.

So that's the way it went: we talked, we laughed, but there was no missing the stiltedness in our conversations, a sense of formality, obligation. It was more like we needed to talk, even though we didn't necessarily want to talk. It's how most people in the world behaved: they are driven to socialize more out of an obligation than desire, cocooning themselves in a false sheath of belonging.

Sometimes, I felt Anya had returned out of pity for me. First, she'd rejected me outright, then blasted me for stalking her and now I was in a hospital for a month, recovering from a coma. She knew I loved her and she didn't. Yes, perhaps pity was the right word.

It's sad when your first love rejects you, devastating when you know you won't be able to change their mind. I was gradually accepting the harshest truth of my life—that Anya and I would never be together.

Once the cloak of sadness for Anya and my doomed relationship lifted, I knew the guilt of Grandma's death would completely engulf me. I'd feel a huge burden in my chest as if someone was trying to squeeze all my organs. It would be very painful, more than any physical pain I'd ever known.

A few months ago I never thought I'd ever miss Grandma. But I did now. If she were alive, despite our differences, she'd have been concerned about my condition. Her forehead would be lined with nervous lines, and she'd have completely devoted herself to my recovery. This I say now because of a conversation I had with Ayush and Shweta.

Both of them would join me in my room right after college. It was a clean, compact room on the fifteenth floor, with plenty of sunshine streaming through the huge glass window that overlooked the city of Shimla. The tall PWD building stood in the distance with a wild, overgrown garden to its right.

Ayush and Shweta gave me a hug and a peck on the cheek before settling themselves on the couch. Ayush had a copy of my report in his hand and went through it. My brain function, Dr Mehta had said, was intact; I was only struggling with the physical activities. I wasn't able to walk unaided and he planned to enrol me for physiotherapy lessons next week.

Ayush put the report down on the small three-legged stool to his right. 'You're going to be out of here soon,' he said. 'I'm so glad.'

After a few pleasantries the conversation shifted to Grandma. Shweta's eyes filled with tears.

'Can I ask you both something?' I propped myself up on my elbows and rested my back against the steel rails of the bed. Ayush stood up to help, but I gestured for him to sit down. 'You have to promise you're going to be honest.'

'Of course,' Shweta said. She'd got herself a pair of round glasses that were pulled too close to her eyes.

I took a deep breath. 'Do you think it was intentional . . . the accident?'

'No,' Ayush said sharply. 'Of course not.' He shook his head. 'I'm sorry, okay. I know I said it that day, but I was angry and sad. I'm sorry. I didn't mean to hold you responsible.'

I shifted my gaze to Shweta.

'Sahil, please, don't do this to yourself. It was not your fault.'

It was too late. I was already fighting the huge lump of sadness that had constricted my throat, giving way to a deep, choking sob. I pressed my hands against my face, covering it entirely, and let the tears lighten my heart.

'It's not your fault,' Shweta persisted. 'It's not your fault, Sahil. It was an accident.'

Ayush was at my side and settled my head under his chin, softly patting my shoulder with his other arm.

Why did I blame him for the accident that day? It was a mistake. I hope it doesn't affect his health.

My mind was spinning now. Ayush wasn't saying anything but I could hear his voice in my head, in deep surround-sound; the words spoken slowly and deliberately.

I was probably hallucinating. I ignored it. 'I . . . I'm so s-sorry,' I managed to stutter between my sobs, 'for Grandma.'

'It was not your fault, Sahil,' said Shweta again. 'Please, don't do this to yourself.'

I couldn't stop the tears. I didn't want to. With every drop I felt lighter.

'It's all right,' Ayush said, planting a kiss on the top of my head. 'Big boys don't cry.'

Despite my sadness, a tiny giggle escaped me. Shweta smiled with me and Ayush too. He ruffled my hair and kissed me once more.

There was a knock on the door and a scrawny man in a green uniform came striding along with my evening tea, some glucose biscuits and a sandwich. I composed myself and wiped my eyes. Ayush settled himself back on the couch and ordered a sandwich, a *samosa* and two coffees.

I quietly drank my tea but I could feel their eyes on me. Ayush cleared his throat. 'I want you to know that Grandma loved you a lot.'

And now I paid heed to his every word. Grandma was worried and concerned about me because, according to her, I had lost my path. Her methods to chasten me might have been harsh, but her intentions were always pure. She wanted only good things for me, nothing else. She always felt Ayush and Shweta would manage to find their place in the world, but I might struggle, not because I was foolish or incompetent but because I had a lot of issues with the world.

And then came the most overwhelming news: Grandma had stashed a few lakhs, her entire savings, in my name; nothing for Ayush or Shweta. She said it was for my writing career or music career or whatever else I planned to pursue.

'Why are you telling me all this now?' I was choking again. It was regret that filled me this time. 'Please don't make me sorrier than I already am.'

Ayush shook his head. 'I'm telling you this because whenever you think of her now, I want you to smile and recall only the good memories.'

22

Blessings

Sometime in the fifth week of my stay at the hospital, I scored a complete fifteen on the Glasgow Coma Scale. Dr Mehta wanted me to stay for another week under close observation to ascertain that all my parameters were normal. Post-breakfast I had two hours of physiotherapy sessions that was conducted in a big, spacious room, a few floors below.

A spent a lot of time reading—in the mornings after physiotherapy, in the afternoons, at night till bedtime.

Ayush had got me a Kindle e-reader—and a get well soon card—and after only a few clicks, and Ayush's credit card details, I had downloaded a dozen books. I read old classics, Agatha Christie crime thrillers, Stephen King, Roald Dahl, a few Sidney Sheldon thrillers, Blyton, Archer and dystopian short stories by Kafka.

It was the only way I could distract myself while confined to the four walls of my room. My own book, the one I was writing, seemed far-fetched now. So much had happened so fast, I'd lost my creative potential. My mind was always crowded with plenty of thoughts and emotions. Despite Ayush and Shweta's convincing appeals that Grandma's death was an accident, a part of me still felt it wasn't. Sometimes that part grew fairly strong, and, like a raging storm out at sea, would drown me in huge waves of self-pity, regret and loathing.

When she was alive, I snubbed Grandma all the time, and now I wanted to hug her and apologize. Stupid human beings that we are, sense dawns on us only when it's too late.

Spending day after day in the hospital, despite the company of loved ones, became excruciatingly boring and monotonous. Lonely, too. What would I do after this? I'd go back to a life of routine: school, music class and home. Where was the excitement in that? Something was missing. Something primary and fundamental. Maybe life itself.

Or was it Anya that was missing?

Sometimes, on an ordinary day, you experience magic. Just when thoughts of her infiltrated my mind, the door to my room opened, and she came trotting inside, smiling, flaunting her dimple, a bored and tired Sameer behind her.

I put my Kindle down. She proceeded to the side of my bed, ducked a little, and gave me a hug. I wrapped my arms around her and buried my head in her hair: her soft, beautiful, strawberry-smelling hair.

This moment, right now, was incredible. If life was frequently sprinkled with moments like these, the human race would survive for a very, very long time.

Thank god, he's all right.

Suddenly Anya's booming voice was in my head. I shivered, unclasped my arms from around her back and retreated to face her. She straightened up and looked down at me with eager eyes.

'Did you just say something?'

She shook her head and took a seat on the couch where Sameer was flipping through a magazine.

I was so sure I had heard her voice. It was loud and resonant, spoken slowly and deliberately. What was happening to me?

I was probably losing my mind, hearing words that were not spoken. Maybe it was a side-effect of the coma.

'When do you get out of here?' Sameer asked.

'Next week,' I said. 'Maybe.' I picked up the Kindle and fiddled with it. 'Sometimes I wonder if I want to.'

'Why?' asked Anya.

'Look what I have done,' I said, waving my hands, as if that answered her. When she looked at me questioningly, I explained, 'I feel bad that I was never nice to Grandma. That I killed her. Maybe I killed my parents too.' I shook my head. 'Ayush says I'm thinking too much, but I feel bad you know . . . about everything. I feel sorry for them also, for Ayush and Shweta . . .'

I traced circles with my right index finger across the bed sheet and I stopped talking, gazing at the imaginary circles. I had their rapt attention, so I continued, 'In the seventeen years of my life I have failed at making a friend. Yesterday Mayur, Nishant and Sammy paid me a visit, but it was forced, formal. They came because they *had* to not because they wanted to. But I don't blame them. I'm hardly a friend to them . . . And the girl I love, I can't even—'

I cut myself short. I couldn't even say it. That is why it was sad and frustrating. Anya had lowered her eyes to the floor but Sameer looked on.

'I wish I had never woken up. I wish I had died.'

At this Anya looked directly at me.

'Maybe suicide is the answer,' I muttered.

In a flash Sameer was at the edge of my bed, concern on his face. 'Don't even think of that!' he warned with a firm finger pointed at me. I'd never seen him so focused. 'What do you think will happen after that?'

'I don't know . . . I'll be free.'

'What if you end up in a world worse than this?'

'What if I don't?'

Sameer smiled and looked over his shoulder at Anya. I couldn't observe the look they exchanged. Then he told me what he'd told Sneha, the girl from our music academy who had attempted suicide a month ago. He'd seen a film on life after suicide that had greatly affected him. The soul, it seems, wandered around helplessly for eternity, unable to talk to loved ones, to sleep or to be at peace. There was a constant ringing in the ears and a perpetual headache. It is a much worse place and people who committed suicide regretted it every second of their afterlife. He went on dissuading me and I hung on to his every word.

I don't know if it was the words he chose, his coherence, his steely expression or his conviction, but he managed to convince me so much so that I shuddered to think of what would become of me if I committed suicide. I decided I wouldn't.

'The next time the thought of suicide comes to you,' he said, 'you must speak to me immediately.' There was nothing but absolute sincerity in his eyes.

'Why do you care so much?'

He sighed. 'Because I have lost a friend to suicide.'

After giving me an appreciative nod for heeding his advice, Sameer left for the cafeteria on the first floor, leaving me befuddled in his wake.

When I shifted my gaze from the door to Anya, she held up a hand. 'Don't ask me,' she said. 'He's a complicated guy.'

So I didn't ask.

She flashed her dimples at me, which made me smile. I think I made her uncomfortable because she looked everywhere but directly at me—out of the window, the ceiling, the bed. Finally, she settled her gaze back on me. Clearing her throat, she said, 'I'm so sorry for what happened to you. I hope you know I'd trade places with you in a heartbeat.'

It was when she said sympathetic words like these, that she annoyed me the most. I didn't doubt her concern, I knew it was genuine, but it was paradoxical. Couldn't she just tell me her secret? Why couldn't she fall in love with me? That saddened and disconcerted me the most: not knowing her completely.

I wanted to say, don't love me, I won't force my love on you, but at least tell me why.

She wouldn't but she continued looking at me with concerned expressions, her lips compressed lips, her eyes filled with tears.

Then I remembered something we'd discussed on our first date three months ago.

'You know, Anya,' I said coolly, 'I wonder why your parents abandoned you. You are such a great girl.'

The comment hit home. If I'd been playing darts, I'd just shot one right in the bullseye. Anya panicked, her hands shivered, her lips trembled.

'No, I'm not,' she managed limply.

'What did you do?' I pressed on.

'I was a bad daughter.'

'Yeah, but *what* did you do?'

She shook her head and her eyes filled so fast I didn't get time to react. Tears came streaming down her cheeks and her hands moved swiftly to wipe them away.

I pulled myself out of bed and settled down beside her. I looped an arm around her shoulder. 'Anya, I didn't mean to . . .' I stopped, deciding to press the issue. 'I'm sorry but I want to know. Don't tell me the other things but I want to know this.'

She continued sobbing and shaking her head. 'I was a very bad daughter.' She cupped her face in her hands as she cried.

Now I wondered if her tears were genuine. I asked a few more times. She didn't answer.

She knew everything about me, but I knew nothing about her. That agitated me.

Ten or twenty minutes later when she returned from the washroom, wiping her face, I gave words to my thoughts. 'Anya, you know everything about me, but I know nothing about you. It annoys me.' I had returned to my bed now.

'Look, Sahil,' her voice downright understanding, 'I know and I'm sorry. My parents just hate me. They don't want to talk to me because I did some horrible things. What else is there to say?'

'But they are alive,' I said, 'unlike mine. I'd give anything in the world just to talk to my parents once.'

Here, I choked. Now Anya came over to the bed and patted my back. I guess it was a day for tears. I cried a little.

'No,' I said wiping my face, 'really. I miss them a lot. But at least you have a—'

'Okay,' she said, 'I know what you should do.' She moved to a drawer by the bed, opened it and searched for something. Then she handed me a pen and a small blank sheet of paper.

'Instead of feeling sad,' she said, 'write a list of five things that you feel blessed to have. It's the best way to feel good about life.'

It could have been the anger, sadness or frustration; it could have also been Anya's hypocrisy or her complete refusal to answer my question which led me to do what I did. I snatched the paper from her hand, crumpled it till it was a tiny ball and hurled it at the wall.

'Anya, just get the hell out of here!'

'What happened?'

'All you have are your damn tips and advice to lead a better life!' I said with my teeth clenched. 'You know what: I don't want any of your bullshit! Just leave me alone with my fucked up life!'

She left without bothering to reply.

23

The Sixth Murder

I woke up the next day with a searing headache and fetched a copy of the *Shimla Times*.

THE MYSTERIOUS MURDERS IN SHIMLA

In an unforeseen turn of events, the police last evening discovered the corpse of another brutally murdered man in the eastern part of the city. The deceased has been identified as Sanjay Singh, son of Mr Brajesh Singh, the leader of the opposition party in Shimla. This is the sixth murder in the last three months, and the police still remain clueless about the killer or the motive for the crime. The forensics team has confirmed that the DNA samples and fingerprints found at the scene of the crime are identical to those found at the previous murder sites. All the six victims were men in the age group of twenty to thirty-five, and were castrated and tortured ruthlessly before being murdered.

The Shimla deputy commissioner, Pramod Mishra, has expressed his disappointment over the failure of his department in solving the case. Senior members of the opposition party are demanding a CBI probe into the murders, saying this is an unmitigated failure on the part of Shimla's police administration.

The Himachal Pradesh governor, Suman Goswami, has rebuffed the intervention of the CBI and has upheld that the state police is competent enough to solve the case. He has sought a detailed report from the police and, adopting a tough stand on the murders, has summoned senior police officials for an immediate action plan. He has also asked the state DGP to present an inquiry report with his comments.

I dropped the paper with a sigh. This murder mystery was growing deeper. I wondered how many more murders would take place before the killer was caught?

When the ward boy brought in my breakfast and tea, I perused the newspaper for further details. It was unanimously accepted it was the same killer with the same modus operandi. The media and the police had filed the murders as hate crimes, although it hadn't been established if they were sectarian in nature or a personal vendetta.

The paper spoke at length about the anguish and anger of Shimlaites. Effigies of Pramod Uncle and the chief minister were being burnt. Outside the police headquarters protests were staged demanding the dismissal of the SP. The police had to use force to dispel the crowd when they turned raucous and hurled stones at the building. Some protestors were injured leading to more agitation.

There was another article in the paper where Brajesh Singh proclaimed that the murders were propaganda by the ruling party; the killing of his son was an attempt to weaken their preparation for the upcoming elections. A senior member of the ruling party responded that it was, to the contrary, propaganda by the opposition party to gain sympathy from the people of Shimla before the elections. 'Mr Brajesh Singh,' he said, 'is willing to go to extreme lengths to come to power, even sacrificing his son.'

In the afternoon when Ayush and Shweta paid me a visit, I asked them about the fifth murder since there wasn't any mention of it in the paper. Ayush said it had been committed in the same brutal manner while I was in the coma.

'By the way, you'll be discharged tomorrow,' Shweta said. The smile on her face was wide.

'Did you speak to Pramod Uncle?' I asked Ayush. 'He must be going through a hellish time.'

'Yeah,' he said, nodding. 'There is a lot of pressure on him. He says the worst part's not knowing what the hell is going on. The victims are all chosen at random.'

'But I remember he had a plan. He'd said it was some kind of satanic ritual.'

Ayush shook his head. 'That plan failed. It is much more than that.'

Shweta added, 'He was saying the manner in which the victims have been murdered has infuriated the people more.'

I recoiled when the images of the two dead Cottonians in the Gaiety theatre flashed in my mind: their bodies twisted, limbs mutilated, drenched in a pool of blood. It was horrifying. At the time it seemed they were the first and the last of such murders.

I wondered when the next murder would occur and who would be the next victim.

* * *

After five weeks and five days in the hospital, I was finally being discharged. Ayush was in attendance all morning and had completed all the paperwork and formalities. Dr Mehta had carried out a general check-up the previous evening. He'd given his approval, assuring me that I was in good enough shape to leave.

After packing, a nurse, tall and gaunt, approached me in my room and handed a feedback form. There was a mournful edge to her expression. Her fingers brushed mine as she explained the columns that I needed to fill.

I hope Sunil comes out of his coma, too.

My hand flew to my head at the loud, distorted sound. I shot her a glance. 'Who's Sunil?'

A stunned pair of eyes glared at me. 'My son,' she said, her hand on her chest. 'But how did you know?'

With chilling intensity it dawned on me that I was somehow able to read minds.

24

The Bus Accident

Winters had arrived in Shimla. It was November and the snowfall would commence within a month. However, cool winds from the north had already gripped the city. The sun hardly made an appearance and people had begun to dress in woollens.

At school I received a warm welcome. It had been a month and a half since I was last there. Students crowded around me, questioning me, one after the other. Mayur, Nishant and Sammy offered me a hug each. After ensuring that I was in the pink of health, Sammy proceeded to the front bench where Gracy awaited him.

As the day wore on, every teacher, upon entering, spent the first two minutes inquiring about my health. During the lunch break, students from other classes who knew me because I was in the school band, continued the Q and A session. I wondered if they cared or were just plain curious.

During classes, I pondered about the mind-reading skill that I had acquired while in a coma. It had happened on three different occasions now. I clearly remember hearing Ayush's and Anya's voices when they hadn't said anything. But when I thought harder I realized there was one catch: to be able to read a person's mind I had to be in physical contact with them. I was crying in Ayush's arms, I had hugged Anya and the nurse yesterday had flicked her fingers against mine. Only then had their thoughts morphed into words in my mind.

My heart filled with joy and fear at the implications of what I could achieve with this newfound power. Joy because I could read Anya's mind and know her secrets, maybe find a way to get her to love me, and fear of discovering something I didn't want to know.

Either way, Anya's secret, whatever it was, wouldn't be a secret for long.

During music class questions were fired from all angles at me. Rajiv was very glad to have me back. Now he could leave the beginners with me and disappear to do his other chores. Mayur, Sammy and I did a 'we're back' piece, a rendition of an old Eagles song, with Rajiv on the flute, and soft applause filled the tiny room when it ended. Anya tried to imitate my swift chord progression but trailed behind. Sameer was lost, his eyes tired and sleepy.

After the class, Anya, Sameer and I met Aditya and Monica. The three of us walked over to the main road where Aditya was waiting with Monica in his blue hatchback. We got in and the engine roared to life.

Aditya drove straight towards Mall Road with Monica giving him directions. Just as we'd got into the car, Aditya, Monica and Sameer expressed their sympathy. I replied with a perfunctory 'Thank you', hoping that was the end, but they carried on, bombarding me with questions about my health until Anya intervened. 'Guys, enough! He's been answering questions all day. He's FINE now!'

I had never felt more grateful.

We had no idea where we were going. We decided to embrace it and termed it my recovery road trip. All around us were hills with narrow roads that wound around them. The sun was about to set, expending the last of its energy in this part of the world. I poked my head out of the window and a fresh, cool breeze snaked through my hair. Birds chirped merrily above us. I settled back and glanced at Anya and she smiled at me. Next to her Sameer had his eyes shut but by the wavering of his eyelids I could tell he wasn't asleep. In front, Monica and Aditya were discussing road accidents on the hills.

I had grazed my shoulder against Anya's so as to hear something. So far there was nothing. Her mind was as empty as a pauper's bank account. Blank. Was I really able to read minds after all?

Suddenly, the three of us seated at the back rammed our heads into the front seats as the car pulled to a screeching halt. Screams ensued from the girls and my heart thudded loudly in my chest at the thought of a probable accident. We looked ahead. There was nothing.

Aditya jumped from his seat, wrenched open the door and sprinted to the back of the car. We whirled in our seats and glanced back. Aditya was nowhere to be seen. Just as we shared confounded looks, a school bus full of children roared past us. I squinted and could see Aditya taking control of the steering wheel of the bus. Sameer climbed into the driver's seat of our car and followed the bus which had started veering uncontrollably ahead of us. And then we saw it just as we approached the bus from the left: the rear tyre of was jutting out, threatening to go over the cliff and take the bus with it. Aditya stopped the bus just in time and parked it on the shoulder of the road. Sameer pulled our car to a stop just behind the bus and we all leapt out.

Aditya dismounted from the bus with the driver. Monica and Anya boarded the bus to comfort the kids.

'Hey, good job!' said Sameer, patting Aditya.

We inspected the tyre assembly and discovered the nuts holding it in place were sheared off, making the entire unit unstable and wobbly.

'Thank God,' Aditya said, lighting a cigarette, 'I was here. This damn thing would have come off and the bus would have fallen off the cliff.'

All this while the question of how he knew vexed me. I looped my arm around his shoulder. 'But hey, Aditya, how the hell did you know such a thing was going to happen? The goddamn bus was behind us.'

He stubbed his cigarette with his foot, looked at the others before peering back at me and mumbled something inaudible under his breath.

I didn't need to pay attention to what he was saying as there it was, loud and clear, Aditya's voice in my head: *Oh god, does he know?*

Something was very wrong here.

* * *

The TV blared in the living room and Ayush and Shweta's eyes were fixated on it. A debate on the mysterious murders of Shimla played out on a popular national news channel. There were five panellists: senior members from both the ruling and opposition parties, an official from the Shimla police department who was Pramod Uncle's sidekick, a veteran Bollywood actor who hailed from Shimla who was very furious and a human rights activist.

The bone of contention was simple: why had the government suddenly woken up only when a politician's son was murdered? No tangible action had been taken until then and, after the sixth murder, the entire police department was running helter-skelter to catch the killer. There were talks of the CBI intervening, the Himachal Pradesh governor was all primed, the state DGP and his forces and been brought in, and Shimla had been put on high alert.

'Why was this not done before? Is the common man not important?'

The debate moderator was articulate, assertive and straightforward, and had not hesitated to convey his point right at the onset of the debate. However, in lieu of answers all we got were glib statements.

Soon, thoughts of the mysterious murders in Shimla were replaced in my mind with thoughts about Anya and her mysterious friends.

Aditya definitely did not see the bus coming. He had no possible clue the bus was heading for an accident. Neither could he have known about the car that almost hit the young family on Mall Road.

How did Sameer know that Sneha was on the roof of our music academy, contemplating suicide?

Monica bothered me with her furtive smiles and glances.

And Anya, the most enigmatic one of them all. Even her name brought a question to my mind. I knew nothing about her other than her insistent declaration that she was a bad daughter and that, from time to time, she would hear something and then disappear mysteriously.

Who the hell were these people?

25

The Game

Annandale, in Shimla, is a top tourist spot. The flat terrain has been developed as a playground for the city: beautiful, lush and green. Years ago it was a pleasure ground for the British and it still preserves the atmosphere of old Shimla. It's just a couple of kilometres from the Ridge, and though mostly people ride to get there, I prefer walking. I prefer walking even more when Anya is by my side.

That day I taught her how to play the classic song *'Neele neele ambar par'* on the guitar—the perfect Hindi song for the instrument, she told me—and she was so thrilled she wanted to spend rest of the evening with me. I more than wholeheartedly agreed.

The previous day as I lay on my bed with just the bedside light on and a book in my hands—a book I barely read—I construed that whatever happened, happened for a reason. My mind-reading skills, for instance, had appeared because I had unanswered questions. I still wouldn't get answers if I didn't use my skills efficiently.

So I thought of a little something to optimize the use of my gift.

There were two basic things I needed to do: establish physical contact—I figured I'd hold her hand—and, I needed to engage her mind. I'd failed the day in the car when her mind was completely blank. So I figured the best way to do that would be to ask questions.

We walked slowly across the ground. There were a hundred different shades of green all around us. Not far from where we were walking there were people playing golf on the well-manicured course. Families relaxed under the late November sun.

Anya suggested visiting the Army Heritage Museum. I refused. Instead I gradually snuck my hand into hers. I started with the index finger of my right hand against the palm of her left hand. When she didn't rebuff me I slid my entire hand in.

If you didn't have very observant eyes, you wouldn't have seen the tiny smile caressing her cheeks, the little depression forming in them, and a subtle nod, an approval, perhaps, saying, 'Okay, holding hands is allowed.'

As much as I was relieved that she let me do that, it struck me with deep-seated annoyance that our whole arrangement was damn odd: we couldn't talk about love but we could hold hands.

Slowly I linked my fingers in hers and squeezed. She followed suit and, at the gesture, my heart skipped a beat. Her hand was cold and soft and delicate. I could have held it for a lifetime.

'Hey,' she said, 'let's just sit there for a bit. There's a beautiful view.' She nodded towards a bench overlooking the valley and the deodar trees.

As we sat, she didn't let go of my hand.

Okay, this was my chance.

'Do you want to play a game?'

'A game?' she asked, arching her eyebrows. 'You want to play a game here? Okay, what game?'

'Truth or dare,' I said. 'Only you can't choose dare.'

'What?' she asked. 'What kind of game is that?'

'My game, my rules.'

She rolled her eyes. 'Why do I get the feeling I made a mistake coming here?'

After a couple minutes spent haggling, we began playing.

I looked away, focused on how to properly frame my question, turning back only once I had it. 'So . . . um . . . what do you love most about yourself?'

I looked into her eyes and concentrated hard, trying to hear something. She was thinking. I concentrated harder. *Changed . . . Help . . . Friend . . .*

'Okay,' she started, still ruminating. 'I love that . . . um . . . I'm happy that I have *changed* myself over the years. I never thought that I could be the person I am now. Trust me, I was a pathetic person earlier. Anyway, that story is for another day. So yeah, I love that about myself—that I was able to transform myself. The other thing I like is that I try to *help* others a lot, and I'm a good *friend*. At least that's what people tell me . . . So did that answer your question?'

'Yeah, yeah,' I said, wondering if that's what I'd heard. 'Yeah, you did. Good.' I raked my hand through my hair. That's exactly what I heard, though fragmented versions of it. But that made sense given that she herself wasn't sure of the answer.

It was her turn next, and she asked me, 'Where do you see yourself five years from now?' I didn't even think about it because I was actually thinking about the next question I would ask her and so I vaguely replied, 'A writer, maybe.'

She winked and said, 'I like the answer.'

'So my turn next,' I said not giving her time to add anything else. 'Tell me your second-biggest regret.'

She was taken aback. 'Second?' she asked. 'Why are you so weird sometimes? Everyone usually asks you your biggest regret, not second-biggest.'

I patted her with my free hand. 'That's because I already know your first.'

'And that is?'

'Your parents, right? You were not a good daughter.'

Her jaw tightened. She nodded.

'So, the second?'

I zoned out everything else I could hear—the clatter of people around us, the rustling of leaves, the honking of cars far away, everything. I wanted to hear this.

I froze when I heard the next word even before she said it: *Pregnant.* I regretted playing this game.

She glanced at me, her expression hollow. 'You might hate me when I say this, but I don't want to hide it from you.' She looked away. 'I was pregnant a few years ago.'

Her words hit me with an almost physical force. I took a deep breath and was saddened by this revelation.

For the next few minutes, there was a deafening silence between us. I wouldn't say she was embarrassed to share this with me, but she grew uneasy. A couple of minutes later she looked at me, smiling that fake smile I knew so well by now and said, 'Okay, now it's my turn to ask.'

When it was my turn again, I warded off all diplomacy. 'How do Aditya and Sameer always happen to know if an accident or suicide is happening in the vicinity? They always reach there before and stop it from happening.'

At that she laughed. 'Why are you asking me about them? They are geniuses, what more can I say.'

'Incorrect answer,' I said and concentrated. Our fingers were still linked.

She didn't reply but I heard something nevertheless, *Shit, he knows.*

'Fine, don't answer that,' I said. 'I'll ask you a replacement question: I want to know about your parents. What did you do to piss them off so badly that they abandoned you?'

Before I could hear anything she jerked her hand away. 'Sahil, this is getting too personal now.' She hiccupped, shook her head and then a couple of tears trickled down her cheeks. She pinched her lips and looked the other way.

I shook my head and sighed. 'Anya, I can't bear to see you like this. You always cry when I talk about your parents. What happened?'

She continued looking away, her hands covering her face. I couldn't tell if she was even listening.

'You have to tell me what the hell happened,' I said. 'I'll help you. I'll go talk to them if you want.'

She cleared her throat. 'You don't understand. There's nothing you can do.'

'Can you at least give me a chance?'

Her red, pudgy eyes now faced me. She sniffled loudly. 'No!' she said tersely.

I moved away and crossed my arms. She was crying now, full-throttle; her hands hid her face. Her shoulders wavered with the gasping of every breath.

'I want to know, Anya.'

I had to wait for a few minutes. She gathered herself slowly and wiped her eyes. 'I'm sorry, but I can't.'

That did it. I pushed myself up angrily. 'Okay,' I said, looking down. 'You said I could never ask for the reason why you couldn't fall in love me. I obliged with much suffering. Now if you can't even tell me what it is that makes you so guilty, it means you don't even think of me as a friend. This whole thing then, between you and me, is utterly meaningless.'

Her silence incited me to say what I said next, even though I regretted it immediately. 'I'm going to ask you one last time. I know you are stubborn, but trust me I'm no less stubborn. If you don't tell me right now I swear I'll walk out of your life, *never* to return. What did you do?'

Nothing.

I felt angry and insulted. 'All right then, bye,' I said, turning on my heels.

I walked no more than twenty metres, when she called out my name. 'Okay,' she said, cupping her hands around her mouth, 'come back. I'll tell you everything.'

26

Anya

Anya was a spoiled brat a few years ago; an 'arrogant bitch' in her words. She was selfish, moody, cynical and hated the world and everyone around her. She got pregnant for the first time at sixteen. Then, twice when she was seventeen. The three abortions, although a cause of constant mortification to her parents, never bothered her. She continued living life on the edge—drinking, partying and sleeping with boys her age; sometimes even men double her age.

In school, she flunked regularly and was a very bad influence on the other kids, as her teachers told her parents during school meetings. She was rusticated more than a couple of times for indecent behaviour. On one instance, she was caught kissing a boy in the washroom while the buttons of her shirt were flung open. When confronted by the teacher who'd caught them, Anya muttered lewd words under her breath, but she later denied having said them. Nonetheless, the principal had issued a two-week suspension from school.

That was only her suspension. She was fourteen at the time. At home her parents launched a tirade at her and locked her in a room. That fuelled the rebellion in her and she grew nastier as she grew older.

Anya never understood why it was such a big deal. She wasn't killing anybody, wasn't hurting anybody. Hell, she was only having a good time. What more was there to do in life, anyway? People never got that. They were all busy moping through their own lives, struggling, fretting over inconsequential things and sulking over the unfairness of it all. They were slaves to their lives, their minds, their families. No one lived for themselves. And they didn't let her live life the way she wanted to.

She had grown increasingly fond of rock music during those days; the louder, the filthier, the better. Her interest in music and the guitar had developed during those days. But she could never get herself to learn how to play or do anything about it. A friend of hers at the time had introduced her to *charas*. Within no time, she became an addict. Life was a roller coaster ride all day.

The first time she became pregnant, it was by a boy she'd met at a local bar. He was a struggling musician, as naïve about everything as her. She was a few months shy of seventeen then. When her parents demanded to know who the father was, she tried very hard but couldn't even recall his name. Her mother was livid and hit her so hard on her face that Anya retaliated and shoved her against the wall, where she hit her head. At the sight of his wife's blood, Anya's father began hitting her. Two days later, she had an abortion.

A year later, she eloped with a man fifteen years older than her. They were lived in a small house by the hills, a few kilometres outside Solan. Her parents, worried and concerned, lodged a missing person's report at the local police station. Anya was so famous, rather infamous, in her small town of Mahdauri in Himachal that the police refused to take up the case. They told her parents that the 'slut' would eventually come back.

They couldn't have been more correct. After a month of debauchery, the man suddenly disappeared. Anya looked for him everywhere but he was gone. For three weeks she remained in that house, doing drugs and drinking before finally proceeding back home. Her parents, indignant and tired, didn't say anything to her.

She was pregnant again. The day she found out, she aborted the baby.

The third pregnancy happened six months later. She was so high that night that she didn't even see the face of the man. Her parents finally threw her out of the house and disowned her.

Anya moved to Shimla and didn't return to her house in Mahdauri again.

27

Anya's Home

Her eyes were sore and puffy from all the crying in the past hour. I initially debated about it but finally put my arm around her shoulder to pacify her. It was futile. She was breathing heavily, choking and coughing. I massaged her back gently until the coughing subsided.

'So now you know,' she croaked. The words came out of her mouth in guttural gasps. Faintly she lifted her head and gazed at me. She looked weak and emaciated.

'I'm sorry,' was all I could muster.

She shook her head. 'I don't know what kind of person I was.'

Silence hung over us for a couple of minutes. It was eerie, distant.

'Hey, you know what?' I said. 'Let's go back to your place. I'll meet your parents and tell them that you are a completely changed person now.'

She shot me a frightening glance. 'No!' she said. 'Never! That can never happen!'

'But why?'

'I don't want to give them any more pain than I already have.'

'They are your parents, Anya,' I said. 'They'll eventually forgive you.'

She shook her head. 'You don't understand.'

'Listen Anya, I don't care what you have to say. I'm going there and telling them that their daughter is a wonderful person and that I love her very much. You can decide if you want to come with me or not.'

Why doesn't he get it? It's not possible. What do I tell him?

'Are you going to come with me?'

Oh god! What do I say?

She surprised me by saying yes.

* * *

The next morning, a Saturday, I took Ayush's permission to borrow our old sedan that we had repaired after the accident. It was dusty and parked under a tree, dried leaves strewn on its roof. I cleaned it up and picked Anya up from Mall Road.

The streets of Shimla were swarming with policemen. There were security checks and barricades, and the entry and exit of every vehicle was monitored. At the last check post I'd held out my driver's licence—a fake—and the car's registration papers. The stout policeman had seized Anya and me up with his brown eyes before nodding and letting us pass.

Anya's home was a little more than fifty kilometres from Shimla. For an hour I drove through the hills before finally hitting the plains. As we crossed an old, bedraggled bridge that hung over a small lake, Anya asked me to pull the car over. She got out and rested her arms on the rusty railing, taking in the fresh air. She stood there for a couple of minutes while I waited in the car at the edge of the road. When she settled back in I asked if she was okay. She said she was and we proceeded.

Mahdauri was a small town and the population density was low. The roads were wide but full of potholes. I had to nudge the breaks several times and weave around them carefully. Anya gave me directions to her place. The houses to my left, I noticed, were mostly old and dilapidated. Over the right was a vast expanse of wild, open land that stretched as far as the eyes could see.

After a few sharp turns to the left, Anya nodded ahead. I pulled over outside the house. It was an old, tawny coloured building; a big, rust-stained gate guarding it. The area around was quiet and there were not too many people out on the wide road. I looked at Anya. She appeared very uncomfortable.

'So are you ready for this?' I asked nodding in the direction of her house.

She shook her head. 'I'm not going in.'

'Why?'

She refused and I couldn't force her. I thought about going in and talking to her parents. I wanted them to forgive her and take her back. Anya was a good person and she deserved this. I had to do this for her.

I got out of the car. Anya was breathing heavily now. She leapt towards the window on my side, rolled it down, and looked at me with nervous eyes.

'Promise me,' she said, 'that you won't tell them I'm here. Don't tell them that and don't talk too much. Come back soon or I'll just go.'

I promised.

I walked towards the house. The gate squeaked as I pushed it open. The ground floor was locked. The windows were dusty and it didn't look like anyone stayed there. I took the stairs to my left. They creaked with each passing step. On the first floor

I rang the bell. A short, pot-bellied man opened the door. He peered down at me in contempt.

'Who are you?' he asked.

'Um—' I looked over my shoulder quickly, 'I'm a friend of Anya's, I . . .'

'Anya?' He bared his teeth. 'What do you want?'

'Well . . . could I come inside?'

He glared at me. A woman, almost as small as him, walked up to the door. Instantly, I could tell she was Anya's mother.

'Who's this boy?' she asked her husband.

He snorted. 'Says he's Anya's friend.'

Her mother ushered me in. I sat on one of the shaky chairs. The furniture was old and tattered. Paint was peeling off the walls and there wasn't any electricity. Anya's father had disappeared inside without saying anything further. Her mother returned with a glass of water.

'Thanks,' I said.

She pulled up a chair and sat down beside me. Her eyes were sad and hollow, and I could make out she hadn't been sleeping well.

'So,' she began, 'what brings you here?'

I placed the glass back on the table and wiped my lips. 'I wanted to talk about her.'

She gave me a weak smile. 'Talk? What do you want to talk about?'

'I'm sorry,' I ventured. 'I know what happened. I'm really sorry for that.'

She stared at me awkwardly.

I cleared my throat. 'Do you miss her?'

She looked at the wall behind me. A picture of Anya hung on the wall with a few other family snaps. 'Of course,' she said. 'Of course I miss her.'

'Have you forgiven her?'

She took a moment to answer, then subtly nodded her head.

'Really?' I was surprised at that revelation. After speaking to Anya I never thought her mother would say that.

'I know she wasn't a good child, but—'

'I don't care about that,' she snapped. 'I miss her and—'

Just then Anya's father barged in. He demanded furiously, 'What's going on here? Madhu, how many times have I told you not to talk about her? All she has given us is pain and nothing else. Just forget her.'

'But—'

'And you! Leave right now!'

'Sir, just one—'

He didn't let me speak. He grabbed me by my shoulder and threw me out. 'We don't want to discuss her! Get out!'

The door was banged shut on my face. I walked towards the car.

'What happened?' Anya asked as I got in.

After getting back on to the main road, I said, 'Your mother still loves you and misses you.'

'Really?' Her eyes sparkled. 'And my father?'

I thought about it. 'I think he misses you more than even your mother.' Perhaps it was a lie, but it brought a smile on her face.

A few hours later when we reached Shimla, she hugged me. It wasn't one of those friendly hugs that we'd shared in the past. She settled her head under my chin and wrapped her arms tightly around my back. It was the most wonderful moment of my life.

'I'm so lucky to have a friend like you,' she said. 'I love you.'

My eyes grew wide at that word.

She giggled and winked. 'Oops,' she said. 'I meant as a friend.'

28

Birthday

I spent the rest of the weekend wondering how else could I put my mind-reading skills to use. I still had to discover a lot about Anya. And about her friends. There was definitely something sneaky going on with them. If I could find out, maybe I'd be able to find the reason for Anya's adamant declaration that love between us wasn't a possibility.

On Saturday evening, Ayush and Shweta invited their friends over and threw a little party in honour of my recovery. I called Mayur, Nishant and Sammy, who although had said yes didn't turn up. I should have called Gracy too. The thought of inviting Anya and her friends did occur to me but I left it at that.

I got books and flowers as presents. Ayush ordered Chinese food from a nearby takeaway and Shweta prepared some home-made snacks that were delicious. Ayush had stacked the fridge with liquor but I was allowed only beer and strictly banned from any hard drinks. Ayush had made that clear and I didn't argue with him.

The party proceeded until midnight and thereafter everybody left, and I retired to my room.

Sunday evening there was another party. It was Monica's birthday. She had invited me to Wake and Bake Café. Anya, Sameer and Aditya were there too.

It being a Sunday the place was over-crowded. Monica had a reservation so we were able to avoid the long queue outside. We took a seat by the window overlooking the valley that was lit up like a wedding hall.

We clapped and sang 'Happy Birthday' when Monica cut the chocolate cake.

'Happy—what—eighteenth?' asked Anya, stuffing cake in Monica's mouth.

'No,' she said at once, chewing and wiping her lips. 'I don't think eighteen is correct.'

The others laughed out loud. I didn't get the joke.

Dinner was served and I tried to get rid of my questions. I wanted to enjoy my time with them. They were the closest friends I had, yet it felt as if I didn't know them.

Anya said with a click of her fingers, 'Hey Sahil! Where are you lost?'

I came back to the present. 'No-nowhere . . .'

'Hey guys, look!' Aditya said, nodding towards two bald, beefy guys to our right. We followed Aditya's gaze. The two boys appeared to be in their twenties but they were strong and staring menacingly at us.

'What are they doing here?' Anya asked, fear apparent in her voice.

I turned my gaze from those boys to my four companions, and saw that sweat had broken out on their faces.

'Who are those guys?' I asked.

No answer.

Aditya rose frantically. 'Move, let's move from here,' he said. 'Come on, quick!'

The other three clumsily jumped from their seats.

'Go, go!' Aditya said, still looking at the two boys in apprehension. 'Let's go!'

'Are they following us?' Monica asked, darting out.

'There's no time for this,' Aditya replied. 'Let's get out of here first.'

They scurried down the stairs. Not sure what to do I followed them, but not without a final glance at the two boys. They were still staring, their eyes following us to the stairs.

Back on the street, I asked, 'What the hell is going on, guys?'

No one uttered a word and the four of them just left, disappearing into the crowd without a trace.

29

Mayur

If life was a suspense thriller, I would have acceded to the current occurrences that had shaped my world. Strange. One after the other.

But life wasn't a suspense thriller. If anything, it was a drama—an agonizingly slow-paced, boring drama.

If I were to ask Anya about the two boys, all she'd do was mumble, 'Oh . . . you know . . . some guys,' and change the topic. I'd never get the answer that way.

This mystery was growing deeper, and I had a feeling I was in for a big surprise.

I was shaken out of my deep reverie by Mayur asking, 'Hey, what are you thinking about?' His jaw moved pointlessly, like a dog's tail, as he strutted up to my desk, Nishant in tow.

'You know what this *stud* is saying?' asked Nishant, adjusting his glasses.

'No,' I said, disinterestedly.

'Pallavi,' he hinted, stealing a glance at her.

'Oh, yeah,' I said. 'Mayur, it's December already. You said by the end of the year you would . . .'

'I know, I know,' he said. 'A few more days; I'm on it.'

'I bet you a thousand rupees she won't do you,' said Nishant. I cackled with him. 'Yeah, count me in.'

'You bastards,' he said. 'Just wait and watch.' His eyes then sought her out, starting at her from across the room. He gawked at her auburn hair, her bra that was made visible under her shirt by the light hitting her back, her healthy bottom, and her neat legs. Mayur's eyes held their position, whether at her bottom or her legs, I wasn't sure.

'If looks could fuck,' said Nishant, and giggled childishly.

Mayur thumped his fist against his chest.

'Let's go to the canteen,' he said. 'I'm hungry.'

'I'm not,' I said. 'You guys carry on.'

They figured the reason was Anya. I had told them more or less everything minus my mind-reading ability.

'You're crazy, man,' Mayur said, 'losing sleep over a girl. There are so many out there.'

'Do you want to bet she'll eventually fall in love with me,' I said.

Mayur shook his head.

'Hey, there's another bet we can make,' said Nishant. 'I saw your uncle on TV yesterday, being asked by a reporter about the killer—you know, his whereabouts, his age and the like.'

'So?'

'Let's guess the age of the psycho killer,' he said.

'Definitely, he's in his thirties,' Mayur said. 'I'd say thirty to thirty-five.'

Nishant looked at me. 'I think twenties,' I said.

'Pick one age guys,' he said. 'The closest one wins.'

'Thirty-four,' Mayur said.

I said twenty-eight.

'I think he's older,' said Nishant. 'You see he's a frustrated man, the way he kills his victims. I like to believe his family left him, he's alone or something like that. I'd pick forty . . . three. Okay, forty-three.'

Mayur clapped. 'Okay,' he said, 'this'll be fun. Let's put down a thousand bucks each. It'll be interesting to see who wins.'

Mayur was the first to find out the age of the killer. But he was never able to tell us.

Because he was the next victim.

30

The Seventh Murder

Mayur died the same way as the other victims. He was tortured and castrated. In his home. His blood was splattered all over the floor and walls of his bedroom.

I'd seen it on the evening news two days after our bet. When Mayur's face was displayed on TV, the dinner plate in my hands fell to the floor with a loud crash. Ayush and Shweta took a seat on the couch, one on either side of me, their arms patting my shoulders. We watched in stunned silence as the reporter presented the news.

The police reported that the time of death was around half past six. Images of his building and his room swarming with khaki uniforms were shown. His parents wailed into the camera. There was an older woman consoling his mother. His father did the talking and informed the reporter that they were at a relative's place. Mayur was alone at home.

The neighbours had confirmed they hadn't seen anyone suspicious around the neighbourhood or entering the flat around the time of the incident.

The police had ascertained it was the same killer, the fingerprints a perfect match to those found at the previous sites.

The toll had now climbed to seven and the media conveniently filed the story under the 'mysterious murders of Shimla' before switching over to the sports news.

I was devastated. Shell-shocked. Why Mayur?

We observed two minutes' silence in the morning assembly in school the next day. Back in our class we were too dumbfounded to speak—Nishant and I—while our classmates hovered around us, some offering condolences, others asking questions and few recounting their theories of how and why it happened.

The classes were restricted to discussions about Mayur. Even the teachers were distraught with grief. Their faces hung low.

Sometime during the third period, some of us—Mayur's friends mostly—were summoned to the principal's office. Her office was on the ground floor, a big and wide room, flanked by staff rooms on either side. On a normal day we'd have felt intimidated to enter it, but our teacher had informed us that the visit was on account of the questions being asked by the media.

Nevertheless, Nishant, Sammy and I entered the room with trepidation. Our principal was a surly, unforgiving old woman. She welcomed us with a small smile and showed us to our seats—an olive couch opposite her desk. There was another lady, a mic in her hands, a fat red *bindi* on her forehead, ingratiatingly smiling at us. A bulky man with a bulky camera and a few helpers also stood around.

The Q and A session took with it everything we knew of Mayur. He was a little skewed, all right, but he was harmless. When Fat Red Bindi asked us if we could provide any reason, clue, as to why he might have been chosen, the three of us shook our heads.

On our way out, we saw half a dozen media vans, antennae on top, cameras and journalists waiting near the main gate. Mayur was the news now.

Nishant finally broke down as we took the stairs to class. Sammy and I, overcome with grief, followed suit with salty tears. We hugged and wiped our eyes before entering class.

After school, Nishant and I paid Mayur's parents a visit. His mother cried inconsolably and his father, despite patting her back, seemingly in control, looked like he'd give out at any time. On the news, nothing of significance was reported; there was absolutely no clue about the killer who still remained at large after four months.

At home, I found out that Ayush had spoken to Pramod Uncle who, along with the entire department, remained befuddled about the crimes and the criminal.

Mayur and I weren't the best of friends but my heart ached every second for his loss. The circumstances of his death—the blood, mutilated limbs, castration—were horrifying. They haunted me for days.

Shweta, who sat at the adjacent seat at the dining table, squeezed my hands when a fresh bout of tears appeared.

'When's Rakesh Uncle coming back?' I asked, blowing my nose into a napkin.

'His ship,' she said, 'is stuck in the Pacific Ocean for a month now. Some engine trouble, he said. It's being towed to an island in Japan. He's completely shattered—Grandma's death, your coma, the murders. He desperately wants to come back but it'll take a few more weeks.'

Ayush gave my hand a tight squeeze. 'Don't worry,' he said. 'I'm here with you.' *Why has life been so unfair to him?* I heard him question silently.

Later, in my room, I resisted but finally gave in to the craving to cut my arms for release.

31

Rape

A little more than a week had passed since Mayur's death. Life wasn't the same again at school. Although Nishant and I talked, there hung that question 'Why Mayur?' in the air between us. We'd glance at his seat with a heavy heart and no sooner would a few tears manage to escape our eyes.

The sadness was further augmented by the complete ineptitude of the police. Newspapers overflowed with articles about the 'mysterious murders of Shimla'; every news channel held debates, interviews, special programmes on the murders; specialists presented their ideas, civilians their anger, reporters their criticism; on the roads of Shimla you could not travel too far before encountering a procession, demonstration or riots, extra policemen were deployed for control; the police headquarters and stations were swamped by angry mobs, *lathi* charges and water cannons had to be effectuated to restrain crowds.

Shimla was a mess; the once peaceful and blissful city was in complete mayhem.

At Musica, Mayur's absence on the drums gnawed at me. I had a tough time concentrating. But he wasn't the only one missing. Anya and Sameer had skipped three classes in a row.

The day she returned, she said she was out of town without my having to interrogate her.

'I'm sure you must have heard about what happened,' I said showing her a few chords to practise.

She shook her head. 'What are you talking about?'

I stopped strumming. 'Oh, you don't know?'

She shook her head again. 'What do I not know?'

I cleared my throat and looked elsewhere for a couple of seconds before turning back to her. 'Mayur . . . um . . .' I fought the lump in my throat. 'Mayur is no more. He was killed.'

'R-really?' Her hands flew to her mouth. 'Oh god! When?'

'Last week.'

She evaded me for the next minute and blankly stared at the book in her lap. Then, she looked back, and said, 'That's bad,' in a nonchalant manner; very casually, as if all I told her was that I couldn't sleep last night or that I had a headache. Oh, a headache, that's bad.

'Do you feel bad for him?'

'I beg your pardon?'

'Do you feel bad about what happened?' I asked harshly.

'Of-of course,' she said. 'When good people die you always feel bad, but—' she stopped abruptly.

'But?' I caught her gaze and didn't let go. 'Are you going to complete that statement?'

'No-no, that's all,' she said, again evading my eyes. 'I wasn't going to say anything else.'

* * *

After class we went over to Gaiety theatre to watch a play. It was Anya's idea. Despite myself I was thrilled as this was the place where we had first met. I told her this gleefully and she rolled her eyes, and said, 'I know! I remember it.'

The play was about a rape victim and her life after the act. It was meant as a social commentary and effectively showed an insight into the psyche of a rape survivor, and society's role in furthering her distress. It was meaningful, certainly, but not entertaining. I was getting very bored but Anya was rapt.

I revelled in the touch of her hand, her fingers firmly closed against mine. I traced a figure of eight with my index finger on the back of her palm.

In the end, the protagonist of the play, unhinged with stress and shame, commits suicide. Anya had tears in her eyes.

Suddenly I could hear her thoughts. *Nobody can know what it feels like, no one, only we know—those who have suffered. I'll kill them, I'll kill them all, all the rapists, like they have been killing. I'll kill them!*

With a sudden gasp I turned to face her. What did she mean when she said, 'I'll kill'?

The sudden realization hit me with an almost physical force! But what I heard next chilled me to the bone and made the hairs on my arms and the back of my neck stand on end.

I'll kill them all, like they killed me!

32

What is Anya?

I was panting, gasping for breath, when we exited the hall.

In shock. Fear. Surprise.

On hearing her thoughts, I had let go of her hand that suddenly felt icy cold in mine. She had managed to compose herself and, instead of tears, there was anger in those eyes, the muscles of her jaw had tightened. I cast a sidelong glance at her from the corner of my eye. She was fuming.

'What are you?' My own question baffled me.

'What?' she asked, frowning.

'You heard me. What are you?'

She shook her head. 'I don't think I understand your question.'

We were making our way towards the parking lot. Anya made it a point to walk a couple of metres ahead of me.

'I know you do,' I called out. I sped up and reached her side. 'I heard everything.'

'What?' She rolled her eyes heavenwards. 'What did you hear?'

'That thing about rapists, about killing, everything.'

She stopped in her tracks. The colour evaporated from her face. In the waning sunshine she suddenly looked pale.

'I didn't even say anything.'

'Yeah, I know, but I heard.' I paused and took a deep breath. 'I can read your mind.'

Her face contorted. 'Rubbish,' she said. 'That's not possible.'

'Of course it is,' I said. 'I can read anyone's mind if I'm in physical contact with them. It's like some magical thing that happened after I woke up from the coma.'

She scowled. 'Really?' She paused. 'So . . . so . . . all this while . . . what did you hear?'

I told her everything.

She took a few short steps, opened the car door and sat. I entered from the other side and took the seat behind the wheel.

'So now can you tell me?' I said, turning on the ignition. 'What are you?'

She pulled back her hair and tied it neatly. She was nervous and confused when her eyes met mine; she swallowed hard and finally said, 'I'm not human.'

33

The Revenants

Aditya, Sameer and Monica were waiting for us at a café near their neighbourhood. Anya had called them and asked me to direct any further questions at them. It was a thirty-minute drive from Gaiety theatre. The sun had set, gulped down by the hills, and the sky was crimson in the horizon and lighter as the eyes travelled upwards.

As I entered the café I felt a shiver that had nothing to do with the cold.

The three of them were smiling as we walked towards them at the far end of the café. The place was buzzing with activity; there were a lot of teenagers around. In fact when I looked closely, there were mostly teenagers.

'It's the only café in the area,' Aditya told me as I scanned the room. 'It's crowded like this all year.'

We sat down and I shot a glance at the other three. They were pretty relaxed and composed unlike Anya.

'Who are you guys?' I fired my question without preamble.

Aditya looked at Anya. 'So he knows everything?'

'Looks like it,' she replied. 'He can read minds, it seems.'

'What have you told him so far?'

'That we are not human.'

I glanced at them, back and forth in bewilderment. 'Stop! Can you just tell me who you guys are?'

'We're ghosts,' Monica said, a big smile playing on her lips.

'No, Monica!' Sameer said, eyeing her with scorn. 'We are not ghosts. We are better than that.'

'Yeah,' she said, 'but only marginally better.'

'No, I don't agree.' It was Anya who said that firmly. 'I think we are much better than that.' She turned to Aditya. 'Do you agree?'

'Absolutely,' he replied. 'At least we have some purpose in life. We spread happiness.'

'Not me!' Anya exclaimed.

'No, also you,' Sameer said, 'you only do it to the bad guys.'

'Arrgh!' I slammed my fist on the table. 'This is not helping. What are you guys talking about?'

A scrawny waiter came running up to our table at the commotion. He took our order—a couple of cappuccinos, a couple of mochas and a black coffee for Anya.

'Okay,' said Aditya, once the waiter had left. 'Who wants to begin?'

'I do.' Monica volunteered with a hand up.

Aditya gave her his assent.

Monica gazed at me and leaned forward. 'So, Sahil,' she said, 'look, you have to listen to this very carefully. All that you have experienced, perceived, felt or read so far in your life'—she paused dramatically—'just forget about it for a moment. This is going to take you by storm. It is going to be a little unrealistic, of course, but it's real.'

'What? Tell me.' I was almost at the edge of my seat.

'Anya is right,' she continued. 'We are not human. There is a name given to us—revenants.' She paused and let it sink in.

'Okay,' I said, 'go on.'

The other three had their eyes glued to me.

'Now, I'm sure you've never heard of it.' She didn't wait for an answer. 'It's a French word which literally means "to return". And that's what we did—revenants. We have returned from the dead.'

'Ha!' I chortled. 'You are joking, right?' I held out my hands. I looked at the other three.

They shook their heads.

'I'm not joking!' Monica protested. 'I know it sounds crazy, but it's true. That's the reason I asked you in the beginning to forget about everything else. Life, as you know it, is limited to what you see, hear or perceive. But that doesn't mean it ends there.'

Aditya took over with a slight wave at her. 'Have you ever heard about parallel worlds, Sahil?'

I grew angrier by the minute. 'I think so.'

'So you can think of us as that,' he said. 'We live in some sort of parallel world that coexists with your world.'

I must have given him a very curious look, which goaded him to bring his hands forward and start again.

'Okay, okay,' he said. 'Let me ask you a question. When you dream, right, suddenly you are transported to a world where you have no control. You are asleep, safely tucked in your bed; but in your dreams you are actually somewhere else.'

'So?'

'Dreams are nothing but a glimpse into our unconscious mind or windows into another world. What if I say you are in a parallel world when you are sleeping and that when you wake up you are back in this world.'

'What bullshit!'

'Okay,' he said. 'Fair enough. Let me give you another example. You have heard about ghosts and zombies and spirits, right? And you would have also heard about their sightings.

So is it not possible that these abandoned souls actually exist somewhere, and you people—humans, I mean—have caught a glimpse into their world. What if that ghost or spirit was alive and doing well in the other world and only humans with special powers could see them.'

'Okay,' I said, 'so parallel worlds exist, and you live in one of them, fine. But that doesn't answer my question: who the hell are you guys? And what do you mean by 'special powers'? Does that mean only I can see you guys? Because I have them?'

Anya took over with a shake of her head. 'No, no,' she said. 'We're not ghosts. You don't need special powers to see us. Anyone can see us. That's how we are different from our so-called peers: ghosts and zombies.'

Then she broke out into a hearty laugh with the others.

'Peers, wow, Anya. Ghosts and zombies, ha ha ha,' Monica said. 'Let's talk about peer pressure.'

Another set of giggles erupted from them.

'But,' Anya continued, taking a couple of sips of her coffee, 'Aditya is right in a way. You can call it a kind of parallel world, you see, because we are all'—she leaned forward and lowered her voice to a murmur—'we're all dead. I died six months ago. Three men raped and tortured me, and then killed me. Sameer here,' she nodded at him, 'committed suicide a couple of months ago. Monica died near a construction site, a year ago. And Aditya—he's been dead for the last five years. He met with a road accident.'

Now it was my turn to laugh. And I did: a deep, loud, hearty laugh that was met by unappreciative looks.

Anya held out an admonishing finger. 'Like I said, let me finish. But we all came back because we were not supposed to die. It was a mistake, an error, whatever you want to call it. Some of us were cynics, nihilists, suicidal.' She again nodded at Sameer. 'Some of us had a mission, maybe, left incomplete on earth, some return to avenge their death, and some simply return because their time on earth isn't complete and the—'

She stopped when a high-pitched giggle escaped me.

'Now, I don't know what makes you not believe me, you dumbo,' she went about in her unrelenting tone, 'but this has been going on for hundreds of years, from the twelfth century, I think. This is not an uncommon occurrence, and—oh my god, you just can't stop laughing!'

I couldn't. I knew she was screwing with me like she always did. The four of them exchanged bitter glances.

'These mysterious murders in Shimla,' said Sameer. 'Who do you think is behind them?'

That sobered me down. I gaped at him.

He pointed a finger at Anya.

'She is.'

34

The Serial Killer

'Who do you think killed your friend Mayur?'

My jaw dropped open.

Sameer again pointed a finger at Anya. 'She did.'

I was stunned by his impudence. 'You asshole,' I said, furious. 'This is the most disgusting joke you could play on anyone. How could you?'

'He's right.' Anya stared at me, sharply, her eyes steady. 'He's right. I'm the one.'

I let out a sigh of anguish. 'What? I mean, how . . . Mayur?'

'I killed him.' It was a cold, stony voice that came out of her.

The other three faintly nodded in assent.

Aditya cleared his throat. 'He was raping a girl in his house, some girl from your school. Had lured her into the house somehow and then—'

'Wait!' I thrust my hand out. 'You killed him!' I was glaring at Anya. 'You killed Mayur and the others?' Suddenly my hands trembled as the gruelling images flashed in my mind. 'And with such brutality? Why would you do that, you bitch?'

A few people craned their necks towards us at my raised voice.

'Hold on,' Aditya said. 'Volume! Let's get out here before he yells again.'

'No one is going anywhere until I know why this bitch killed them.' I was softer this time.

Anya's face puckered with contempt. She gnashed her teeth. 'I can't stand rapists, so I kill them. I can't stand the injustice that is doled out to the victims—all the pain, suffering and accusatory fingers, while the motherfuckers who do it roam scot free because our impotent government is too fucking lazy and indifferent to act. I do it because if I don't, we'll never get justice. Did you know that those three men who raped me, after they were done, they shoved objects inside me—scissors, knives—would you believe it? They wanted to remove their semen that was inside me to conceal any evidence against them. They scraped and pierced while I screamed . . . I screamed in unimaginable pain and squirmed like an animal. Then they dumped me on the road to die, and I did—a few hours later. I killed those bastards a few months ago.'

She took a shaky breath. I could see tears well up in her eyes. Aditya handed her a tissue. 'Those other animals,' she continued after wiping her eyes, 'they were all raping someone, when I killed them. I can hear the screams, the painful wails of women, when I'm around them. So I rush to help. I give these animals the same pain, the same treatment, they give us. I torture them, castrate them before their death. Mayur was doing the same thing. Ask that girl in your class, the tall, red-haired girl—Pallavi, I think her name is.'

I was shaking. I dabbed at the sweat on my forehead. I asked Aditya, 'Is she telling the truth?'

'She is.'

'So those twin murders at Gaiety theatre?'

'I did it,' said Anya calmly. 'Those two boys had got hold of a girl and had forcefully dragged her to the men's washroom.

I was not too far from there—a few kilometres at the most—
when I heard her wails. That is when I rushed to the sight and
saw this boy pushing himself inside her from behind while the
other clasped her mouth to muffle her screams.'

'But *how* did you hear her?'

Monica jumped in. 'We have er . . . you could call them
special powers. We can see, hear and perceive what's not around
us.' She smiled with pride.

'Extra-sensory perception, it's called,' Aditya quipped.
'It's simple, I'll explain. Basically, it works like this: we have
heightened senses when it comes to the ways in which we died.'

I felt a shiver. 'What the hell?'

'I wasn't supposed to die,' Sameer said. 'I killed myself, so
here I am today. I can sense when people are about to commit
suicide; I can hear all their inner voices, turmoil, agitation.
Probably,' he shrugged, 'that's my mission here; that's why I
returned.'

Anya added, 'And I am supposed to save girls who are about
to be raped and killed like me. But I take it a little further. I kill
the rapists as well.'

Aditya arched his brow. 'Me: road accidents.' He paused.
'So that answers all the questions you've been asking us over the
last few months—how I saw the car coming, the bus, Anya's
disappearances, Sameer's suicidal talk, blah, blah, blah.'

He peered at me, probably wondering if I believed him. I
didn't think I did. 'And I'm sure what your next question will
be so let me answer that. Yes, we are all clairvoyant, we've got
pre-cognitive powers, as in we see visions, a short while into the
future and mostly in our vicinity. For that time we become very
powerful, so powerful we can overcome anything. For example,
Anya when she hears these screams, can just fly through the
air at breakneck speed and be there to help. It's the same with
Sameer, me and all of us.'

'So you guys can teleport?'

All of them nodded, but Monica's nod was the firmest.

'What other powers do you have?'

'That's it, dumbo,' said Anya licking her lips. 'We're not god.'

'But, how do you do what you do?' I asked her, making a face. 'I mean, the castration and tearing away of the limbs and all. Some of them were really strong men.' I felt ill at ease even looking at Anya now.

'Like I said,' Aditya jumped in, 'we become extremely powerful during the act. We can fly, lift tonnes of weight, move aside trucks and buses with a shove of a hand, kill dozens of people at the drop of a hat—you want more?'

A little shriek escaped me. 'Are you serious?'

'Try me some day,' Anya said, her voice full of malice, her head rocking slightly.

There was a silence, a long, but not uncomfortable one, as I quietly absorbed all of it.

'Okay, one more question,' I said when another doubt struck me. 'So basically you are telling me that if I kill myself now, I'll be one of you, a reven-what?'

'A revenant,' Monica replied. 'The answer is no. I mean maybe, not necessarily. It primarily depends on one condition: whether your time on earth is complete.'

'So how do I know?'

'You don't need to know,' Aditya said. He looked at the empty cups before us. 'More coffee?' He looked around.

'Okay,' they chimed.

'Sahil?'

'Yeah, whatever, just continue what you were saying.'

'Repeat the order,' he told the waiter and settled his eyes back on me. 'So yeah, you don't need to know. Sahil, there are so many things in this world that are inexplicable—you just can't find logic in them. I guess this is just one of those things. You cannot know if you would become one of us; you wouldn't want to, but that is an issue to ponder on another day.' He exchanged glances with the others and they nodded. 'If you commit suicide, you may or may not become a revenant. Maybe your time on earth is complete and you were supposed to die that way, maybe not. Nobody knows. So that's condition number one: those who become revenants mostly die in their youth due to an accident. The second condition we discussed earlier: were you an asshole when you were a human? You know, a cynic, a wrongdoer, causing pain and agony to others, having complete disregard for life and other people. Were you left with some unfinished business? Do you have to avenge your death? There could be so many reasons.'

'So now you know,' Anya said. 'Sorry for interrupting, Aditya.' When Aditya gave her a wave, she continued, 'Why have I been insisting that you respect life, love your family, appreciate the little joys, count your blessings and stop wallowing in misery and cutting yourself? We all were like you when we were human. When I first met you I saw my life in yours, you were like a mirror—a clear, gleaming mirror of my own screwed-up human life. I didn't want a revenant life for you: a life of suffering.'

My head was spinning now. 'Suffering?'

Sameer said, 'We'll explain that in the next class. I think that's enough for today. He can't take it any more, guys.'

They agreed. We drank the rest of our coffee in silence and it still felt like a cruel joke. Maybe it was, maybe they would suddenly scream *'Bakra'* or 'April fool', anything. This whole thing was too hard to fathom.

Before leaving the café, I glanced at Anya, and said in dread, 'God, you killed Mayur?'

35

The Revenant Lore

I returned home and simply retired to my room and lay down on the bed. I told Ayush I had eaten dinner and he didn't badger me. In any case I didn't want to speak to him or Shweta, lest I gave something away.

About the revenants.

About the serial-killer of Shimla.

I folded my hands and placed them beneath my head. Listlessly, I gazed at the ceiling. Damn, was it all true? Revenants? Did Anya really kill all those men?

And if all that was true, what the hell was I doing with these people, no ghosts, sorry, revenants, I mean. I shook my head. Actually what difference did it make anyway—'revenant' is just a euphemism for 'ghost'. They were all a subset of the undead.

I let out a short burst of laughter when suddenly it occurred to me that I had fallen in love with a dead girl, a brutal murderer at that. I laughed again, this time a restrained one, when my heart raced at the realization that I perhaps was still in love with her.

I sat upright, alarmed, and despite the cold, I felt sweat crawling on my forehead. I dabbed at it. I poured myself some water and drank it.

Now, then, seriously were there such things as revenants? A part of me still felt they were joking. But how else could you explain those life-saving incidents that had me vexed for the past few months? Those murders? The clueless police?

Maybe there was something I could do to be sure after all.

The answer was Pallavi.

After the morning assembly in school the next day, I walked over to her desk. She sat alone, staring at the blank whiteboard, her hands in the side pockets of her coat.

'Hey,' I said.

She glanced up at me and nodded.

It was awkward given that I couldn't think of a single conversation I had had with her since she joined school last year, a few hellos and polite nods notwithstanding.

'So . . . um . . . can we talk?'

She nodded again.

'Listen, I-I was meaning to tell you that Mayur, you know, he really liked you.'

I saw the panic. It was clear as crystal: her eyes, hands, a little swallow, the look of aversion.

'I didn't do anything,' she said. 'I swear.'

'What did you not do?'

'His murder,' she said. 'If that's what you think.'

'No, no.' I shook my head. 'I know you didn't. I want to know who did.'

She flushed. I could see her eyes move with nervousness. 'How did you know?'

'I don't . . . I'm asking you.'

'No, you do,' she insisted. 'That's why you came here to talk. We've never talked before.'

I sniffed loudly. 'Okay, fine,' I said. 'This girl . . . er . . . who . . . I-I think I know her. Could you tell me what happened that day.'

She eyed me sceptically. Nevertheless, she answered, 'That asshole, your friend Mayur, tricked me into coming to his place. I'd told him earlier about my struggle with maths and he said he'd help me. Suddenly in his study room his hand crawled up my thigh. He thought I was a slut, a whore, who would do as he pleased. When I declined and got my stuff together to leave, he leapt at me and shoved me on the bed. I screamed and he began undressing me, and kissing and licking my face. He was strong; I couldn't stop him. And then suddenly—no, magically—this girl was there. Don't ask me how, the door was locked . . . she was . . . she was just there . . . somehow . . . She hurled him off me and banged him against the wall. His head was crushed and blood splattered on the wall. She grabbed his scrotum and then . . . then she-she just plucked it out like it was some kind of rotten fruit. Ew! He screamed in agony. It was awful to see that blood pouring out of him . . . I threw up. She lifted him and threw him at the wall a few times, tore out his arm, twisted his body out of shape . . . god, she killed him mercilessly. I was too stunned to stop her. Then she told me, "Run, get away from here, and don't tell anyone." I did as told out of fear and in the morning I saw the story on the news but remained silent.'

* * *

The Shimla State Library housed over a million books. It was located in the southern part of the city. It was a formidable looking edifice, built of square grey stone during the British era.

I walked up to the reception and entered my name in the register. An old woman, grey haired and bespectacled, smiled at me from behind the desk.

I took the stairs to the first floor. The room was big and wide, flanked by steel bookshelves on either side, with two rows in the middle. I located the history section and began my search. There were books about the establishment of the Mughal empire, the German invasion, the British Raj and others.

I picked up a book called *Parallel Worlds: An Insight*, but on realizing that it was not what I was looking for, I put it back after a desultory peek. There were some thick books about ghosts, apparitions, spirits, but nothing on revenants. The four of them had said clearly that they weren't ghosts.

A few minutes later I found a book called *The Undead*. I took it out and placed it on the desk behind me. I continued my search to find something specifically about revenants.

Over the next hour I scanned the entire four rows and found nothing. *Anya, you cunning bitch, so you were screwing with me, weren't you?* Relief washed over me. I curled my lips and let a breath whoosh out. Damn, these people. It must have been her and Aditya's idea, definitely. Monica and Sameer were too sweet to pull off a joke like this on their own.

I smiled and shook my head as I took a seat and opened *The Undead*. There was pin-drop silence in the room. The screeching sound of my chair against the floor resonated through the room and half a dozen faces looked at me in annoyance. I held out a hand and mouthed 'sorry'.

The Undead was written by a French author in the nineteenth century and translated into English.

It was a non-fiction book and spoke unabashedly about the sightings of spirits, zombies, apparitions and ghosts during the time.

Two chapters later I saw the word 'revenant'.

I froze. My knees buckled and head wobbled. I clutched the edge of the desk and read through the passage.

Many stories about revenants were documented by English historians in the Middle Ages. The stories were very personal;

always about a specific individual who had died, and they
shared a number of common features. Like zombies, revenants
were undead and horrible creatures from an unholy source.

I stopped reading and walked towards the water cooler. It took
two glasses of cold water to soothe my parched throat. The lump
that had established itself there, refused to budge. Terror seized
me and my heart throbbed against my chest in loud, pulsating
rhythms. I kneeled against the wall and tried to calm myself:
deep breaths, in, out, in and out.

I crushed the plastic glass, dropped it in the bin and rushed
back to my seat.

Medieval stories of revenants have common features. Those
who returned from the dead were wrongdoers in their
lifetime. Often, revenants are associated with the spreading
of disease among the living.

My hands shaking, I hurriedly turned the pages.

The chapter mostly spoke about William Parvus, a twelfth
century English historian, and his major work, the incomplete
book *Historia*—a history of England from 1066 to 1198.
The book was a major source of stories of medieval revenants,
including early vampire stories. In *Historia*, William Parvus briefly
recounted stories he had heard about revenants.

William's first story took place in Buckinghamshire where
a man returned from the grave and assaulted his wife for
several nights. He 'not only terrified her on awaking, but
nearly crushed her due to the insupportable weight of his
body'. Finally, she appealed to her family members only to
have the corpse return to terrorize both her family and her
neighbours. Only a letter of forgiveness, written by the local

priest and placed on the corpse, could bind the body to the grave.

Two runaway peasants from around 1090 died suddenly of unknown causes and were buried; but the very same day, they appeared, carrying on their shoulders the wooden coffins in which they had been buried. The following night they walked the paths and fields of the village. They spoke to the other peasants, banging on the walls of their houses shouting, 'Move quickly, move! Get going! Come!' The villagers became sick and started dying, but eventually the bodies of the two revenants were exhumed, their heads cut off and their hearts removed, which put an end to the spread of the sickness.

A wealthy merchant in Northumberland, England, had become rich by evil deeds. After his death, he was seen to rise again and wander the streets at night. Wherever he went, dogs would howl and whoever met him would freeze with terror. The great and good of Berwick met to discuss what could be done. They decided not to fight the revenant as it would cause much injury to them but they could not leave it as it would spread plague and pollute the air like the other revenants were known to have done. Finally, they decided that ten brave men would exhume the corpse and dismember it, this they did immediately; afterwards each part was thrown in a furnace and burnt.

On my computer at home, I opened my browser and logged on to Google. I typed the word 'revenant'.

With close to a million search results, I couldn't turn my back on the ugliest truth of my life: I was in love with a dead girl.

A revenant.

36

Love?

Anya had a freakishly crafty smile plastered on her face when I made my way into the music academy two days later. It could be due to relief because the barrage of questions from me would end now that I knew who they were or simply because she somehow knew a part of me was terrified of her.

'Your eyes,' she chuckled as I settled down. 'You should have seen them darting about. Are you scared of me or something?'

'No,' I said, tuning the guitar. 'Not really. You are just a ghost, after all. A dead, blood-sucking vampire. You've killed a dozen people, you torture and castrate them. You've brought the Himachal police to their knees. Scared? Why do you ask?'

She laughed. 'Asshole.'

* * *

Later, after class, we went for a stroll to Lakkar Bazaar as she said she wanted to shop for her home.

'You mean your graveyard?' I teased her. 'Since when do ghosts live in homes?'

She punched me—a firm, solid punch on my shoulder. 'Don't you dare mock me.' Then her lips parted and her teeth shone.

Lakkar Bazaar was a market extending off the Ridge, famous for its souvenirs and wooden crafts, carpets and rugs, intricately designed beaded and metal jewellery, embroidered handkerchiefs and handheld fans, gloves and caps, shawls and leather belts and shoes. It was a famous tourist spot—a place to buy something to take back home after the vacation was over, along with memories of this beautiful city, rich in its tradition and culture.

Anya caught hold of my hand as we snaked through the densely crowded alleys and corners, through the sounds of haggling and hawking, amidst beggars and paupers, past shops and shacks.

Surprisingly, it felt the same, her touch, the touch of a normal human hand, of a pretty teenage girl, of Anya, but damn, she was a revenant. Clumsily, I freed my hand as I felt odd and squeamish.

'Good,' she said, blowing a tuft of her raven-black hair back. 'This way you won't be able to read my mind.'

I grabbed her hand. I didn't want to miss a thing.

This time she let it go. 'You know you can ask me anything, right?' Then, smiling, she held out her hand and we interlinked our fingers. I couldn't stave off the fact that my heart still skipped a beat for her.

We were standing next to a carpet shop. Behind the hoardes of floral rugs sat the bald shopkeeper, smiling ingratiatingly at us. We entered the narrow aisle and sat on squeaky steel chairs.

Anya asked for a subtle light-coloured rug before we could be presented with all sorts of varieties and shades of rugs. She cast a cursory look, twitched her nose and shook her head, and both the assistant and the shop owner, without losing enthusiasm, rolled out different rugs, one after the other.

'So do all you reve—I mean people stay together?' I asked.

'Not here, dumbo,' she said smiling at the baldy.

Anya eventually chose two rugs and asked for them to be delivered at an extra cost. She wrote her address on a piece of paper and handed it over. I stole a glance at it and it surprised me that she resided in an affluent neighbourhood.

'You stay in Johor Bagh?' I asked as we stepped out.

She nodded. 'We have three bungalows there. All of us stay there.'

'How many of you are there?'

'Seventy-eight.'

I swallowed, shocked. Anya told me they dwelt with the humans in the neighbourhood peacefully. Obviously the humans didn't know the truth about their neighbours and it worked well for both the groups. I told her I wanted to visit her place someday and she said humans weren't allowed into a revenant house.

'But I'll make an exception for you,' she said.

'I hope it's not one of those *bhoot banglas* from our Bollywood movies; you know, where invariably there'll be a frightened old *chowkidaar* recounting haunted stories, smoke billowing, curtains swaying, big tinkling chandeliers and all?'

She gave me an irritated gaze.

'Sorry,' I said with a restrained smile.

It was a cold day but not chilly and sometimes the sun managed to find its way out through the dense clouds. It would peek at us from time to time before a drifting cloud shrouded it.

We stopped at a fast-food joint and ordered two plates of steamed chicken momos. That was the good thing about Mall Road; there were plenty of shops and delicious eateries all along. We sat in the makeshift restaurant on red plastic chairs and tables.

'Listen, um . . .' said Anya, squeezing my hand on the wobbly table. 'I wanted to apologize to you.'

'For what?'

'For everything,' she said. 'For hiding who I was, for the lies I've been telling you, killing your friend, everything really.'

I withdrew my hand and crossed my arms across my chest. 'I don't know, Anya,' I said. 'Sometimes I wonder what I am doing with you.'

'You love me,' she said. 'Don't you?'

I gave out a short laugh. 'So *now* you're comfortable talking about love, you revenant? That's funny!'

She smiled, exposing her dimple. I pondered on her question. Did I love her? Really? She a revenant, me a human.

She released the sky-blue ribbon that held back her hair and the gorgeous curtain cascaded down her shoulders, like frothy water down a valley. She cleared her hair off her face and tucked it behind her ear. Then she smiled once more, her dimple saying hello.

Pins, needles and the quick flutter of my heart gave me the answer.

I realized then that love isn't a decision, love isn't even a choice and love certainly can't be based on conditions. It's a breathing, living being that seeps into our lives, spreads and gradually takes full control of it. It brings immense joy and sorrow in equal measure, but, once infected by it, we can never be the same again.

Yes, I loved her.

The momos arrived, and after taking a bite Anya told me that her friendship with a human was against their code: it could hamper their existence. In fact, right from the beginning Aditya and the others had been coercing her to cut off all ties with me.

'There were two reasons why I didn't,' she said.

The cold was getting to me. I asked for a hot coffee.

'Reason one,' she said, 'I told you earlier was that I didn't want you to become one of us. You definitely were on that path, what with the suicidal talk, the cutting and all. I wanted you to see the world through a different pair of eyes.'

'And what was the second reason?'

'I lied to you earlier,' she said and then fell silent.

'The second reason, Anya?' I pressed.

'The second reason is,' she said, hesitantly, 'that I was in love with you, too.'

37

Sameer

Sameer was eleven years old when his mother passed away. His father became an inveterate alcoholic and would seek pleasure in hitting his only son. He had his reasons. His wife had died while walking down a road with her son when a speeding car had hit them from behind.

Sameer should have been more alert. His mother was deaf.

Sameer grew up a lean, reticent boy, afraid of crowds, afraid of his teachers, afraid of going back home to his father—afraid of living. He was good at one thing though—his studies. His father liked that. He didn't hit him the day he got his results because Sameer would always manage to be in the top five of his class.

That became Sameer's reprieve. He'd hide behind his books when his father returned home and was spared a thrashing. But there was nothing else to do anyway. He was a bored teenager, he had no friends, no hobbies; his classmates would mock him for his timidity.

Cutting was his only hobby. Out of frustration he'd cut himself on his arms, calves, thighs, anywhere he could find a clean spot. He loved the physical pain; it helped him forget his inner tumult.

But it wasn't long before this ended.

When he was sixteen years old, he fared badly in his final examinations. He knew it even before the results were out. Somewhere down the line, concentration had become a difficult pursuit. He couldn't find a particular reason for it. Maybe it was that girl, Parul, in his class who had outright rejected him when he'd proposed to her, stuttering from the nerves. Or maybe it was the constant mocking that his classmates subjected him to even weeks after the incident, imitating his words, his stutter, and laughing and whistling to his face, making fun of his centre-parted hair, his bushy eyebrows, his hairy arms, his temerity to propose to the prettiest girl in the class. Or maybe it was because his new stepmother of the past few months wouldn't even look his way, as though he didn't exist.

So when the results were out and he'd managed an 'F' in some of his subjects, he didn't go home for fear of the physical assault that would be inflicted on him.

Instead he walked down the main road, through dense traffic, his mind imagining all sorts of terrible outcomes for his future. It did occur to him that this might not be the best decision. What if he ended up in a place worse than this? But as soon as he answered that question with 'no place could be worse than this life', he didn't hesitate. He looked over his shoulder. There was a massive truck speeding down the road, horn blaring, its brute energy sending the smaller vehicles scurrying out of its way.

Sameer timed his jump well.

Later, the police found it impossible to assemble all the parts of his body together.

38

Aditya

Aditya couldn't stop wondering why he wasn't able to save the teenage boy from the accident. It was horrific; body parts flying everywhere. He wasn't too far from the site. These kinds of cases were textbook—he'd see flashes of the future, the exact place of the incident, the to-be victim, the speeding vehicle, and he'd assemble the pieces together and prevent the accidents.

But not that day. That day he didn't get a single vision.

It was only when the boy became one of them that Aditya realized the reason. It was a suicide and preventing suicides wasn't his forté. That was his troubled friend Majumdar's arena. But Majumdar had completed his time as a revenant and was 'gone'.

Aditya had welcomed a confused Sameer to their abode.

When he was human, Aditya was often told he was a mean, money-grabbing bastard, who would even sell his mother and sister if he got a good bargain.

He knew these opinions and statements were not unfounded. But he swallowed all these accusations with pride. After all, it took a lot of brains to be that successful.

Throughout his early twenties, Aditya had made forays into various business ventures—a small insurance firm where the

179

clients were mostly his family and friends, all of whom turned hostile in a few months when they lost their investments due to a 'change in the RBI policies'; a PR agency where he promoted his agency using his clients' money; a wholesale fruits and vegetables enterprise built with the money from his few remaining friends who had the 'risk-taking ability and the audacity to do something of their own'; a money-laundering business that really kicked off where he'd launder the money of small businessmen and shop owners, petty drug dealers and arms' vendors, bookies and gamblers, but his clients rarely saw any rewards because 'the income tax department has never been so strict and vigilant, they track and seize a *lot* of money, not to mention the bribes'.

By the time he'd reached his late twenties, Aditya had earned enough money to last a lifetime. He now wanted to settle down.

He looked at all the single daughters of wealthy businessmen in his city, approaching it like one would a research project. In his diary he kept a track of the 'accessible' ones. There were at least four who were in his league. He was, after all, a decent looking, tall, well-spoken, well-off man. He used his sly, glib tongue to his full advantage.

Two weeks before his engagement to a girl named Tulip he was on his way to see another girl, Sheena, just to be sure he'd made the right choice. Tulip was more beautiful but Sheena's father had more money.

His Kawasaki Ninja 650 bike rammed into a Fortuner when the driver of the SUV had suddenly applied the brakes to avoid a meandering cow on the road.

Later, passers-by reported to the authorities that they had seen the man on the fancy bike flying through the air and landing dozens of metres ahead.

Aditya wasn't wearing a helmet.

39

Monica

Monica had always been embarrassed about her height. She was an inch shy of five feet, but when inquired would say, 'Five feet and two inches.'

She had a slight crookedness to her gait; some said there was a boyish edge to her that was also visible in her manner of speech, and she found it easier to be friends with boys rather than the hypocritical girls of her class. She was the tomboy of her school. She was called 'small tomboy' and the term never affected her much.

Monica had a charming face, bright, sparkling eyes and her shoulder-length hair rolled into small curls at the end. She was mostly perceived as a happy-go-lucky girl.

But she was not.

She was madly in love with Madhur, a tall, handsome guy in her class, and Madhur was madly in love with a beautiful girl, Meher, who was in a different section.

What really peeved Monica was that Madhur used her as a guinea pig, trying out different techniques to woo Meher on her.

'Come on, Monica,' he'd say. 'You are my best friend. If you don't help me, who will?'

He would rehearse with her—the best way to say 'I love you', how to hold her hand, how to nonchalantly loop his arm around her shoulder. He would step up these efforts every time Meher was around to induce some jealousy in her.

Jealousy spawns love, he thought, and it worked. Soon Meher began casting coquettish smiles his way, inviting smiles, pleading smiles and, within no time, Monica was out of Madhur's life. He had no time for her any more. He was always with Meher—before classes began, in the intervals between classes, during the lunch break and every other time they managed to sneak away.

Monica was furious and sad, but more sad than furious.

It wasn't fair. Was it right what Madhur had done? Using her to get to Meher—that bitch, that plastic-faced, wiry bitch. That long-haired, condescending bitch who teased Monica, telling her how Madhur and she would often talk about her, laughing at what a gullible person she was.

Something had to be done. She had to be taught a lesson.

The acid was stronger than Monica had anticipated. One splash and Meher's face had deflated like a balloon. Flecks of skin peeled off from every place where the acid made contact; in less than a minute her eyes were popping out because the skin below them had melted. There was a hissing sound that was soon engulfed by Meher's painful screams. Monica watched as she squirmed on the road and considered helping her, but then she kicked her hard in the belly and walked away.

It was a good thing no one saw her otherwise she'd have had to spend her life in prison.

Meher died in hospital the next day.

What Monica didn't anticipate was losing Madhur in the process. He never found out but the depression from losing Meher was such that he spent the next year in the psychiatry ward of Max Hospital in Delhi.

Before he could be declared fit and discharged, Monica had become a revenant.

It was a sunny day in Gurgaon. Monica and her parents were out looking at prospective property to buy.

Nobody saw it coming. At the construction site where her parents were contemplating purchasing a flat, the front wall of the newly built eleventh floor collapsed.

Monica and a few workers were buried alive.

Moments before her life seeped out of her, she thought it was a good thing this had happened.

She had been dying of guilt anyway.

40

The Revenant Rules

'I don't want to listen to any more of this,' I said. 'Can you answer my question now?'

'Trust me,' Anya said. 'I'm doing just that.'

I sighed. 'No, you're not.'

'Okay,' she said. 'I'm coming to it.'

'Then do it now,' I said. 'If you were in love with me as well, why the hell did you lie to me?'

I rose from my seat, leaned across the table between us, and planted a quick kiss on her lips.

She smiled. 'What was that for?'

I took a bite of the momos. 'Your punishment for lying.' Then I felt my lips.

'What are you checking?' she asked.

'Kissing a ghost's lips,' I said, 'could have consequences. God, I can't believe I did that. Love makes you do crazy things.'

She rolled her eyes. 'I'm not a ghost.'

'Yeah, revenant, whatever, same-same.'

She rose and kissed me back.

'What was that for?' I asked, surprised but enormously pleased.

'I love you,' she said.

My heart raced and my pulse quickened. It's the best feeling in the world: to hear those three magic words from the person you love. It didn't fail to impinge upon my mind though that Anya wasn't really a person.

After eating our momos we figured we had a lot to discuss. We decided to have dinner together. But before that she did some more shopping. She bought herself some beaded, artificial jewellery from a small shop, two coffee mugs with 'I love Shimla' intricately carved on them, a few bronze showpieces and some other stuff.

I called Ayush and told him I wouldn't be eating dinner at home since I was going to a friend's birthday party. He said, 'Enjoy yourself,' and hung up. Ever since Grandma's death, he'd been very accommodating, I had to give him that. Shweta, too, was all smiles when I was around her. Perhaps, they still felt sorry for me.

I, on the other hand, was still coping with the after-effects of the coma—the mind-reading and the revenants. If it wasn't for the former, I would never have known about the latter. Anya and her friends would have made sure of that.

And I had just realized that all this happened while Anya was in love with me too.

She still hadn't answered my question and was taking a circuitous route. She said I had to know them first—the revenants, their rules—before I could so much as comprehend her reasoning.

It came as a shocker to know about her three friends, the lives they had lived as humans. But if it hadn't been for all this, Anya said they would never have become revenants. Monica, my god, she *killed* someone.

Anya had warned me that after she spilled the beans on her and their lives, I wouldn't love her any more. Like love was some kind of contract.

'The worst is yet to come,' she said. 'You know nothing about us yet and, when you do, maybe you'll realize it was a good thing that I lied.'

'I'm all ears.'

We sat in Domino's Pizza and ordered pizzas, garlic bread and Coke. The place was noisy and that was good thing because there was no danger of being overheard. Outside, the sky had darkened and Mall Road was beautifully lit.

'Remember, a few days ago I'd said we were suffering?'

I nodded hesitantly.

She'd stopped chewing and her eyes were brimming with tears. 'It's time you knew.'

She was quiet for a minute before continuing. 'Living a revenant's life isn't easy,' she said. 'It cannot be easy or the purpose won't be served.'

'What purpose?'

'We are here to suffer, Sahil, for the wrongs we have done, for hurting people all along our way, for taking life and relationships for granted. A human life is some sort of examination for what lies ahead in this vast universe. And a revenant's life is their second chance to get it right. It is some kind of limbo between life and the afterlife. But it lasts a very long, long time because we don't age like humans.'

The pizza slice fell from my hand.

A revenant, she told me, aged four times slower than a human. They were not immortal, though. The time left in your life when you die as a human has to be lived four-fold.

'Serves us right, don't you think?' she said. 'It's the best punishment for we hated to live and, now, we have to live four times as long.'

She said that with a shake of her head.

'But that's not all,' she said, blinking back her tears. She took a long sip of the Coke and composed herself. 'We are stripped off all the luxuries we had as humans.'

'Luxuries?' I asked. 'What luxuries?'

A weak, restrained smile played on her lips. 'That's the irony,' she said. 'We never realized they were luxuries when we were human.'

Revenants have limited vision. They can only see partially and what is seen is usually hazy and blurred. And they cannot see colours. They weren't just colour-blind, Anya asserted. They can't see any colours; the world to them is black-and-white, like an old noir film.

Revenants don't have a sense of smell—good or bad, nothing. They cannot smell the fragrance of flowers, the aroma of home-cooked food, rain, the grass wet with dew, nothing at all. Their taste buds are completely wiped-out, with no trace. Burnt. Erased.

Revenants cannot sleep for more than a couple of hours every day, leaving them with perpetual headaches through the course of their lives. Those who commit suicide can never sleep.

Those who commit suicide, in addition to the headaches, have to deal with a constant ringing sound, not unlike a group of flies buzzing in your ears, only much louder.

Revenants are not visible to the people who knew them as humans—family, friends, colleagues, neighbours. They cannot be heard by them either. It's as if they are in a parallel world.

Revenant can also never be aroused. Their sex organs are impaired.

'It's a luxury,' Anya said, helplessly sniffing and crying. 'It's a luxury to be human.'

41

Anya

It was a Saturday evening. It had been raining all day in Shimla. Anya was living with her doper friend Nisha in a small flat in Mehrauli, in the eastern part of Shimla. She had vowed she'd never return to her town when her parents threw her out of the house after her third pregnancy.

Life wasn't complicated here. They drank liquor, smoked some charas and spent their time listening to psychedelic music. Other friends joined them, amateur musicians and, sometimes in the evenings, they'd try composing music. Anya was learning how to play the guitar those days but could never bring herself to play a single chord. All she could manage were twangy sounds. Then she turned to composing lyrics. She wrote about teenage angst, adolescent passion, sexuality. Scandalous mostly, but some of them had insight.

Like a far-off dim light in the horizon, it was her dream to be part of a band, make music, travel the world. All she managed was the disposition of a rocker—her wardrobe was stuffed with only black and grey clothes, dark kohl lined her eyes, black paint on her nails, thin streaks of purple in her hair, thick bangs that shrouded part of her forehead and a whining, capricious temper.

The three guys were friends of friends or friends of friends of friends, she didn't care at the time. That evening, her small flat was overcrowded with people in every corner; loud music, lots of booze, twirls of smoke in the air. A few hours into the party the three guys broached the idea of a long drive. They had a long blue sedan with a sun-roof. Although inebriated, Anya agreed; Nisha was far too stoned.

The roads of Shimla were slimy and deserted. After driving around aimlessly till midnight, they car pulled to a stop near an abandoned building complex.

It was sudden, the onslaught, and Anya was appalled at three pairs of hands undoing her clothes. She resisted, screamed, but when one of them pulled out a gun and ordered her to let it happen peacefully, she succumbed. She squirmed in the back seat of the car, the cold muzzle of the gun firmly against her forehead as they took turns to penetrate her. Two of them were violent, squeezing her breasts, their nails digging into her skin. She struggled and screamed but it only arouse them further. They slapped her while they climaxed, and hollered and laughed.

After the three of them were done and blood returned to their brains, they debated the next step while a naked Anya lying next to them struggled to calm her shaking body. Her eyes were sore, the mascara smudged all over her face and her dishevelled hair hung off the side of the seat.

The one with the gun was a local MLA's son and he told the other two this matter needed to be hushed. They spent five minutes digging around the glove box and the trunk of the car.

Then Anya's screams turned to shrieks. They pierced the humid air in the car—keening cries of excruciating pain. Her arms and legs were held down by the two stronger boys as the third burrowed inside her. He first used a Philips screwdriver, then a knife. Soon his hands were red but he continued digging.

'Make sure there's no trace of semen left,' one of them barked, then slammed his hand across Anya's face. She was screaming too loudly.

Later that night, a couple passing by came upon the naked, bloodied body of a girl, screaming and trembling, by the road. Terrified, they slowed the car to a halt, shot a quick glance at the girl, wrinkled their noses in disgust, swore under their breath and sped off. No one helped. It was a police case.

Anya's dying wish was to kill those three animals.

42

A Good Life

Anya was quietly sobbing, her face buried in her hands. 'Whenever I think of that day . . .' She trailed off and shook her head.

'But you told me once you become a revenant, people who knew you as a human couldn't see you.'

Here she managed a smile—a slight malicious one. She cocked her eyebrow.

'Of course,' she said. 'Those bastards never knew what happened.'

Two months after her death, Anya shoved a rag into the fuel tank of their blue sedan when the three of them were driving down the hills. She flew to their speeding car; she used that specific word 'flew'. Then she lit the dangling end of the rag.

'Peace,' she said. 'That's what I felt when I heard the explosion. The three of them were burnt alive.' She paused. 'And then I thought all rapists deserve the same ending.'

I remembered reading in the library that revenants could be seen by those who knew them as humans, which went against what Anya told me. In fact, some of them had returned to haunt and terrorize their own families. I asked her about this.

'Yeah,' she replied. 'I'm sure you must have read it.'

'And?'

'The laws of the universe keep changing.' she said. 'Nothing is permanent.'

We had finished our food and drinks by then. I asked her if she wanted something else. She said some dessert would be nice. I ordered two pieces of chocolate cake.

'So can we talk about it now?' I asked. 'Enough time has gone by.'

She nodded, feebly digging into her cake.

'Oh and, by the way, how can you taste that?' I asked, pointing to the cake.

She stopped, then shook her head slowly from side to side.

'You can't see colours, you don't have a sense of smell and—'

'Yes, Sahil,' she said. 'All that's true. Suffering is synonymous with a revenant's life.'

'Oh, Anya,' I said, reaching for her hands across the table. 'I'm so, so sorry.'

I couldn't believe I'd brought this up so soon after she told me about the awful and deplorable state of revenants when even the thought of it had pained her so much she'd wanted to defer the subject for as long as she could. She spoke about her death instead.

For the first time in my life I felt killing someone could be justified. What those three guys did to her was reprehensible, but the police and courts didn't think so. When her friend Nisha told the authorities she'd seen Anya last with them, they dismissed her. The charges Nisha pressed against them were dropped and the three of them were acquitted. They had laughed their way out of it.

I waved my hand slowly in front of her.

She made a face. 'I can see that, you dumbo.'

'Clearly?'

She let out a humbled sigh. 'Not very,' she said. 'But I can make out it's your hand.'

I shook my head. 'But I-I don't understand . . . all this while you've been telling me, "Oh, look at the sunset, isn't it beautiful?", "Enjoy your food, it's so delicious", "Isn't this lovely?", "Isn't that lovely?". What was all that about?'

She took her time finishing the cake, swirling the spoon slowly around, not leaving a scrap. Then she drank some water. Wiped her lips. Finally she looked at me.

'Why do you think I did that?'

I fell back on my seat when it hit me. I should have realized it earlier.

'You did that . . . you did that—you were lying? You did that so I could—'

'Bingo!' she said before pausing and holding her gaze at me. 'Between the two of us, I wanted at least one to live a good life.'

43

Boyfriend–Girlfriend

It must have been close to ten by the time we left Domino's though I didn't check the time. The entire evening had been a roller coaster, an evening of surprising revelations. One of them had been really pleasant—Anya had been in love with me right through. But the others felt like a story straight out of a fantasy book. But fantasy, she said, was nothing more than a manifestation of our thoughts, and thoughts emerged from the things we saw and heard. So couldn't fantasies be real?

A cool burst of wind hit us when we pushed the glass doors open. My teeth chattered and I clenched my fists at the bracing cold. The black-and-white checked overcoat that Anya had carried around all evening was finally brought to use. She unfolded it and wore it, fastening the big black buttons. It matched her high-heeled boots perfectly.

She looped an arm around my waist and I placed mine around her shoulders. She tilted her head slightly on to my shoulder, her warm breath hitting my cheek. At that moment I really wondered how it mattered, revenant or human, all I knew was I loved her madly. Everything else was inconsequential.

I kissed the top of her head. 'Love you, babe.'

'Love you too,' she said. 'But . . . why?'

'Why what?'

She lifted her head from my shoulder and cast me a sidelong glance. 'I'm a revenant, you idiot. Don't you get it? The reason I lied, why I kept you away from me. Why do you love me? You deserve better.' She hesitated, then said, 'You deserve a human.'

I stopped in my tracks and held her elbows. In the cool breeze, her hair flew about. Her eyelids were heavy, desperate for sleep. Her lips, full and inviting. I kissed them.

'Now *you* listen to me, dumbo,' I said. 'You told me you slept around, got pregnant thrice, whatever—did it change my feelings for you? No, I loved you all the same. Then you told me that you were a revenant, a serial killer, that you killed my friend. Did anything change? No, ma'am, not again. And now you say all your "luxuries"'—I made quotation marks with my fingers—'have been taken away. You know what, that's fine with me, too. You love me and that's all I'll ever want.'

Her eyes shone and a crooked smile formed on her lips. 'Oh really,' she said, 'think again.'

I thought again. 'Um . . . yeah . . . the arousal part, is that also true?'

She thumped my chest and the crooked smile transformed into a wide grin. 'I knew it. That's what you were going to say. Gosh, all you guys are the same.'

It was fine, manageable.

She tried to dissuade me further. The ageing factor, for instance, she said, was a deterrent. If anything, I told her, it was the best thing a man could ask for. Imagine as he aged, his woman remained young, aged four times slower, remained pretty and dynamic.

'Ha!' I said, pumping my fist in the air.

We strolled easily back and forth down Mall Road. The crowd had thinned, the lights dimmed. The sky was dark save for the full moon right above us: a big white ball suspended against an ebony backdrop, a company of lonely stars sprawled around it. Its silvery light lit the streets and the trees, a few stars twinkling in approval. In the distance a dog howled.

Our hands were clasped together and I'd closed my eyes to listen.

How can this be—

She wrenched her hand from my grip. 'Are you trying to read my mind?'

'Old habits!' I exclaimed.

'I've got to be careful,' she said, smiling. 'Anyway, I was just thinking, this is insane. We shouldn't be together, Sahil. I'm dead, I kill people. My life is like a prison, I've got to complete my time. Please understand.'

I took her hand back in mine. 'For me, you're that pretty and smart and confident girl I fell in love with. Nothing else. Let's give us a shot at least. Please.'

'It's a crazy idea,' she said.

'That's the cool part,' I said. 'That it's crazy. If it wasn't crazy, it wouldn't be love, now, would it?'

She nodded and pondered on this for a minute or two. 'Okay then,' she said finally, 'boyfriend.'

'Girlfriend.'

We moved towards each other and our lips met. This time they lingered for a while, exploring. A shot of heat rose below my ears all the way down to the back of my neck. My heart swelled, tightening my chest. Our lips still together, I moved closer, coursed my hand through her hair, settling a lock behind her ear. We closed our eyes. Our lips moved swiftly. My pulse rose. My heart beat louder.

When we parted, I noticed a deep flush had risen to her cheeks. Her eyes were lowered as she slowly moved backwards.

'So, girlfriend,' I said quickly, to mitigate the tension in the air. 'There's something I don't like about you.'

'Ha!' she said, looking back up, now as comfortable as a bee in a hive. 'One long kiss and "there's something I don't like about you"!'

I smiled. 'No, no, nothing to do with the kiss. I was wondering if you could stop killing.'

'Not kill the rapists, you mean?' she asked.

I shrugged.

'Okay, boyfriend,' she said. 'I won't if you promise me the victims will get justice and the animals a death sentence without delay, because currently our country sucks in this department.'

I shrugged once more.

'See, there you go. Those bastards, in my opinion, should be brought out on the streets, castrated, stoned to death, whatever. And this happens in some countries, by the way. If that starts happening in our country, I promise I'll stop.'

'So basically,' I said, summing it up, 'you won't.'

This time she shrugged.

I'd been thinking about this for a while.

'Okay, girlfriend,' I said, cupping her face in my hands. 'Listen. The next time you fly off on such a mission, take me along. I might have an idea.'

44

Apologies

It had been almost a month since I had woken up from the coma. The book that I had been working on so religiously before the accident stayed untouched on page ninety-six of my journal. I'd reached midway at about twenty-seven thousand words and, for a first timer, I thought that wasn't bad. What was bad though was my complete inability to progress. I'd tried half a dozen times over the last month, but all I managed was a single, dangling line:

Nirvaan spent the entire night wondering if the dagger he'd jabbed into the man's ribs was real.

After thirty minutes I tossed the pen on the desk and flipped the journal shut. School was closed for winter vacations and, I figured, I'd have plenty of time to write in the coming three weeks.

Three days ago, on the last day before vacations, Nishant had sauntered over to my desk in class. The anger on his face was visible.

'Can you believe it?' he said, throwing up his arms. 'That son of a bitch killer still hasn't been caught. Mayur deserves justice.'

He'd caught me off-guard with that statement and I tried my best to maintain a poker face.

I rose to my feet. 'The police is full of dumbasses,' I said.

He shook his head. 'I don't know if they are even working on the case any more.'

'They are, for sure. Ayush speaks to Pramod Uncle often. They can't get a lead it seems.'

He shook his head, this time vigorously. 'There are so many barricades and police checks on the roads all over, what's the point of all that?'

They are looking for a dead girl, I wanted to tell him. They'll never find her. A few days ago I'd asked Anya: what if they catch you some day? Anya was cool about it. She said the fingerprints and other evidence that they'd found at the scenes of the crimes could not be traced to anyone alive. And nobody pursues dead people.

The police, however, was trying tooth and nail to nab the killer. Security had been augmented at all strategic locations across the city, including the entry and exit points; extra police force had been summoned to Shimla; through the media, civilians had been asked to be alert and report any suspicious activity to the nearest SHO; the newspapers were full of reports and articles on the 'mysterious murders of Shimla' as was the TV. It was all the people of Shimla talked about.

Sometimes a shiver shot through me thinking about all of this.

I placed a comforting hand on Nishant's shoulder. 'It's going to be all right.'

What does he care? He never got along with Mayur anyway. Mayur was my friend.

The same evening at home, Ayush and Shweta, during dinner-time, were hooked to the TV. Another debate, another slinging match, questions hurled at the authorities, glib replies, angry calls and demands from civilians across Shimla. More anger, more drama, but the end result was the same: nothing.

We exchanged a few pleasantries, my siblings and I, but that was it. They didn't ask me many questions and I didn't venture any details either. Before proceeding to my room I stopped in front of Grandma's picture in the living room. The frame was a reasonable size with brass counters at the edges. A garland was draped over it. Grandma was smiling into the camera. I ran my hand across her face. I stared at the picture before taking a deep breath and trudging off to my room.

Over the next few days I learnt a lot more about revenants. The first time I'd met Aditya at Jakhoo Hill he'd intimidated me, asking me a question about a certain place I might have visited. Samra, near Kullu valley. A place about 200 kilometres north of Shimla.

That was where the bad revenants resided.

'The bad revenants?' I asked Anya.

'Yes, sweetheart,' she said, nodding. 'They are our arch-nemesis. We call them "the Others".'

The revenants, for centuries, had been an antidote to the Others. They killed, while the revenants saved; they caused havoc, the revenants spread peace; they celebrated their longevity of live, the revenants regretted it; the revenants wanted to atone for the sins committed in their human lives, the Others committed more sins. The Others were happy to be who they were, the revenants repented every minute of their existence.

Both the groups, however, had similar attributes, stripped off their human luxuries, for instance, and were born out of the same rationality: to suffer.

'In simple words,' Anya said, 'we are different sides of the same coin.'

The Others had been around for over a hundred years, as long as the revenants. The two groups had been at war for centuries but for the last five decades a truce had been established between them. A truce that was beginning to dwindle.

On Monica's birthday at Wake and Bake Café, the two bald, beefy guys who'd been staring at us with malice were the Others. They were meant to be lookouts, cautious scouts.

Anya told me that was all I needed to know for now. But I couldn't shake off a stiff feeling that there was a lot more.

Something dark. Ominous.

While talking about the Others, Anya's lips quivered and her fingers, that are always steady, trembled.

Aditya and the gang had initially perceived me to be one of the Others, some kind of a conduit, an informant. They'd asked Anya to keep clear of me, but Anya insisted I was 'harmless'. Aditya did a background check on me for a week. After the Jakhoo Hill visit he'd been tailing me, keeping an eye on my activities, the people I met, my home, family. The sneaky bastard must have done a damn good job for I had no inkling.

When I'd proposed Anya, all of them had a hearty laugh. Aditya told Anya it was one of the reasons he'd asked her to stay away from a human. He'd paraphrased a dialogue from an old Bollywood film: 'A boy and a girl can never be just friends.' They'd all had another hearty laugh and Anya had avoided me for the next week, quietly weeping at the unfairness of it all.

I finally got the joke about Monica's eighteenth birthday. It would have been her eighteenth had she been a human, but in the revenant world she'd have to serve three more years before she turned eighteen. Although she'd laughed at the time, once home, Anya told me, she'd broken into a fit of sobs.

Anya, herself, broke into a visceral fit of sobs after our Mahdauri visit. Her parents were right there, she wanted to apologize, hug them, tell them how much she loved and missed them. All she could do was to wait in the car, her fingers crossed, that I didn't find out she was dead.

Of course, I would have if she'd accompanied me to the house. She wasn't visible to them.

Although strange, it was one of the pivotal revenant rules. But, according to Anya, it was befitting for two reasons. One: if the dead could be seen by their family, death would serve no purpose; and two: it was the best or rather the worst punishment for taking relationships for granted.

Anya visited her family often. She roamed the hallway of her home, watching her father read the newspaper, horn-rimmed glasses on his nose, watch TV, pour himself drinks in the evening, while her mother was in the kitchen, squatting in the bathroom washing clothes, sweeping floors, sometimes sneaking a look at Anya's picture on the wall with teary eyes. Anya would sit next to her, her weightless head resting on her mother's shoulder, sometimes in her lap, her arms around her, shedding lonesome tears.

Sometimes she would saunter to her room and be struck both with revulsion and reminiscence. Nothing had changed. Her mother had not removed a single item from the room. The walls were still adorned with posters of her favourite heavy-metal bands, albeit some were peeling off, her Gibson guitar kneeling by the wall with the second string broken, her wardrobe at the far end still housed her clothes—a motley collections of blacks and greys, the first drawer of the chest strewn with images of tattoos that she'd planned to get, the dark lamp shade by the bed, the ashtray on the desk. It was all there.

Anya could never fight the lump that would lodge in her throat every time she stood at the threshold to her room. With a heavy heart she would trudge inside, watching her steps, as though treading in dangerous waters. She would sit on the edge of her bed, her head bent and gaze at the walls. She would hear the voices of her parents in the adjacent room, polite conversations, at other times heated exchanges of words that were sometimes about her. Her chest would tighten, cinching at every mention of her name, her eyes crying bucketfuls of tears.

All her life she'd turned them down, antagonized them, disrespected them, now she'd do anything to spend just one normal day with them.

And say sorry.

'But apologies,' she told me, 'have an expiry date. If you wait long enough they lose their magic.'

45

The Eighth Murder

It happened two days before New Year's Eve. Anya and I were strolling past Scandal Point, on the west end of Mall Road. The sky was dull and overcast.

I asked Anya if she knew the history of this place. When she shook her head I told her the name arose when the daughter of the then British viceroy allegedly eloped with the maharaja of Patiala. The British authorities banished the maharaja from entering Shimla.

'Love stories,' she said. 'Always tricky.'

Then she stopped abruptly, pulled her hand clumsily out of my grip and pressed her temples. Her eyes squeezed shut. Despite us not being in physical contact, I could read her mind. It was happening. I stood facing her in horror, watching the nuances of her expression. Sad. Worried. Her nose scrunched up. Her forehead furrowed. And then anger.

Her eyes flew open. 'We have to go,' she said, panting loudly. 'Do you want to come?'

I nodded. 'But first we need to make a stop.'

'Quick, quick,' she said, one hand pressed to her temple, her eyes partly shut.

As quickly as I could I bought a can of black spray paint from the nearest store.

It's difficult to explain what happened next. No sooner than I had the paint in my hands, she looped an arm around my waist and started galloping, taking insanely large steps. I had never run so fast in my life; people and shops passed behind me in a blur, like a montage of images, as if someone was flicking through the pictures hastily, one after the other, on their iPhone. As the crowd thinned out, we ran faster, only this time we were not really running, but zipping through the roads of Shimla, the images now hazy.

And then it happened. Our feet first slowly lifted off the ground, Anya's grip tightened around me. Soon we were flying. I had both my arms around her waist. One of her arms hung in mid-air, guiding and manoeuvring us to the correct elevation and direction. All of this happened so fast it was as good as dematerializing.

We whooshed past tall buildings, rising all the time, the air thick and cold on my cheeks, piercing my eyes and deafening me, billowing Anya's hair in angry, rebellious waves all over her face. My heart thudded in my ribcage when I cast a glance below us. Everything looked small and insignificant. What if we fell? It was frightening, yet monumentally exciting.

This had to be a dream, all of it; definitely a dream.

Anya tilted her arm slightly towards the west, into the setting sun, and then downwards. There were a cluster of similar-looking homes below us, red-walled with landscaped lawns and backyards. We fell sharply downwards, and after settling back on our feet, we stared at the thick chestnut door of the house in front of us.

The next second Anya threw it open with a hard kick of her leg. The door crumbled. She usually never did this, she told me. The walls were permeable for her, and had it not been for me, she could just as easily have passed through them.

We were twenty-two kilometres north-west of Mall Road. It had taken us less than two minutes to get there.

We followed the screams that filled the two-storied house. They originated on the first floor. Anya hopped up the stairs, five at a time, and I tried to catch up with her. When I entered the room there was a girl, fair-skinned with a small, cute face, cowering behind the bed, the bed sheet flimsily covering her naked body. Her brown hair was dishevelled and eyes filled with dread as she choked back her sobs.

Anya was on the other side of the bed, clobbering the face of a portly man who naked from the waist down. She kept at it till his face was a squashed reddish mess. He screamed the entire time, begging Anya to stop. The girl, now more petrified, buried her head in the mattress, her hands covering her ears.

The man's howl when Anya dismembered his arm with one yank was so painfully loud, I was sure it would ring in my ears for days to come. She flung his arm at the wall and it fell with a plunk to the floor, streaks of blood splattered against the walls like graffiti.

Anya made a move towards his crotch and tore it all off with a single twisting motion of her hand. Once more the man howled, only this time it was much louder. She threw his genitals across the room and they came hurtling towards me.

I cringed and slid out of the way.

My stomach churned and out came its contents with a quick, raspy retch. I leaned by the window and vomited on the curtains. The girl sat still, her face down, her hands clamped tighter over her ears.

One last heave of Anya's right leg in a powerful blow on the man's abdomen and his entrails flew out of his mouth.

After wriggling on the floor for a minute, his body came to a rest.

'Do what you have to do now!' Anya said to me, wiping her face with a swipe of her arm, which only made it dirtier, bloodier. 'And make it quick!' Then to the girl she said, 'Put on your clothes and get out of here!'

I tried to stop shaking before slowly walking towards the wall. I averted my eyes to avoid even a glimpse at the floor. I opened the lid of the can and sprayed across the wall, as neatly and clearly as I could.

'You really think that'll help?'

I turned to look at the words again.

I WAS A RAPIST
GOD DEALT WITH ME

'I sure hope so.'

Before the girl left the room, with one hand cupping the side of her face, Anya stopped her.

'You tell anyone about this, anyone about him,' Anya pointed a finger at me, 'or about me. I'll find you, and then I'll kill you, just like I killed him!'

The girl gave a frightened nod.

'You saw nothing, you know nothing.'

The girl slowly nodded again.

'Say the words!'

The girl swallowed. 'I-I saw nothing, I know-know nothing.'

'Good,' Anya said. 'You can leave now.'

With the girl gone, Anya looked at me. 'So, boyfriend,' she said, a sly smile reaching her eyes, 'how about a kiss now?'

46

The Miraculous Murders of Shimla

I couldn't sleep that night or the next night or the two nights after that. The images flashing in my mind were morbid, the screams still stinging my ears. It was one thing to see it on TV, quite another to witness the act.

We'd planned on spending New Year's Eve together, Ayush, Shweta and I, on the Ridge. Every year the place is thronged with cheerful, excited faces; there are celebrations, dance and music, varieties of food stalls; whoops and hollers culminating in a collective countdown to midnight. The noise reaches a crescendo, people shake hands with complete strangers, wishing their best and congratulating each other for stepping into a new year, before dispersing slowly into the night.

After contemplating it for a few days I'd decided to introduce Anya to my siblings that evening, not with all her secrets, of course, but as my girl.

But all I could do on New Year's Eve was lie in bed, two blankets pulled up to my face and hope for some sleep. My head throbbed with pain and I'd caught a chronic cold with a hacking cough. Ayush and Shweta celebrated their evening at home with some of their friends. They checked in on me often, softly tapping on the door, poking their heads in. I'd raise an arm and tell them I was fine.

I was not.

Anya was ruthless. I understood her intentions, but no killing could be justified, definitely not one that was done in such a horrible manner.

It was all over the TV the following day. I was leaning against the couch in the living room, legs resting on the centre table, a blanket draped over me. Shweta had prepared a hot cup of ginger tea for me. I dipped a Marie biscuit into the tea and chewed the soft end absently as Ayush tuned into the evening news. A bespectacled, young woman seated behind a blue desk spoke to us.

'In a major turn of events in the case of the mysterious murders of Shimla that have rocked the city for the last five months, another murder, the eighth, was reported in the north-western part of the city. The victim's name was Virendra Kumar. He was forty-two years old. Like all the other victims in this gruesome murderous rampage, he was tortured and castrated before his death. With what is being referred to as the latest development, the police have found a note scrawled on the wall of the room where the victim breathed his last.'

I shifted in my seat when an image of the wall was flashed on the TV screen. The paint had dribbled down slightly from the words I had written.

Ayush turned to me. 'Rapist? What the hell is wrong with this bastard?'

The image changed to a policeman in broad daylight. 'We are investigating this message and viewing the murders from a new angle,' he said into the mics being thrust into his face outside the police station.

The newsreader was back. 'Meanwhile, the people of Shimla, furious and agitated, have launched a fresh demonstration outside the police headquarters, repeatedly addressing the law officials as "incompetent". There have been reports of protests on the streets in other parts of the city as well.

'In other news, refugees . . .'

Ayush pressed the mute button on the TV remote. 'Pathetic,' he swore under his breath. He swung his massive legs off the table and straightened his back. He picked up his mobile, unlocked the screen and scrolled through his contacts list. 'Should I call Pramod Uncle?'

Shweta raked a hand through her hair. 'What's the point, brother?' she said with a little curve of her right hand. 'Ever since Grandma's death he has barely talked to us. All I know is that the police needs to find him fast.'

'Him?' I asked. 'How do you know it's a him?'

'It has to be a him,' she said. 'Only men could commit such gruesome acts.'

* * *

A week before school reopened, I finally felt better. For the past five days as I lay in bed, I did some reading and some thinking, mostly thinking, and it was limited to just one thing: confronting Anya.

She couldn't do this any more. Didn't the revenant world keep track of her sins?

'Have you forgotten what they did to me?' she said when I finally spoke to her.

'Doesn't the revenant world keep a track of your sins?' I stuck to my approach.

'Cleansing the world is not a sin!' She held my hand. We stood on the street outside our academy. It was noisy. 'Besides I'm beginning to think more and more that your idea wasn't that bad after all.'

'What do you mean?'

Over the next two weeks she killed two more people, taking the victim count to ten. I didn't dare accompany her but she took the spray paint along.

The two lines that I'd scripted were all over the newspapers, TV, Internet, and were scrutinized, dissected, debated in every way possible. Was it really an act of god? Or an evil execution masked in a sheath of vigilante justice?

The spiritual gurus spoke unabashedly that it was clearly stated in *Upanishads* that during Kalyug, when evil powers reached extreme levels, god would descend on Earth and takes matters into his own hands.

Brajesh Singh, the opposition party leader, when questioned was quick to rebuff this 'sheer nonsense' and proclaim that his son, Sanjay Singh, was no rapist and insisted that he was a noble man. He maintained his position that this was all propaganda by the ruling party meant to defile him. The media did a short piece on the affluent and promiscuous life of Sanjay Singh suggesting that he wasn't entirely incapable of a forceful sexcapade.

No one knew how but the news spread quickly across Shimla that some lunatic hated rapists and had killed ten of them. It could have been an intentional or unwitting attempt by the police and the media collectively to frighten them.

By the third week of January the 'mysterious murders of Shimla' had been altered to the 'miraculous murders of Shimla'.

Social media helped augment this popularity with hashtags such as #RapistsBeware trending on Twitter and a page on Facebook by the same name.

It is amazing what people can be made to believe.

47

The Home of the Revenants

Snow had been pounding Shimla with all its fury. On the third Monday of the month, meteorologists reported an average snowfall of twenty-two inches, the highest in January over the last ten years. A thick blanket of white had enveloped the entire city. Even the trees were not spared. The branches and leaves of the deodars were sprinkled liberally with fistfuls of snow.

The sun had lost its vigour and visited us intermittently only for a few hours in the day before surrendering to the dense, dreary clouds and eventually being swallowed by them. Gusts of wind travelling from the north ensured that the temperature hovered below freezing point during the night.

No matter how many layers of woollen clothes we wore, the biting cold would find its way to our skin. So, in the fourth week of January, when I took the bus from outside my house to visit the revenants' abode in Johor Bagh, I was already regretting my decision.

Anya had been inviting me for the last few days—'You'd be the first human', 'I had to take so many permissions'—but I had been deferring it for various reasons—the cold, my health, but mostly because I felt scared. I was afraid to enter a house full of revenants, full of dead people.

As the door swung open and I stepped off the bus, a rush of frigid air slapped my cheeks. I felt my nose and it was frozen at the tip. I stepped on to the footpath along the periphery of a well-manicured garden. I walked slowly, my head bent, the hood of my leather jacket drawn over it.

The wealthiest people of Shimla resided in Johor Bagh. The houses were the biggest here, their grandeur eliciting envy; the streets were wide and spectacularly clean, with luxury cars speeding on them; the parks green and lush, rows of maples and cedars lining them.

The houses in the area were arranged in a square, with a massive park in the centre.

I encountered no difficulty in locating their house. It was on the southern edge of a park, the third from the left, and sat on a few acres of land. Damn! And Anya had said they owned three bungalows here.

I stood outside the house, awe-struck, and took in the place for a minute. It was a three-storied building, green vines dangling from the roof. There was a driveway, wide enough to accommodate at least ten cars. I spotted a Mercedes, a Porsche and an Audi resting under the shade of deodar trees on the outer periphery of the driveway.

In front of the house was a landscaped garden with a neat row of flowers of various colours—lilies and tulips, neatly trimmed rosebushes. There was a mechanical swing that could easily seat four, a cream-white antique set of garden furniture, shrubs that had been modelled like animals—a giraffe, an elephant, a deer.

The house proved even more impressive once I stepped inside. The first thing I noticed was the high ceiling. Then the tasteful choice of furnishings neatly positioned, the pleated burgundy drapes framing the glass door on the far end that opened on to another garden, the home theatre system, the spotless marble floor. Everything in the room was polished to a shine, free of dust.

An old, primly dressed gentleman descended down the stairs to my left.

'Hello,' he said, offering his hand. 'I'm Ibrahim and you must be Sahil.'

I shook his cold, nimble hand. 'Yes, sir.'

I hadn't intended to call him 'sir' but it stumbled out of my mouth at the sight of his impeccable clothes and conduct, and his assertive, confident eyes shining as brightly as a star. Anya stood next to me, her arm coiled in mine, but at that moment, it was only his eminent presence that I felt.

He was bald and his head shone with such a powerful gleam, I wondered if I might see my reflection if I moved closer; slender pince-nez glasses sat comfortably on his nose; a perfectly trimmed French beard, mostly black with some grey thrown in, graced his face; and his clothes—there wasn't a single fold or wrinkle in his crisp striped blue shirt that was tucked neatly into black trousers and held by a belt with a shiny, chrome buckle. His black shoes were polished. They were shining, too.

It rarely happened to me but I suddenly grew extremely self-conscious in my ill-fitting jeans, checked shirt, leather jacket and loafers.

'Please call me Ibrahim.'

'Yes, sir—Ibrahim.'

He led me towards the cream-coloured couch that looked straight out of a high-end interiors magazine. The three of us took a seat, Anya and I on the couch and Ibrahim on the adjoining single-seater chair to my side.

'Um . . .' I ventured. 'Are you also a . . .'

'Revenant? Yes.' He nodded. 'All of us in this house are.'

Then, silence.

I grinned like a donkey and allowed my gaze to drift. There was a massive black-and-white oil painting on the wall across us. It was of a woman with a pot on her head, her shoulders stooped forward, on her way to a small hut in the distance, her two toddlers in her wake. At the top right corner of the painting, a full moon cast an ominous stream of light over the darkened village.

'If you'll excuse me,' Ibrahim said, rising, 'I'll get some refreshments organized.'

'That won't be necessa—' I started to say, but he was already walking towards the stairs.

Once he'd disappeared from earshot, Anya kissed me on my cheek. 'Relax, monkey. Why are you so stressed?'

I let out a sharp breath in a hiss and relaxed. I held her hand and we laced our fingers. 'Why does it feel like he's your father and I'm here to ask for your hand in marriage?'

She rolled her eyes. 'In your dreams, boyfriend.'

'Oh, girlfriend.'

We shared a soft, short kiss.

I didn't hide my wonder at the opulence of the house. 'You guys are so rich.'

She shook her head. 'Ibrahim is. It all belongs to him.'

Anya told me Ibrahim was a very wealthy man when he was human. He had enough money to last him ten lifetimes. But then he died.

Now he used his money for the well-being of the revenants. Ibrahim had a few more houses in Ooty, Cochin and Panchgani where other revenants resided.

'Other revenants?'

So Shimla wasn't the only home for the revenants. In order to avoid the suspicions of their neighbours and the people they worked with, the revenants relocated two to three times during the span of their lives.

Despite having enough money to accommodate close to two hundred revenants all over the country, some worked in government offices, banks and private companies. It made them feel human.

Some of them made human friends. But no one was allowed in the house. Ibrahim was strictly against that and against any romantic liaisons with humans.

'But we have done both,' I said with a wink.

'That was because you found out, dumbo. Remember?' She melodramatically turned her index finger in circles at her temple. 'Why do you think I was avoiding you? It wasn't allowed.'

I kissed her cheek. 'Well, in that case, it's good that I can read minds.'

'Do you still do it?'

'I don't need to,' I said, matter-of-factly. 'You don't lie any more.'

At that moment, Aditya, Sameer and Monica came hopping down the stairs and told me that they were pleased to have me over.

'Oh, wow,' Monica chortled. 'A human in the house. How often does that happen?' Her tomboyish gait reminded me of her story. My heart skipped a beat. Small tomboy.

'Don't these guys look cute together, Monica?' There was a playful mocking edge to Aditya's voice.

'Oh,' she replied, 'you mean the virgins?'

Anya and I exchanged a quick glance.

'The what?' she said.

'The virgins,' Aditya said, pleased. 'Monica coined this term for you since, you know, you'll never be able to . . .'

Anya tipped her head. 'I'm not a virgin, trust me.'

'Yeah,' I said. 'Me neither.'

'Okay,' Monica and Aditya said in unison, laughing loudly and high-fiving each other, pleased at having annoyed us.

Sameer, the good boy, smiled softly to himself.

They sat on the beige divan to our left, Sameer on the outermost side. His eyes were so tired and red and, now that I knew, I felt sorry for him. Plus, the headache, that constant buzzing sound, Anya had told me. No wonder he was always so distracted.

'Listen, Sameer,' I began, 'um . . . Anya told me. I'm so sorry for what you have to go through, and, of course, thank you, for convincing me against, uh, suicide.'

Sameer dramatically took a bow, very uncharacteristically. 'Always a pleasure.'

'I'm sorry, again. You know, I always wondered why you were so distant, aloof, your eyes always red and brooding. I have to admit, regretfully, that I thought you were boring, and I'm sorry for that. I really am. We shouldn't judge people we barely know.'

He nodded. 'It's okay. I'm sorry too for what I did. I always felt pathetic when I was alive. I thought suicide was the solution, and now—' He took a deep breath. 'I would do anything to go back to that wonderful, wonderful life. I wish people knew, suicide is not the solution, it's the problem.'

All of us nodded gravely.

'So how do you do it? I mean, convince people not to kill themselves.'

'Thanks to these powers I know when and where it'll happen, and then I just talk them out of it. No magic there.'

'How? You're saying people are convinced just by your words?'

He cocked his head. 'Words are very powerful, Sahil. When chosen correctly and articulated well, they can even change governments.'

I smiled. 'True that.' Then to Aditya I said, 'So, how many of you live in this house?'

'There are twenty-three of us here,' Aditya replied immediately, glad that I had changed the topic. 'We have about twelve rooms on three floors. The rest stay in the bungalows next door. Plus, we have some who live outside Shimla.'

'I told him about that,' Anya said.

'You guys are so filthy rich,' I said. 'Damn, I'm jealous. I wish I was one of you.'

When she was alive, Grandma always told us, 'Think before you talk.' I wish I had heeded her advice.

Now, Monica leaned forward, her eyes glazed with tears. 'Trust me,' she said with a sniff, 'you don't want to be one of us.'

48

Guilt

The refreshments arrived after few minutes. We said thanks to the lean man with a pencil moustache and the grey-haired woman. Not just for the refreshments, I thought, but also for softening the uncomfortable air around us.

They got us tiny fried samosas, chicken nuggets, *dhokla*, cookies and soft drinks. They placed spotless plates with thin gold lining in front of us.

As they left, we said thanks again. I helped myself to both the samosa and dhokla.

'Servants, are they?' I inquired, curious.

Aditya shook his head. He held a long glass of Fanta. 'Nobody's a servant here. We're all equal.'

'It's an egalitarian society,' Anya added. 'That's what Ibrahim likes to call it. We're free to do whatever we want. Those two like kitchen work.'

I stole a glance at Monica. The small tomboy was subdued. 'Are you okay, Monica?'

'Uh-huh,' she said, picking up a glass of Coke. 'Actually . . . about earlier, why did you say you wanted to be one of us?'

I exchanged a quick glance with Anya and Aditya. 'Monica,' I said, 'it was a joke.'

'It'd better be.'

'Come to think of it,' I added, my hands motioning at their home, 'it wouldn't be so bad living in a palace, fancy cars parked out front, gardens with flowers and fruit trees; the cramped three BHK flat I live in is a far cry from this.'

There, I had done it again. Wherever she was, Grandma was wrinkling her nose at me.

Monica was in a very bad mood that day. She leaned forward and kept her glass on the table. Tears glazed her eyes again.

'Do you really think so?' she said. She looked once each at Aditya, Anya and Sameer. When they didn't give her more than a raised eyebrow—Sameer didn't even give her that—she went on. 'That Coke, you know what, I can't taste a damn thing. How about that? It's just cold, aerated water. This palace you talk about, it could be a dungeon for all I care. I see only black and white, anyway. And what gardens and flowers? We don't get their scent, they might as well be dead.' She shook her head. 'Our neighbour from across the street, Mrs Nehra, told me one day when I was in the park, "Oh look, Monica, what a beautiful rainbow, so full and complete."'

She managed to banish the tears but her face was like stone, her eyes expressionless, staring at the glass door unblinkingly. 'I want to see a rainbow someday, with all its colours.' And then came the tears in an uncontrollable flurry.

Aditya threw his arm around Monica and pulled her to his side. 'We have discussed this, haven't we, Monica? Please. We're all in this together.'

'Why do you do this to yourself, Monica?' Anya's face was stony as well.

Sameer quietly nibbled a biscuit, his head lowered.

She let her tears run out. Her shaking body slowly came to a halt. 'I feel bad, that's why,' Monica replied. When she finally lifted her head from her hands, her eyes were as red as a fireball. 'Every day I think of what I did. Guilt is the heaviest burden.'

A claw tightened around my throat. All I had to do was keep my mouth shut.

Now she fixed her gaze at me. She wiped her eyes and sniffed once. 'You know, Sahil, I always thought I'd get away with what I did, nobody would find out. But there is a journal maintained somewhere upstairs of all our deeds, good and bad, and we'll pay for all our sins before we depart from this world.'

49

Money

The revenants usually had an early dinner. When summoned, we mounted the stairs to the first floor and I was struck, once again, by the grandeur of the place.

In front of me was a massive dining table, a fine blue silk table runner across its entire length. Two dozen chairs were neatly arranged along the table. The dining hall was the centre around which the other rooms were laid out. To the right, a corridor led to an open kitchen, where I could see the lean man and the old, grey-haired woman. In front of us was a dull yellow-brick wall, but after staring at it for a while, the yellow didn't appear dull at all. It gelled perfectly with the aura of the hall, which was at once calm and pleasing. The interior designer would have been paid a handsome sum.

There was a healthy murmur from the twenty-three revenants and, as I walked in, they turned to glance at me. It was a solicitous glance, a non-judgemental, cordial one. Anya and Aditya walked me over for an introduction.

I met a guy named Chinna, in his thirties, short and dark; Tandel who smiled in your face, wholesome teeth on full display; Dilsheraz, a tiny little teenager; Aakriti, a fair, pleasant-looking woman; Mihika, with the roundest face I'd ever seen, and those were all the names I could remember. All of them were kind and courteous, and welcomed me warmly.

Ibrahim joined us, emerging from a room to the left. He took a seat at the head of the table, and the others promptly joined him. The lean man with the pencil moustache and the old, grey-haired woman, after taking one last look at the table, satisfied, sat down. I sat between Anya and Aditya, two seats from Ibrahim. Monica and Sameer sat across the table from us. The food on the table surprised me with its normalcy. Not that I was expecting human meat or blood.

I let my eyes run through the items one by one. It was an eclectic mix of Indian cuisine—idli and sambar, mutton biryani, rice and dal, chicken curry, *chapattis*, a fresh green salad, *papad* and pickle.

It was normal human food!

The murmur died when Ibrahim cleared his throat. Like clockwork, they brought their hands together, closed their eyes, and bent their heads in reverence. A little prayer echoed through the room.

'Thank you, Lord, for today, for the meal and for the companionship. Forgive our sins for we are weak and ignorant.'

And then everyone began serving themselves. I ladled a spoonful of biryani on to my plate. Anya helped herself to lots of salad, and some dal.

'That's it?'

'That's it,' she said.

'You're a health-conscious ghost.'

She jabbed her elbow into my ribs. 'You ass.'

We laughed softly under our breath. I took a small bite of the biryani. It wasn't the best biryani I had had, but it was definitely savoury. Without being able to taste it, the man and the woman had done their job well. But then I grew curious once more.

'Forgive me for asking,' I said to Ibrahim, while the revenants on the other side of the table were engaged within themselves, 'but why go through so much trouble? I mean with good food and all, when you can't taste . . .'

'Because we like to lead human lives,' Ibrahim replied before I could complete my sentence.

'That's true,' Aditya said, his fork and knife clinking on his plate.

Ibrahim reached for the glass next to his plate, lifted the jug and poured some water. Before taking a sip, he said, 'We like to enjoy what we do and try not to make the same mistake twice.'

Chinna and another fat revenant whose name I couldn't remember smiled benevolently, absorbed in their meal.

The noise level at the table was neither loud nor soft, but a good-natured banter. The revenants had a lot to talk about.

'Could I ask another question?'

Ibrahim nodded.

'What did you do?'

Here, he threw his head back and laughed heartily. 'The question is what did I not do.' He wiped the corner of his mouth with his napkin. 'I did very well for myself when I was human; surely you can see that. All I ever wanted was to earn money, so much that I could pile it all up and make a whole bed of money.' He flicked his right wrist. 'I was the bad guy.'

When he didn't add more, I pressed, 'So what did you not do?'

'My family,' he replied. 'I never had time for them. They meant nothing to me then: my wife, two kids—a daughter and a son.'

Something gave way. The smile had left his face and a hard steeliness took over. He drummed his fingers on the table while absently chewing on the last morsels on his plate.

I turned to Anya; she winked at me, a don't-worry-he'll-be-fine wink.

Ibrahim took another sip of water. 'You know, my wife would always ask me, "Ibrahim, just how much is enough?" All I would answer was, "More". When she realized lives were being destroyed, she left with the kids. I didn't even try to stop her.' He picked up his fork again. 'Anyway, that's my life's irony: I have tons of money today which I'd happily give up just to spend a few minutes with them.' He allowed the smile to return to his face, a rueful smile.

Silence slowly mushroomed, then enveloped the hall. Everyone's head was turned to Ibrahim. His was looking directly at me.

'It's simple enough,' he said. 'The only thing that money provides us is freedom: the freedom to do what we want to and the freedom to not do what we don't want to. To expect anything else from it is the root cause of all misery.'

50

Ibrahim

Ibrahim was born in 1863, the year the Viceroy of India decided to shift the summer capital of the British Raj to Shimla. He was born to a teenage mother and a high-ranking Indian official in the government.

His father hated Indians. In 1876, when they started preparing Shimla for the move, a hunt began for a suitable place for a viceregal lodge, the current Rashtrapati Niwas. Ibrahim's father suggested they clear an area where a large population of Indians lived, what is now Upper Bazaar. This was adhered to and the place was burned down and the natives forced to shift to the Middle and Lower Bazaars on the lower terraces that descended down the steep slopes from the Ridge.

Violence ensued. Many people died. In retribution, a high-ranking Indian official was killed. Ibrahim's father.

Years later, his mother would think that her son turned out to be more crooked than her husband.

Ibrahim continued his father's legacy: persecuting the natives and ingratiating himself with the Whites. With his father's contacts at the highest levels of the government, as well as his black money, Ibrahim was successful in establishing a thriving drug business. Hands were greased, files cleared, people who posed threats were 'taken care of'.

The labourers were made to toil in inhumane conditions, those who resisted were fired. Ibrahim had a horde of loyal goons working under him.

By the close of the nineteenth century, the presence of many single men and women, mostly Whites escaping the heat, created the perfect atmosphere for adultery in Shimla. Ibrahim had a multitude of affairs with young British women, before finally tying the knot with Samreen, a young, confident woman, when he was thirty. She was the daughter of a wealthy merchant in the neighbouring town.

Samreen never knew about her husband's line of work. To her, he was a merchant, as straight an arrow as her father. Ibrahim never thought of enlightening her either.

Over the next two years Samreen bore Ibrahim two kids—a boy and a girl.

Things were smooth for the first few years of their marriage. Then, one summer day, she witnessed the killing of a skinny man in their factory. Ibrahim couldn't twist the facts any more. She gave him a chance to undo his past, threatened to leave, take the kids away. Ibrahim showed her the way to the door.

'We have everything,' she cried. 'How much more do you want?'

'I want to build an empire, you stupid woman!'

Eventually, he did build an empire, the biggest drug cartel in north India. But he never saw his wife and kids again, and was butchered to death in 1901.

Upon his death one of his goons took over his empire.

51

The Body and the Soul

A chill crawled all the way up my spine. Gooseflesh prickled at my skin. My heart battered against my chest.

Ibrahim had died in 1901, more than a century ago!

Yet, he was here. In flesh and blood. Smiling. I took a bite of the cold *rasagulla* served in oval-shaped bowls. The main course had since long been cleared as Ibrahim recounted his story.

I did the mental maths. Ibrahim was thirty-eight when he died. Had he been human he would now be a hundred and fifty years old. But he was not human. He aged four times slower after his death a hundred and twelve years ago, so that would be twenty-eight years of life as a revenant.

I peered at him. He was sixty-six now! Assuming a life-span of eighty human years, he'd have to live for approximately fifty-six more years as a revenant.

Two centuries, then, give or take. The world would see Ibrahim for two centuries! I quickly glanced around. A shudder shot through me and ended in a gasp. All of them, including my Anya, would have to wait that long for . . . for . . .

'Um . . . sorry, but what happens once you complete your . . . you know, your time as a revenant?' I asked, hesitantly.

'We're done,' Aditya replied.

'Of course you are,' I said. 'But what *happens*, you know, technically?'

The good-natured banter had returned to the table as the revenants dug into their rasagullas. The tone on our side of the table had softened.

'We die just like humans do,' Monica said, shrugging from across the table. Her spoon dug little bored grooves into her dessert. 'If we were to die of old age as humans, we would slowly struggle our way till then and—' She dramatically sliced her hand across her neck.

'But we have a long time to go before that,' Sameer spoke up.

A stupid idea then floated into my mind. Nonetheless, I thought of sharing it. 'But why can't you just finish your life like . . .'

'Suicide?' Sameer gawked at me in shock.

I nodded, warily.

'Great idea, dumbo,' Anya said with a shake of her head. 'And end up in a place, perhaps, worse than this?'

I bit my lip. 'I'm sorry.'

'There's one other way,' Aditya said. Then, when he had everyone's attention, he continued. 'What if we were killed?'

'Killed by whom, Aditya?'

Aditya cleared his throat and leaned forward, his gaze on Ibrahim. 'I saw them again, last evening by the gate. They are here.'

I saw a flash of concern in Ibrahim's eyes as they darted back and forth from Aditya to Anya.

'The Brothers, you mean?'

Aditya nodded. 'It seems your little old treaty is withering away.'

When I inquired Aditya replied in what seemed like a measured, careful manner. The two bald, beefy guys at Wake and

Bake Café were the Brothers. They were not related, but looked similar—bald, heavily-built, violent animals. Their leader had christened them. They were the most dangerous of the Others.

'Okay,' I said, 'but what do they want?'

Anya said, squeezing my hand, 'In simple words, they want to kill some of us.'

'Why? I thought a truce had been established between you guys?'

I said this rising to my feet. The plates were being cleared and after wishing us goodnight, the revenants excused themselves, one by one. Sameer and Monica, too, retired to their rooms. Along with Ibrahim and Aditya, Anya and I went down the stairs and took our original seats.

'So, why do they want to kill you?' I asked as soon as we sat down.

Ibrahim held out of his hand. 'Let me explain. Sahil, the good and bad revenants have existed for thousands of years, fighting amongst each other, establishing territories, usurping power, resulting in bloodshed and so on. Let me just say that when I became a revenant there were a lot more of us all over the country. However, we kept fighting and when both sides realized there was too much collateral damage, we hung up our boots, so to speak.

'This was in the seventies and by then I was more or less heading operations for the good revenants. A rat named Damiyan was the leader of the Others. Both of us agreed to a peace treaty and for more than forty years we never crossed each other's paths. Now that Damiyan and some of his cronies are getting old, they want to kill a few of us. Initially it was perceived to be a myth, but it has been proven true over years of observation: when a revenant kills another he acquires his soul, his powers and the years left of his life.'

'Sahil,' said Anya placing a hand on my thigh, 'do you remember I told you that as much as we regret being who we are, the Others love it; in fact, they want to be immortal. Well, they can't be, but killing us can certainly give them extra years.'

I shook my head. 'But I don't understand. If they suffer like you, why would they want to be immortal.'

'Think about it,' she said. 'That's what power and money do—rule out the rationale in you.'

I shook my head again. 'Wait . . . how does a good revenant become good and a bad revenant a bad one in the first place? Is there some kind of a . . . I don't know . . . background check?'

The three of them laughed.

'No, there isn't,' replied Aditya. 'It's just a matter of choice.'

'But when you die, right,' I turned to Anya 'for example, when you died and then . . . whatever . . . woke up . . . how did you know which team to join? Or how did you find them?' I nodded towards Ibrahim.

'That's a long story,' she said. 'Okay, obviously I only remember fragments of this, my memory is like a huge collage of inter-connected images, but whenever I try to put them all together, some pieces don't fit. So what happened was this: I died on my way to the hospital when finally someone took mercy on me and called an ambulance. It was the perfect out-of-body experience in the hospital, staring down at my bloodied, lifeless corpse. A few hours later, my parents came storming through the door and, at the sight of my body, first sank in shock, and then wailed, you know, those ear-splitting, piercing wails of pain. It was so heartbreaking. I stood there, right next to them, my arm around my mother, telling her, "I'm fine, I'm here", but her wails didn't stop.

'Sometime later, now I don't know when exactly, or what happened in the middle—missing pieces, like I said earlier—I was kind of flying at breakneck speed into what seemed like a deep and terrifyingly long white tunnel towards a very bright blinding light. Sometime during this journey I heard a loud thundering voice of which I remember only fragments, "Your time is not up. You must go back!"

'And then, just like that, I wasn't flying any more. Instead I was walking on a previously untrodden path. It could have been days, months later, I don't know, but, finally, I found them. It really was like that. I found them. We, the revenants, can recognize each other. One exchange of a glance and we know. Ibrahim took me under his wing and then, well, here I am.'

'But what if you had found the Others first?'

'It can happen.' Aditya took over from her. 'I had a friend, Majumdar, suicide case, good guy. I don't know what drove him to kill himself. Anyway, he found them first. Lived with them for a few months, struggled, then came looking for us, the good revenants. I was not a revenant then. This was about two decades ago.'

'And where is he now?'

'Oh, he's gone,' Aditya replied. 'He didn't do a lot of time. About twenty years as a revenant.'

'So that means,' I said, turning to Anya and back to Aditya, 'correct me if I'm wrong—had he not killed himself as a human, he would have have lived for only five more years anyway?'

'Bingo!' both of them said in unison, a spark in their eyes.

I shook my head incredulously. 'Unbelievable,' I said. 'All of it.'

Ibrahim was smiling to himself. 'Well,' he said, 'believe it or not, that's the way it works.'

He said this with an air of finality. *Believe it or not, that's the way it works.* It could have been construed as: listen, ignorant human, just because you don't know something, doesn't invalidate its existence.

'Okay, here's another thing,' I went on, speaking to Anya, 'you just said your body was gone, right? Of course, you were dead so . . . but, now you have it. You are as corporeal as I am. How the hell did you get that back?'

'Body?' Ibrahim said in distaste, wrinkling his nose. 'You really think it has any significance? The soul is everything, the all-important matter of the universe. The body is temporary; a disintegrating mass of refuse. Get this straight: you are your soul, not your body. Okay, let me ask you a question: how do you address your arm, your leg or your face? You say "my arm", "my leg", "my face". Do you ever refer to it as "me arm" or "me leg"?' He shook his head. 'You don't. Why? Because you are not your body, you are your soul. You are separate from your body. So coming back to your question, how hard do you think it is to acquire a damn body?'

'Not hard at all,' Anya replied for me.

52

'They Are Here'

The moon was right above us, its silvery stream lighting the gravelled driveway as Anya and I slowly traipsed across it. Despite the parked cars, there was enough space to walk.

I checked my wristwatch, 9.47 p.m. I should be leaving soon, I thought.

The cold was fierce. As we exhaled, plumes of white mist danced in front of us before making way for the next batch. Anya's right hand was frigid against mine. She was resting her head on my shoulder. I noticed with great delight, not for the first time, that the difference in our heights afforded her head to sit just perfectly on my shoulder. We're made for each other, I had once remarked.

'You know,' she said, 'you're the one supposed to be reading minds, but I know what you're thinking.'

I smiled. 'What am I thinking?'

'Something on the lines of "how weird".'

I raised her hand to my lips and kissed it. 'You're right.'

We reached the main gate and turned around.

'Seriously,' I continued, 'everything about the evening was so damn weird. I mean, you guys eating proper human food—biryani and chicken curry and all that—and I thought ghosts and vampires or whatever drank blood and feasted on human flesh.'

She stopped, then turned to me. 'Actually, we do that too.'

When I started to smile and shake my head, she said she was serious.

'I'm not lying,' she said. Her eyes had caught the gleam of the moon, and presently they shone like two bright bulbs. 'When we told you about the Others wanting to kill us, what do you think goes on?'

'What goes on?'

She took a deep breath and then snorted it out, clouds of vapour gushing out to accompany the sound. 'Okay, so . . . um . . . it's not as easy as what we told you. I mean, they kill us and they get our years and all, because if it was that way Ibrahim would live for thousands of years. Trust me, he's killed a lot of them back in the day when there was a massive war between the two groups.

'Anyway, a ritual needs to be performed. A revenant cannot just die from a gunshot or a dagger. What happens is we are subdued, we become unconscious. At that point our bodies need to be burnt right down to ashes within fifteen minutes. If more time is taken, our wounds heal by themselves and we sort of just awaken. Now, in order to acquire the remaining years, the revenant who is performing this ritual, before burning the body, needs to drain the blood and, you know, drink it. Only then is the soul trapped within him.'

I frowned. 'You have got to be kidding me, girlfriend.'

'Not one word, boyfriend.'

Her eyes corroborated her words.

Each time I thought I had wrapped my head around the mysteries surrounding the revenants, another eerie fact popped up. This one filled me with a mounting sense of dread.

'Sameer, once,' she continued ignoring my queasiness, 'thought of handing himself over to them. He was finding it difficult to survive in his initial days as a revenant. When we told him that that didn't provide an exit from this life, his soul would still sort of hang in there, he changed his mind. That's why when you first met us, we always hung out together, Sameer and I. He was really disturbed those days. I was trying to help him, calm him down, tell him he had to pay for his mistakes, there's no easy way out.'

I let out a little smile of amusement. 'I don't know, Anya. Somehow you manage to freak me out every time I think it's no big deal.'

'So you have doubts about—'

'No, no,' I said. 'God, no, I love you. That's all that matters.'

I moved closer and wrapped my arms around her. I felt her arms moving across my back. I kissed her softly on her head and withdrew after a minute.

'I could never have doubts about us, Anya,' I whispered. 'I just hope you'll be fine.' I caught hold of a few strands of her hair and tucked them in place behind her ear.

'Trust me,' she said. 'They won't get us.'

I cupped her face in my hands. 'I hope so. I don't know what I'd do without you. I love you.'

'I love you, too, Sahil. Everything's going to be fine.'

I nodded. 'All right, I must go now. Ayush would be waiting. And, oh yeah, about earlier, just tell Monica I said I was sorry. Can you imagine I made *her* cry, the ever-smiling tomboy?'

She waved an arm. 'It's not your fault. She has been off all day. We all have our days when the regret and sadness really gets to us.'

A door creaked open and Aditya strutted over to us. 'Hey virgins, what are you doing out here in the cold?'

Anya wagged a menacing finger at him. 'Don't you call us that!'

He laughed, tilting his head back, happy his teasing worked. 'Be of some help,' Anya said. 'Can you drop Sahil back?'

'No, no, it's—' I started to protest but Aditya caught hold of my hand before I could say anything else and sat me down in the outermost car. It was a white Verna. I rolled the window down and kissed Anya's hand. Slowly, we drove off.

Once we reached my neighbourhood Aditya pulled the car to a sudden halt a few metres from my house.

'My house is over there.'

'Look ahead!' Aditya said, sweat crawling across his forehead. 'They are here!'

My eyes hunted in the dark till they settled on two familiar figures. My heart stopped and I felt a sudden rush of adrenaline. 'Oh my god!'

The Brothers were standing outside my building.

'Sahil,' Aditya said, regretfully, 'your life is in danger.'

53

Ayush and Shweta

Nothing happened that week. Or the week after.

What did happen was that I completed my book—I had a lot of time over the past two weeks. It was a great feeling to pen the last sentence of the book, a feeling of wild contentment and of closure.

The night I visited the revenants' home for the first time, Aditya and I climbed out of the car and slowly walked down the street towards my house. The Brothers were standing under a lamppost, its yellow light cast sinister shadows across their faces. They were leaning against the rusty gate of the park. They did nothing, said nothing, they just stared.

I was drop-dead frightened. My heart throbbed in my chest and my feet were unsteady on the ground.

Aditya had fixed them with a piercing gaze. Just when we drew level with them and rounded the corner for the stairway to my flat, Aditya said, 'This is between us. Don't involve him!'

Slowly, the Brothers turned to each other, shared a stolid glance, then continued staring at us.

Aditya and I held our ground for a minute, waiting for them to respond. When no words were forthcoming, we continued to walk towards the stairway to our right.

'You share our secrets with the world, dimwit, and tell us he's not *involved*?'

Dread crawled down my back. Now my heart hammered against my ribs.

Aditya snorted and turned on his heels. 'We had a deal, remember?'

Again the deafening silence. Only the cold stares.

Aditya shook his head. I could see a fine coat of perspiration spread evenly on his face. He walked me to the second floor. Only once I was inside, did he leave.

Over, the last two weeks whenever I drew the curtains to my room, I saw a revenant, the good kind, sitting on a green bench in the park across my flat, keeping a sharp lookout. Aditya and Anya had been petrified that the Others were planning to get to them through me. They were each keeping an eight-hour watch—Aditya, Anya and Titlu, the fat revenant I remembered from the dinner table—round the clock. Anya had assured me she wouldn't let anything happen to me; their threat, she said, was nothing more than a fart in the breeze.

The Brothers would visit my neighbourhood often. They would walk around slowly, drawing minimum attention, their upturned faces sometimes surveying my flat. The revenant keeping watch would quickly trot over to them; they'd exchange a silent glance and the Brothers would then leave.

Anya had told me the Others wouldn't risk killing me in public as that would draw immense attention to them, something they didn't want as it would affect their lives. But whenever I left my house to go to school or the music academy, one of the Brothers would trail me.

It was slightly nerve-racking for the first few days—I was constantly looking over my shoulder—but I eventually calmed down. All the Brothers ever did was stare ominously at me. Besides, after witnessing Anya in action, I knew what she was capable of.

Ayush and Shweta never found out. I never told them. It would have been a mess if they did. Pramod Uncle would have got involved, and then Anya and her comrades would be in trouble.

On Sunday afternoon, a week later—I was feeling safe and comfortable by then—the three of us were having lunch. I had just returned from my room, after giving Anya a flying kiss through my window. Anya was reading my manuscript, which I had handed over with much reluctance.

'Nice *rajma chawal*,' I said. 'Did you make it, Shweta?'

Shweta and Ayush exchanged a puzzled glance.

'No, I didn't,' she said. 'The cook made it. Why?'

I shrugged. 'No, I was just, you know, curious.'

'So you *like* it?'

'I love it,' I said. 'It's the best rajma chawal I've ever had.'

One more puzzled glance between them.

Ayush smiled a little. 'The cook hasn't changed in years, Sahil. You're eating this same dish for probably the thousandth time.'

'Yeah, but,' I smiled sheepishly, 'it's good.'

'Okay.'

After a couple of more delicious bites, I said, 'So what's going on in your lives?'

A third puzzled glance between them.

'Sahil,' said Shweta, putting her spoon aside. 'Are you okay? You *actually* want to know what's going on in our lives?'

I glanced at them, back and forth a few times. 'Yeah, why not?'

Now Shweta smiled. 'Something's wrong with you today, Sahil. You barely talk to us.' Then to Ayush she said, 'Can you believe it?'

Ayush shook his head. 'Sahil, what's the matter?'

I was struck by the strangeness of this conversation. 'Guys, you are my siblings. What's wrong if I want to know how you've been?'

'Yeah, but, Shweta is right. You barely talk to us and now you want to know about our lives!'

'Yes!'

They finally started talking. It was the last year of Ayush's medical course and the pressure was immense. He was studying eighteen hours a day. And then the bummer: Mehek had broken up with him.

A hand flew to my mouth. 'I'm so sorry. When?'

A streak of sadness crossed his face. I realized later it was more to do with my ignorance than the break up. 'It's been three months now, Sahil. Good morning,' he said, sarcastically.

'Don't tell me you never noticed?' Shweta was saying, leaning forward. 'He's been a mess ever since. Look at how much weight he has lost.'

'No, I mean, yes, I-I, of course I noticed.' I grabbed the water jug and poured some in a glass and drank. 'I'm sorry, Ayush. Really, I am. I always thought you guys would—' I stopped myself.

He shrugged it off. 'It's okay, shit happens.'

Shweta was enjoying her course. She was in her first year at St Bede's College. Her course had just the right energy and excitement.

'I'm sorry, Shweta. What . . . I mean . . . what course are you . . .'

'Mass communication!' Shweta rolled her eyes. 'God, you don't even know that! I'm going to complete a year now.'

When my turn came, I managed to resist the urge to tell them about Anya. They would never understand. Or believe me, for that matter. Besides, what good would it do?

Some other time maybe, I thought.

After lunch, while we were clearing the table, I said, hesitatingly, 'Guys, listen, I wanted to tell you something. I know I haven't said this enough, or probably ever, but I-I love both of you very much. I really do. Thank you for being there for me always.'

They shared a fourth puzzled glance that afternoon.

'Sahil, brother,' Ayush replied, bemused, 'there's something *definitely* wrong with you today.'

54

Blessings

After lunch I at stopped at Grandma's picture and, after a glance, kissed her forehead, before proceeding to my room. My eyes fell on the drawer where I housed the instruments of my temporary escape. I pulled it open, picked up the few blades and threw them out of the window.

From the park across the street, Anya gave me a thumbs-up sign. It was her idea.

The next Sunday evening, we strolled over to the Ridge. We sat on the pavement looking out at Christ Church in the distance.

The cold had withered slightly, but was still enough to induce a shiver from time to time. In the western part of the sky, the sun was a subdued orange ball.

Anya placed her left elbow on my shoulder. We'd been discussing my manuscript.

'You definitely have a knack for storytelling,' she told me.

'I'm glad to hear you say that.'

'Are you sending it out to publishers?'

I thought about this in apprehension. 'I would,' I said, 'but they are nasty. I don't think they'll give a newbie a chance. I'll probably have to self-publish it.'

'But this is a good story,' she said, with some protest. She took her elbow off my shoulder.

I placed my right elbow on her shoulder. 'Okay, but if they reject it, promise me you'll dole out the same treatment to them that you reserve for rapists.'

She laughed.

'Which reminds me, did you read today's paper?'

She shook her head.

'You know what the headlines were? "Shimla—A Rape-Free City?" Apparently there haven't been any rapes, or even attempted rapes, or eve-teasing, none of those things, in Shimla. After the ten murders, the report said, these hooligans are scared for their lives. And how long has it been, just three weeks have passed, right, since your last murder? You did it, Anya.'

'No,' she corrected me. '*We* did it.'

The consequences of the murders were apparent across the city. Security had eased and there was a general perception that as long as you didn't rape anyone, you were safe. Even the media highlighted this substantially. On the Internet, the 'Rapists Beware' Facebook page and hashtag had gone viral.

It was a win-win situation for all. I was happy because Anya wouldn't be killing any more.

However, very soon I would realize, I couldn't have been more wrong.

* * *

The sun was setting slowly behind the hills, leaving in its wake a deep orange-coloured sky with liberal streaks of red, yellow and indigo across it. If god was a painter, he did his job well. It was idyllic; my eyes slowly traced the sky, admiring the painting.

'Look, Anya,' I said, my eyes never leaving the sky, 'it's so beautiful.' As soon as the words were out, I bit my lip.

She looked up, squinted her eyes. 'All I see is a charcoal-coloured sky and a small charcoal-coloured ball.'

She took a deep breath and turned to me. Her eyes glinted with tears. 'I can't see any colours, Sahil. Don't you remember?'

I slipped an arm around her shoulder and pulled her close. I kissed her ear and whispered, 'It's not that pretty, anyway.' A chuckle rose out of her. I kissed her again.

She wiped her eyes with the back of her hand. 'I miss living,' she said sadly. 'Sometimes, it feels so bad. I wish I was given another chance.'

I took her hand. 'I'm with you, Anya, always. Just close your eyes.'

She pinched them shut.

I turned back to the sky. 'Just above the wood-coloured hills, the orange sun is loosely suspended, happy in its solitude. All around it are bright streaks of red and orange and yellow, as if god took his gigantic paintbrush, dipped it whimsically in huge pots of these colours and splashed them across the sky. A few birds are flying past—'

Her eyes flew open. 'I can see *that*. The birds are black, dumbo.'

We giggled a little.

Then, I asked, 'Why do I love you so much, girlfriend?'

She drew closer and wrapped her arms around me, her head settled on my shoulder. We sat that way for a while. The weather was pleasant and the number of people increased gradually as the evening wore on. Pictures were clicked, street-food gobbled, hugs exchanged, and a feeling of contentment washed over me.

Life was good.

'Hey Anya,' I said, shifting. 'I've got something for you.'

I retrieved a piece of paper from my jacket and handed it to her.

'What's this?' she asked. She slowly unfurled the paper.

Her face broke out into a wide smile, her dimple came to life. I kissed her.

'In the hospital,' I said, 'when I was just out of the coma, you told me to do this, remember?'

She nodded and read.

My Five Blessings

5. I live in a wonderful city.
4. I'm healthy and alive. I can see, smell, taste and savour.
3. I've got wonderful siblings.
2. I have a dream—to be a great storyteller.
1. I fell in love with you.

55

The List

The Brothers never really planned on hurting me. They only paid visits to my neighbourhood, sometimes to the music academy, but all they ever did was to stare quietly. They did that for a little more than two weeks. But we could never figure out why.

We only realized it two days later. Tailing me was a ploy, a distraction.

They never wanted me. All they wanted were the young revenants. And they got them.

Sameer was killed.

Along with Chinna and Aakriti.

Anya had been sobbing all morning. Aditya drove to my school and, citing a family emergency, got me out.

The revenant house was quiet, a mournful air had seeped into every nook and cranny. Long, desolate faces greeted me. Anya sprinted across the hallway and hugged me at the door, sobbing loudly.

I met Ibrahim and Monica. They sat on the couch, where a couple of weeks before Anya and I had sat. Monica's face was burrowed deep in his chest; Ibrahim's hand softly patted her head. The few tears on his face sparkled in the sunlight streaming in through the window on the other side.

'I'm terribly sorry,' I muttered, settling down. 'But, how did this happen?'

The revenants, although aware of the notoriety of their peers, hadn't seen the attack coming. All they ever anticipated was the threat to me. The Others took advantage of this and kidnapped Sameer, Chinna and Aakriti not too far from their neighbourhood.

'They must have subdued them, perhaps shot them or handcuffed them and I think by now—' Ibrahim's voice shook. 'I think they would have already performed the ritual.'

A painful sob rose from Monica.

'When did this happen?'

'This morning,' Ibrahim replied.

A few hours ago The Others had called the house. Apart from the three revenants that they took, they had given a list of five more to be surrendered to them.

'That bastard Damiyan said nothing would happen to the rest of us.' Aditya's voice was raspy, full of anger.

'And who *was* on that list?' I asked, apprehensively.

'The youngest ones,' Ibrahim said, the desperation on his face obvious.

I turned to Anya. When she slowly nodded, a shudder shot through me. I bolted from my seat. 'This can't happen!'

'Sahil, listen,' Ibrahim said, 'please, we don't want to involve you in this. We'll figure something out.'

'By that if you mean you'll just hand Anya and the four others over to them, then I'm sorry, I won't let that happen. Let me help.'

'You can't be of any help,' Aditya cried out. 'You'll get yourself killed.'

'Then so be it.' I hugged Anya. 'I can't lose her.'

Anya kissed me and squeezed my hand. She wiped her tears away and said, 'Please Sahil, there's nothing you can do. Just stay safe and go home.'

I looked at them, one by one. I'd never been so unyielding in my life. 'There's always something I can do. You guys can be the brawn, let me be the brain.'

56

The End: Part 1

The air was putrid. It stank of rats, urine and sodden walls. There was a steady whirr of a fan somewhere close to my right, probably an exhaust or a table fan. Other than that, there was no other sound. I didn't know where I was, but whatever this place was, it had to be a badly ventilated basement because I found it difficult to breathe.

I was blindfolded with a rough cloth, my arms were tied to the back of the chair I was sitting on with an abrasive rope, its loose strands jagged against my skin.

My throat was dry and I collected the saliva in my mouth and let it drip down. My stomach growled; I hadn't had anything to eat all day. The school blazer and sweater that I was wearing had increased my body temperature considerably. Sweat beaded on my forehead before crawling down the length of my face to my chin and below. I felt an overpowering urge to free my arms and wipe my face.

It must have been at least six hours since I was kidnapped.

The Others had got me.

I would say I made it easy for them. Aditya and I had encountered them a few kilometres to the west of the Ridge.

There were four of them: the Brothers and two others with stained yellow teeth. Aditya had asked me to stop but I was so furious about them not only killing Sameer but planning to kill Anya too, that I didn't heed Aditya's advice.

A stupid, impulsive act, but you truly fall in love only once.

The Brothers were surprised to see me head in their direction. I confronted them first, then requested, then begged them to stop this madness. I told them I loved Anya. The four of them sniggered and smirked at me. Then, before I knew what was happening, I was being yanked into their SUV, legs first, as I helplessly squirmed and protested.

I was blindfolded next, the engines started and after thirty minutes or so, I was dumped in this place. The Brothers had told me to wait, without making a sound, until Damiyan showed up and decided my fate. One sound from me, one of them had warned, and a bullet would find a nice spot in my brain.

'I don't want to die, please,' I told them. 'I'll do whatever you ask me to.'

They nodded and left me in the gloom.

Footsteps. I heard the sound of footsteps, somewhere behind me, descending down the stairs. It, or they, approached me. A hand pulled off the blindfold. I slowly let my eyes open and adjust to the light. Three figures loomed in front of me. The Brothers in black leather jackets, their arms crossed at their chests, their faces emotionless, peering down at me. The third was perhaps . . .

'I'm Damiyan,' the third man said.

He was tall and thin; he had small eyes with a scar that ran from underneath his left eye to the bridge of his nose. His hair was thin and grey, wet, and pulled back very tightly to form a small ponytail. His cheeks were almost hollow, his jaw prominent and there was a forbidding air about him. From time to time he flicked his tongue out, like a lizard, and licked his lips. He wore a steel-grey overcoat, long enough to reach his knees.

'They will be here any minute,' he said. Out came the tongue, licked the lips and slunk back inside. 'You be a good boy and I promise to give you a quick death.'

'What?' I asked, shocked, looking at the Brothers before turning to him. 'But . . . but I thought it was supposed to be an exchange. Me for the five revenants you'd asked for.'

Damiyan snickered. The Brothers joined him.

'You stupid human!' he barked. 'You really thought I'd let you walk out of here alive?'

'Please, please,' I begged. 'My brother and sister will be shattered. Please don't kill me.'

He flicked his tongue again and snickered. The Brothers, although smiling, looked at me in contempt.

One of them said, 'He said he loves that—who is that rape girl? Anya!'

'Oh, she's pretty,' Damiyan leered. 'Let's hope her blood is nice and warm too.'

Hopelessness permeated every muscle in my body. 'Why are you doing this?' I cried 'What will you do with more years? You can't enjoy anything. You're stripped of all your luxuries anyway!'

Damiyan pulled out a long knife from inside his shirt. He came over to me and placed it against my neck. I screamed in pain as he slowly slid it across my neck, grazing my skin. I felt warm blood trickling out.

'I'm sorry, I'm sorry. Please don't—'

'Don't you dare say that again!'

A voice, loud and harsh, from above, echoed in the room. 'Damiyan, they are here!'

He continued sliding the knife across my neck, slowly, piercing my skin, letting the blood ooze out, but never going in completely. His face puckered in contempt, the small eyes burnt in rage; his hot, unpleasant breath hit my cheeks as I sat motionless, fists curled up tight to counter some of the pain.

Then, he withdrew the knife. 'Get him up!' he said, walking over to the stairs.

The Brothers untied the rope. My hand flew to my neck and pressed against the gash. Although it was a superficial wound, blood continued trickling out and the pain didn't ease. My white school-uniform shirt was stained at the collar with some of the blood. I kept the gash pressed tight when one of them jerked me up and pushed me towards the stairs.

I cast a look around the room where I'd spent the last six hours. The four walls had been left unpainted, cement and bricks on display. Water had seeped into some of its edges. The ceiling was bare. Apart from the chair there was a table at the far end of the room, a small fan atop it.

They pushed me up the bare stairs. The world upstairs was in complete contrast to the dingy basement—brightly painted walls, elite furniture, a big, sparkling chandelier. They pushed me across the length of the room, through the door and out into the open.

My jaw dropped at the sight of a helpless Anya. She gazed at me in sympathy, her eyes lingering on my neck and the blood-stained shirt. Monica and Ibrahim were at her side. There were three other teenage revenants I didn't recognize, perhaps from the other two bungalows that I hadn't visited—a petite girl, her face creased with worry, and two boys, one frail, the other of medium build.

I looked around. We were in the middle of nowhere. All my eyes could see were the endless mountains and dense forest. There was, however, a small cluster of habitation to the south-west, far from us. Our screams would never reach them. Behind me the two-storied bungalow stood alone in the wilderness; it was the perfect place for the ritual.

Apart from the Brothers and Damiyan, there were five Others, their faces in a permanent sulk, automatic rifles in their hands.

'Check them!' Damiyan ordered.

The Brothers walked over and frisked the revenants, one by one. The Others were keeping a sharp lookout and had ensured that, apart from the five and Ibrahim, there were no other revenants sneaking around.

'No weapons,' one said.

'All right then!' Damiyan shouted, although the revenants stood just a few metres across him on the open patch of land. 'The five of you walk towards me and say your goodbyes. And remember: one foolish act and I'll,' he gestured, pointing two fingers at my forehead, 'blow his brains out.'

Ibrahim nodded and the five revenants started towards him.

'Ibrahim, wait!' I said. 'He will not hold up his end of the deal. They plan to kill me after the exchange.'

Damiyan rammed his elbow into my face, and I yelped. It struck the side of my nose; there was a crunching sound and then a lot of blood.

'You bastard!' Anya screamed. 'Leave him alone!'

Ibrahim held out a hand. 'Damiyan, listen, you let this go peacefully, take these five and let me and Sahil walk out of here, and we forget this ever happened. Otherwise there will be consequences. Remember, there are more of us than you.'

Damiyan put his hands in the pockets of his overcoat and looked at his fellows, his tongue flicking his lips. 'What do you say?'

Three of them nodded. He turned to the Brothers. There was nothing but impudence in their expressions. They were glancing at the five revenants who were ready to sacrifice their lives for me.

'Okay,' Damiyan said. 'Let him go.'

The bald, sturdy bastard, who held my hand, released me. With one hand on my nose and the other on my neck, I slowly walked over to the revenants, to Anya. She took a step forward.

'Are you okay?' she asked, hugging me.

I embraced her, my arms slowly moving around her; a cry of despair emanated from me. Soon she would be meal for Damiyan. Killed. Stripped of her blood. Then burnt. So would Monica and the other three.

'Enough!' Damiyan said. 'Now, come on, walk over.'

I withdrew from her embrace and cupped her face. 'Just remember, I will love you no matter what happens.'

'I know,' she said.

Then she, along with Monica and the three other revenants, walked over to Damiyan.

'Give me the gun!' He snatched one from a dark, moustachioed Other. 'I'll shoot them.'

He placed the nozzle of the rifle against the chest of the petite girl and fired. There was a loud, booming noise. A flock of birds, hiding in the trees, took flight, rustling the leaves of the oaks and the deodars behind them. The gunshot reverberated, the echoes finally petering out. With a small yelp, the petite girl fell to the ground; a puddle of her blood soaked into the mud.

Then the two boys.

Then Monica.

Anya, before going down, looked over her shoulder, sent me a kiss. A knot tightened in my stomach.

Then she fell with a thud.

57

Prelude to the Plan

Two days earlier

'There's always something I can do. You guys can be the brawn, let me be the brain.'

Aditya and Ibrahim shared a quick glance. 'Okay, genius,' said Aditya. 'What's your plan?'

'Have you read *The Art of War*?' I asked.

Ibrahim, Aditya, Anya and Monica shook their head.

'I thought so,' I said. 'It was written by a Chinese writer, Sun Tzu, in the thirteenth century. Warriors swear by it. It's the perfect guide to war. *This* is war!'

I saw them sharing puzzled glances with each other. Finally, Anya turned to me. 'So?'

'He insisted on two things. First: know your enemy, and second: all warfare is based on deception.'

'Okay,' Aditya said, in rapt attention. 'Go on.'

'We need to give them a false notion that they are winning. But first,' I said, turning to Ibrahim, 'tell me everything you know about the Others.'

58

Damiyan

Damiyan would never have killed Ibrahim if he had been *nice* to him. More than a decade of working for him and Ibrahim still treated him, along with his other goons, as slaves. Agreed they were mostly lower castes, Shudras, but some respect was all Damiyan asked for.

After all, he had killed at least fifty people at Ibrahim's behest.

Damiyan first started working for Ibrahim back in 1887. Those days he was just a small crook, killing for paltry sums of money, but feared throughout the district of Solan. He had two younger brothers, both equally notorious, and the three had ganged up, leaving suffering and death in their wake.

Ibrahim, always on the hunt for hot-headed thugs, hired the three of them at the first opportunity. Their job, within the drug cartel, was simple: to get the work done. The dread that they spread within the labour class was so profound that not once, since they had been put in charge, did the labourers complain. Not against the eighteen-hour shifts, or the inhumane working conditions, sometimes not even at the non-remittal of their wages. Damiyan and his brothers were not only known for killing, but killing mercilessly. They were passionate about killing. They loved killing.

Very soon, Damiyan was assisting Ibrahim in operations, downsizing competition and expansion. It was then that Damiyan realized the true worth of the empire and the tendrils of greed began taking root inside him.

He would have resisted his greed but he, along with his brothers, were finding it hard to swallow the repeated insults, some implied, some direct: making him wait outside while he dined and confabulated with the Whites, calling him names, treating him and his brothers like dirt.

In the end, it was easy. All Damiyan did was drive a stake through Ibrahim's heart. It wasn't planned; it was an impulse, after yet another snooty remark.

No one retaliated. No one questioned it when he took over the empire in 1901.

Fifteen years later, he was shot dead.

Damiyan and Ibrahim met again. Both hated the other with equal magnitude. Ibrahim had changed; he wanted to pay for his sins. Damiyan hadn't had enough of them.

Both the groups fought and attacked each other, but this was a centuries-old war. In the 1970s, when it became obvious there wasn't much to gain, the two groups decided to co-exist and a truce at Ibrahim's suggestion was established. Damiyan was not in a position to disagree. There were barely fifty Others left; the number of revenants was well in excess of two hundred.

Besides, the Others had a lot of wealth accumulated through years of drug trafficking, black-marketeering and prostitution. Damiyan figured it wouldn't be a bad idea to leave the revenants for a while and focus on humans instead.

Unlike the revenants, the Others didn't move around to hide their identity. If suspicion arose, they killed. If heads turned, they killed. If people pried, they killed. The officials who worked hand-in-glove with them, facilitating their deals, couldn't be killed, so their palms were adequately greased.

The Others lived in Samra, near the Kullu valley, in a mansion no less than a palace, occupying a few hundred acres, armed humans guarding the endless boundary round the clock.

They countered impotence with sexual violence—more women had disappeared in Samra than anywhere else in the rest of the country—the lack of taste buds with warm blood, and the lack of coloured sight and a sense of smell with more violence.

Damiyan constantly told his people, 'It's not such a bad life, after all.'

59

The Brothers

The Brothers were not the brothers of Damiyan back when he was a human and they were certainly not related.

Few decades ago, they had caught hold of two women on a deserted road. Damiyan had found their whims too similar to not share a bloodline. It was after that incident he decided they'd rather be called Brothers; with only an inch difference in their height and a similar stout structure with a bald head, it's not as if they looked much different anyway.

The bodies of the two women (one with each Brother) were later found naked dumped by the side of the road drained of their blood in entirety.

60

The Plan

'They are animals, I'm telling you,' said Anya.

'And with all your powers, you never tried to stop them?' I asked.

Ibrahim cleared his throat. 'Okay, two things,' he said. 'Firstly, our powers only come into play when we try to save someone, not kill them. And secondly, why do you think we've been at war for such a long time?'

The Others wanted to kill the revenants for their lifespans. Period. There was no other motive. The revenants wanted to kill the Others, firstly, in defence and, secondly, to mitigate some of their violence and terror.

'It's not like we don't want to kill them,' Aditya said with distaste, 'and stop all their killings, their rampages, but we risk putting our people's lives in danger.'

'But now they are coming after *you*,' I stated the obvious.

He nodded.

I turned to Anya. She had a helpless, a slightly forlorn appearance.

'Come on, guys,' I said. 'You realize you can't just sit here and wait for them to kill you? It's better to be the pursuer than the pursued.'

'You were saying something about deception,' said Aditya. 'Go on. Complete your thought.'

'Why can't the five of you on the list go to their place and surrender while the rest of you take them by surprise and attack from a vantage point?'

Ibrahim considered it. Then he shook his head slowly. 'Not possible. You should see their mansion. They have an army guarding it. There is no way we could pull off a sneak act.'

'Wait a minute!' Aditya said, his eyes suddenly bright. 'The place where they hold the ritual is in the middle of nowhere, right?'

'But why would they . . .' Ibrahim trailed off and stared at the painting ahead. 'You're right. They'll surely ask us to surrender there.' He turned to Anya. 'What if the five of you surrendered there and just before they subdued you—' he stopped suddenly. 'But Aditya, I'm sure they'll do a thorough check for any weapons.'

'But what if *we* carry the guns?' I suggested.

'Who's "we"?' Anya asked.

'Me and maybe you, Ibrahim.'

'What would *you* be doing there?' Anya asked. 'Please Sahil, don't involve yourself in this. It's too dangerous.'

I appreciated her concern but this had to be done. If I didn't do this, they would kill Anya and I couldn't let that happen. I'd lost enough loved ones already and couldn't afford to lose another. I realized I might lose my life in the process. But it didn't matter. It's amazing what a man will do when properly motivated.

'What if I get myself kidnapped?' I presented the idea, loving it already. 'What if the five of you are not there for a meek surrender, but instead, for an exchange? An exchange for me? There are two advantages to this. First, I would already be there and, second, they'd think they were in control.'

'And why the hell do you think they'll want to kidnap you? A human?' said Anya, visibly angry.

'That,' I said, throwing an arm around her, 'you leave to me. If they don't want to kidnap me, I'll manipulate them into wanting to kidnap me.'

61

The Kidnapping

If everything went as per the plan, not only would we manage to save Anya and the four revenants, but we would kill a significant number of Others too.

That being said, a sinking feeling had taken residence in the pit of my stomach by early the next day. After all, it wasn't every day that I planned to get myself kidnapped by a bunch of blood-sucking cannibals.

Aditya had told me I might encounter the Brothers west of the Ridge in the evening. They had a buyer there and they visited the place regularly to deliver consignments. Aditya and I hunkered behind a straggly bush, ahead of us was a large ramshackle factory of some sort. The Brothers emerged through a small door to the left of a large iron gate, shaking hands with people who looked like humans.

Before I could ask Aditya confirmed they weren't revenants. The Brothers headed for their Land Cruiser parked on the other side of the road.

'Are you sure about this?' Aditya asked as I stood up and manoeuvred my way out of the bushes.

'Never been surer,' I said over my shoulder and ventured on to the road, my heart thudding in my chest.

There were two more Others near the car and, as they saw me approaching, the four of them maintained their stance and held my gaze.

'What the heck are you doing here?' the shorter Brother asked.

'Please don't hurt Anya,' I begged. 'Please, I love her.'

Laughter rose in quick bursts from the Brothers. The other two snickered.

Once they were done, the taller Brother held out his hand. 'Yesterday Ibrahim refused to hand her over along with the four other revenants we'd asked for. So that's exactly what we are going to do, one way or the other.'

'Please, please, leave her. Take me if you want to.'

'What will we do with a damn human?' the taller Brother replied. 'You're worthless to us.'

The shorter Brother nodded in assent while the other two ominously gazed at me.

'Why are you staring me like that?' I asked. 'Please don't kidnap me. If you plan to use me as a bargaining chip, trust me it won't work. Though Anya loves me, she'd never want to exchange her life for mine.'

The puzzled glance shared between the four of them was quick.

As they shoved me inside the car, a blindfold taut across my eyes, I heard one of the Brothers remark, 'He's such a fool!'

62

The End: Part 2

My chest tightened as Anya crashed to the ground, a bullet perforating her chest. After the last echo died down there was a deafening calm in the air. There was a look of intense gratification on Damiyan's face as he cocked his head sideways to one of his sidekicks to clear the mess.

Then I allowed myself to take a deep breath and think clearly. So far, so good. The plan was working. Ibrahim and I had less than fifteen minutes for our next step.

Damiyan and his clan would want to perform their ritual within that time else the five revenants they had just killed would awaken.

Now, one by one, their bodies were pulled into the house.

'Can we leave now?' Ibrahim asked Damiyan who flicked his right hand disinterestedly.

'Get the hell out of here quickly,' he said. 'I don't want to have to kill you twice.'

Then he laughed.

Ibrahim looked at me and nodded. We turned on our heels and slowly walked away. Once out of sight, we started sprinting.

'*So you'll get yourself kidnapped, somehow, okay,*' said Aditya, still finding my idea hard to execute. '*But how will Ibrahim get there?*'

It was not a bad question.

'*Wait a minute,*' Ibrahim intervened, '*but Sahil, are you sure you want me to tell Damiyan we won't hand over the five revenants?*'

'*Positive,*' I said. '*Why else would they kidnap me?*' Then I turned to Aditya. '*Ibrahim will get there in this manner: when he gets a call from Damiyan for the exchange, Ibrahim will say he'll also be there to ensure I get out of there alive.*'

'*Okay, that's one part of the plan,*' Monica said, smiling. Somehow she was enjoying this. '*Did you think of the next part, Sahil? How will you kill them?*'

'*We need guns,*' I said, '*that's all. When they are not expecting us, that's when we'll get them.*'

'*But how?*' Anya asked. '*Surely we can't have the guns on us; they'll check us.*'

'*Then maybe hidden, in a place close by.*'

Ibrahim and I dug the earth under an oak tree a kilometre south. Aditya and Ibrahim had planted guns there yesterday. We retrieved a .22 calibre rifle and a 9mm Glock pistol.

'*Just one problem,*' I said. '*I've never used a gun.*'

'*Get him a 9mm pistol,*' Ibrahim said.

To our left, on the far side, was a large cabinet that I hadn't noticed before. Aditya opened it and I was flummoxed at the sight of a wide collection of guns—rifles, pistols, handguns of varying shapes and sizes.

'*I had a thing for guns when I was human,*' Ibrahim said. '*I loved collecting them.*'

'*So this one's for you,*' he continued, when Aditya handed it over. The pistol was a black, shiny piece of metal that I had seen in movies. It was slightly heavy and I revelled in the feeling of a gun in my hand.

'It's a 9 mm pistol, fairly simple to use. Press this button on the side of the grip here and out comes the magazine. Now these bullets you insert one at a time with the rounded side facing forward. Re-insert the magazine and you'll hear a click when it locks into place. After that—' Ibrahim took the pistol in his hand, '—disengage the safety by pushing down this lever and pull back this slide at the top of the barrel to load the bullet into the firing chamber. Now, you're ready to shoot.'

'Do you realize,' I said, 'I've never fired a gun. How the hell will I hit a target?'

'You don't have to,' said Ibrahim. 'Just be my backup and I'll do the rest.'

I looked at Anya.

'I'm sure you'll do it,' she said.

When we reached the house where I had been held captive, the first thing I noticed was blood splattered on the ground. Anya's blood. I recoiled and felt the urge to shoot Damiyan with my pistol and burn him to death.

The house bore a deserted look; the Others must be preparing for the ritual.

The door to the entrance was ajar and we tiptoed our way towards it, slowly making an entry. All I had to do, Ibrahim had told me, was to fire my gun and distract the Others while he shot the bastards one by one. There were seventeen rounds in my pistol and I hoped at least two would land in the right place.

We tiptoed further across the living room to the left where we could hear voices. Time was limited; the shortest delay and I risked losing Anya forever.

Ibrahim gestured and I followed him silently as he slid through another door. There was a faint creak and for a moment we held our position, our backs against the wall, weapons drawn out front. When nothing happened, we continued crossing the room, this one bare, save for a few paintings on the wall.

The voices we could hear were now louder. Through a chink in the door Ibrahim peeked in and when he withdrew he nodded. I leaned forward and could see a vast room, bodies on the floor; Damiyan, the Brothers and two Others sitting beside them. In the middle was a crackling fire and somebody whom I couldn't see was reciting verses I couldn't fathom.

The room was large enough so that when Ibrahim and I slowly entered it and took our positions behind two pillars, no one took notice. From here I could observe the proceedings. There was an old bearded man, a priest perhaps, a revenant, Ibrahim mouthed, in charge of the ritual, sitting cross-legged at the head of the fire. Damiyan held a long, lustrous dagger in his right hand; Monica's numb body by his side. Anya was lying next to a Brother who held another dagger which looked similar to the one in Damiyan's hand, presumably from a collection for revenant killings.

Five Others were sitting on the floor, another five standing around them, three more watching over.

I checked my watch. I had set a timer for fifteen minutes and presently the digits read 09:48. I turned sideways to Ibrahim and there was a slight nod.

It was time.

I slid the barrel at the top of the pistol and fired at Damiyan. It missed and hit the vase to his left. Just when the Others realized what was happening Ibrahim opened fire. He struck one of the Brothers and an Other sitting opposite him.

Panic ensued and the Others scrambled for cover as bullets flew in the air, hitting three more. Over the sound of the bullets Ibrahim asked me to stop firing and hold on to my rounds while he kept the trigger of his rifle busy. Two more Others fell to the floor.

By now Damiyan, one of the Brothers and four Others had found cover. Ibrahim stopped firing and assessed the situation. I whispered to him that only Damiyan and an Other had guns, while the other weapons were sprawled on the floor by the subdued bodies. At his instruction I re-loaded my magazine with the ammunition in my coat pocket. When he nodded I began firing aimlessly, providing him cover, while he quickly crossed the floor and crouched behind a chair to his right and opened fire. The remaining Brother and two Others were clearly in the trajectory and the bullets easily found them.

Three more to go.

Damiyan emerged from his hiding position behind the couch and fired. I shielded myself behind the pillar and kept an eye on Ibrahim who hunkered down and waited. The bullets missed. Ibrahim, his position unchanged, drew out his rifle and fired in the air, and nodded towards me. I did the same while continuing to hide behind the pillar.

When in control, Ibrahim and I peeked out for a quick scan and saw that Damiyan and two of his people were escaping, closing the door behind them. We stepped out from our hiding positions and made a dash for the door. Anya and Monica woke up, along with the three other revenants, and we breathed a sigh of relief. We spent a moment with them.

'Prepare to burn these bastards while we get them!' Ibrahim ordered, sprinting towards the door. I followed him, casting a quick glance at Anya. She looked fragile.

Past the door there wasn't any trail. We ran up to the front yard and, apart from the dense trees and mountains far ahead, there was nothing.

'Shit!' Ibrahim said. 'We lost them.'

'Ibrahim,' I said, 'we killed ten of them and managed to save our people. I think we did okay.'

'We haven't killed them yet,' he said. 'Come, let's quickly burn the ones we killed.'

Inside the room the fire had intensified as more combustible items and fuel were added to it. One by one, we hurled the bodies of the Others into the fire and watched them melt. These weren't human bodies and they disintegrated quickly.

With the last body in the fire, I walked over to Anya and hugged her.

'We did it, girlfriend.'

'No,' she said, shaking her head. 'You did it! Thanks.'

'No thanks necessary,' I said. 'I did it for us.'

We shared a kiss before Ibrahim interrupted us. 'Kiddos, later. First let's get out of here.'

No sooner had he said this, there was a flurry of gunshots. This time we ran for cover, hastily collecting the weapons from the floor and hiding where the Others had hidden ten minutes ago.

Ibrahim, after a quick reload of his rifle, fired away and charged towards. The two male revenants followed him.

I wanted to join them but I could feel a burning sensation near my heart. As I raised an arm, I saw it.

I had caught a bullet.

Blood trickled out and a sudden dizziness washed over me. I was kneeling behind the couch and suddenly I crashed to the floor. Anya came running over from behind a pillar.

'Sahil! Oh my god! Are you okay?'

She raised my head and rested it on her knees. Monica and the petite girl slowly helped me lie down. By then my entire shirt and coat were smeared with blood. The pain was excruciating. Everything was slowly fading. All I could see was Anya's face above me, screaming, kissing me, crying.

'You're going to be okay! Just hold on . . . Please hold on . . .'

I managed to utter, 'I love you, Anya. We . . . our . . . story can't end this way.' Then my eyes closed.

'Sahil, no! You can't leave me . . . Sahil . . . Sahil, please open your eyes . . .'

Epilogue

What happened? What's going on? Why can't they see me?

'Ayush . . . Ayush, Shweta, guys I'm here.'

Why is everything blurry? Black and white?

'Ayush, can you hear me? Shweta? Ayush, listen I'm here, right behind you . . .'